Westobou Gold

By
Hawk MacKinney

BOOK II:

MOCCASIN HOLLOW MYSTERY SERIES

Westobou Gold

Hawk MacKinney

Westobou Gold

Edited by Jake George www.sagewordsservices.com

Cover artwork by Sage Words Services   www.sagewordsservices.com

A Sage Words Publishing Book

www.sagewordspublishing.com

ISBN-13: 978-0997096231
ISBN-10: 0997096233

Cover image credit: Copyright: <a href='http://www.123rf.com/profile_fowler5338'>fowler5338 / 123RF Stock Photo</a>

Printed in the United States of America

Westobou Gold

Prologue

The young Cutifachiqui queen peered cautiously from a heavy cover of thick brushwood. She watched the bearded ones clothed in shiny hard metal that her warriors' arrows could not pierce. The brushwood so dense they had to walk leading their big horses. Like a newborn fawn, she kept very still. The thunder sticks of these barbarians killed at a great distance.

On first hearing that the hairy-faced ones were coming, she had gathered with her Westobou peoples near the ceremonial spots on the high shell bluffs that rose above the river of the Westoe's. They had greeted the newcomers with a royal feast only to be rewarded with the plunder of her peoples. Her warriors' words proved of little meaning when she was seized and threatened by these unclean strangers. By her command her enraged warriors had only watched as these invaders took her and left. It was her duty to protect her people. She would not have their certain death from the thunder sticks. Rather, she let herself be taken away from her peoples. The one who spoke of himself as *de Soto* was on a great trek for the yellow metal. Knowing the back-trails through the tall pine forests between the trading centers of the Cacique, through the lands of the great Chief Ocute and the Cacia, the lands of the Patofa and other settlements, she would wait for her chance; and slip away without having revealed the secret location of her peoples' hidden treasure. A treasure the Spaniards desperately sought. A guarded secret they never knew she concealed.

She clutched the bark and reed wrappings bound belly-tight beneath her fur cape. In the chill of the frost-nipped sun-down she shivered more with what they would do to her if she were caught. Her thoughts were on ways to deceive these cruel marauders. Her trembling fingers dug at the damp chilled soil beneath the thick layers of brown long needles from the pines searching for the thin grit of sand and granite outcrops that would drain away the moist wetness of the slick clay. She must escape, but first—in case they caught her—she must hide it. Satisfied that she had left no visible trace, she left another of her unspoken signs along this trail. The twisted branches and patterned leaves with the small tuft of down would warn the Muscogee Coosa of the metal-clothed ones who pillaged for treasure and dispensed death. These invaders would not have what had been entrusted to her. No matter, even if it meant her death, they would not have it.

Chapter 1

His life would have been a lot longer if Johnny Crockett had ever learned that just about anybody could do things the easy way. Blessed with brains, no-boundaries imagination, and little-to-no street sense, it made the shortcuts too easy. He never worked for things he liked, 'specially if it meant he had to sweat. Johnny was made for trouble. Johnny was greedy. The more money he had, the bigger a man it made him.

He slowed the old pickup to a stop at the edge of the canebrake clearing. Sea-blue shifty-mean eyes cut sharp and cunning as he checked for any uninvited snooping eyes. He brushed the sandy brown lock of hair back from a rugged face that had been called handsome. It was a damning gift, one he bent to his advantage anytime he wanted someone else to cover his backside.

The slippery red-clay ruts mired in a once-upon-a-time gravel road curved up toward the house. The extended eaves of the porches of the great age-worn house that was Redcliffe shadowed its tall windows. Gaunt un-curtained windows gaped like empty eye sockets in a sun-bleached skull. Johnny couldn't keep his bone-deep trepidations at bay. The old lady had been dead for a number of years, but her cantankerous overseer was very much alive. Crockett half expected the wrinkled, toothless old man to burst out one of the doors, carrying the same long-barrel shotgun as last time. The man had threatened to gut-shoot him if Johnny trespassed again. Johnny hadn't forgotten. He kept Redcliffe and the peeling stucco hunting lodge located behind it at a distance.

The hunting lodge was the first Redcliffe built nearly a hundred years ago. Eventually the mixed-up facts of the new Redcliffe and the old yard became known to the locals as Ardochy, named after a long forgotten Scottish grandmother whose maiden name was McArdy.

Folks there'bouts still talked about the McArdy family. "Whole McArdy clan was tetched in the head. Comes from bedding down with too many cousins. Kids're funny looking, pinch-nosed and squat necked with wrinkly, whitish, chicken-skin bodies."

Folks talked. "Was a god-sent blessin' most'a them died 'fore they hardly could walk." Chugged a big swaller of a cold beer, "Never could'a growed into nuthin' what could take care of itself."

During afternoon teas church ladies abuzz amid dainty sips of Methodist cough medicine or homebrew brandy, their talk had nothing to do with facts. They just liked to ogle while they tittle-tattled.

Johnny didn't trust barely nobody, and except for a few, most didn't trust Johnny Crockett. He should've stuck to what he knew best—bein' lazy and sneaking beers from the cases on the delivery truck making its daily runs to local joints, including Mother's Bar.

Johnny climbed out of the pickup, and slowly skirted around the boggier bayou-edge of the sand bar shoal where Horse Creek spilled into the Savannah River. A mosquito hummed in his ear. He slapped at it; the smack clapped gunshot loud. He spotted the caretaker's old bird dog flopped asleep on the front porch, one droopy ear hanging down. Somewhere off in the birch grove came the springtime exaltation of a mockingbird, its singular clarity out-singing the babble of blue jays and red birds and the raspy irritation of a pair of wrens.

He moved careful back toward the truck, trying to look out for beaver traps buried in dark cypress-stained water along the shallow edges of the bogs. Besides beaver traps, wading in the warm, sun-dappled knee-deep marsh of the shoal, he kept an eye out for basking gators. Locals in these parts swore big ones hung back in the mossy wetlands of Hollow Creek. With another quick glance at Redcliffe, he sloshed out of the murky water and climbed into the truck, careful not to slam the door and alert the old dog. Thoughts about the first time he even heard of this god-forsaken place came to mind. His squad had been on field maneuvers in the outback underbrush of Fort Gordon when they came across the man and his gun.

Man claimed he was trailing a wounded deer that straggled onto the fort. "Deer must'a crossed the parish line at the Brier Creek end of the fort," he said, claiming he lived some place between the south end of the army base and some dried-up railroad stop farther south on Dirty Spoon Road.

Johnny felt certain the man was lying. He'd never heard of Dirty Spoon Road. A body'd have to be dead and twict stump-dumb to miss Brier Creek. The creek wasn't no trickle; it was a plenty-big.

Emmett Whitfield, Johnny's army bunkmate trouble-hunter from Alabama snickered, "He's not chasin' no deer. He's running shine out of the bottoms down in these hollers. Good place, too. Plenty water to brew a batch. Seen it before back home in Alabama." Their green lieutenant gave them the high sign. Lieutenant didn't want a *civilian incident* with all the paperwork reports.

Johnny didn't care too much for backcountry types. Him and Emmett were scheduled to get discharged about the same time. With no other place to go, they'd talked about settling in the area. Johnny hadn't figured to ever wind up in a one-stop wide spot in the road on the far side of some bridge across another river. Gas station and quick-burger places reminded him of home. Never in his wildest fancies did he ever think how much fun the night was going to be that payday Friday. They'd planned on getting a cheap motel room in the string along the Gordon Highway along with a bottle of cheap booze and plenty beer chaser. They'd have a fun time consecrating their survival of Mother Army. After a couple of bar stops he and Emmett hit the road with another six-pack. They got bleary streets and befuddled bridges mixed up and crossed the river into South Carolina where they found themselves on the Charleston highway. After they turned around to find their way back, they made another liquored-up wrong turn and discovered another out-of-the-way rundown neon-sign joint on an unpaved back road. They were horny, thirsty, prowling studlies counting down the remaining days till their discharge originals cleared Personnel Division. They wanted to party it up; get laid; and they didn't give a damn about Medical Corps scare stories about AIDS, clap, or sundry STD. Johnny never used a rubber—didn't like 'em.

5

Johnny never had a problem convincing foxy chicks and lonely wives what a champ he was. He preferred lonely wives. They was easier and ready; knew what they wanted, and taught Johnny some new tricks. Booze, broads and good times rolled free and easy for Johnny Crockett. Stocky, not muscle-pumped but well developed, good shoulders, stout, tight butt and golden fizzed thighs promised a good fuck. He was a lean, mean GQ Kansas beef, steak-and-potatoes with a million-dollar smile that broke bedroom battlefields into dazzling promises of robust fun. The only giveaway about Johnny Crockett was his slinking scheming eyes.

The cheap watered-down whisky-night rolled uninterrupted. Her name was Janella. He never did know whether it was Jan Ella or a one-word name, and didn't care. "You work here all the time?"

One-word name Janella said, "I'm just fillin' in. My reg'lar job is bartending at Mother's Bar. Sort of a regular irregular job. You two ought'a come by."

"I know where Mother's is," Johnny said. "Keep their beer good an' cold."

Janella said, "We always got plenty cold beer on any hot day."

Emmett grinned at Johnny, then back at her—all three knowing exactly what her business was. She liked the promises of these two well enough to supply them one setup after another.

Johnny and Emmett made ribald brags about threesomes, switch-hitting stories, humping their hips and making sucking sounds with their lips. Johnny never figured in his whole life to land in something this crazy-easy. Didn't matter to him what any of the other pool players and bar huggers thought. Do it if it felt good—Johnny's main rule. Good times sure was rolling.

She snuggled closer to Johnny, "After the bar closes you two want to come to a party?"

"Heck yeh," Emmett blurted. Grinned another double boilermaker straight-shot grin at Johnny. Neither of them was about to turn down free liquor.

It didn't matter when the bartender began turning off the lights. They were the party. Little more than a mile from what ever'body called the Bomb Plant she said, "Turn right here," and pointed.

Johnny squinted. Flashed the high beams, "Don't look to be much of a road."

The trailer was unlit except for one feeble bulb glaring by the front door. Janella stumbled inside. More beers, the long night, an assorted ménage. Barely dawn-light morning came with a crack-of-doom hangovers—or was it afternoon? Johnny couldn't tell. Emmett sprawled one naked thigh between hers. His slobbery lips drooled asleep in a half-wadded pillow. Johnny's head ached in places he didn't know he had. That was before he heard a car door bang. Emmett jerked bolt upright; sat up in a gawked still-asleep, unsure of exactly where or what was happening.

Unworried Janella said, "It's only my husband."

Johnny about shit when the door opened to frame a South Carolina Highway Patrol uniform. In a butt-flurry of naked arms and legs, and sheets smelling of stale beer, cigarette butts, and musty sweaty bodies, Johnny slurred an inaudible frantic, "... fuck!"

Janella, indifferent, glanced at Johnny, "His name is Purvis. He don't care."

"Well Honeybun," the uniform smirked, "You done gone an' started the party without me. Got us a couple of horny snot-nosed kids. Just the kind you like for us to make a movie." He stripped away his tie and began unbuttoning his shirt. She put on her best prim and coy smile that came out in a floosy-toothed leer. Uniform didn't care. Nobody cared.

It was the first sex tag-team video Johnny and Emmett made across the bedsheet-stage with Janella, and it was the last video stardom threesome for Johnny. After that her husband made sure he was there with his camcorder, powdery white powder, and plenty of needles. It was more powder than Johnny and Emmett and Janella could ever snort up their noses in any free-for-all sunrise-afternoon delight. Husband introduced Johnny and Emmett to rock crack and meth. Johnny liked it all—a combo of skin and bleary fantasies. It was better than beer and shooters. After each taping they halfway messed around and watched reruns and each other as bare-ass Janella flounced between sofa and kitchen keeping the hot buttered popcorn and the shots of homebrew white lightenin' a'comin', nothing in short supply.

7

Husband Purvis said, "You two got any buddies who'd like to come to one of our parties? We could have us a blow-out in Charleston or Atlanta."

Janella added, "They better be as good as you two." She snickered, "Emmett, you look just like that Hollywood actor with them two teenage hookers. He was cute."

"You ain't half bad yourself." Emmett blushed a bleary rubberneck at Johnny with no idea who she was talking about. Johnny was quick on the pickup, "We might know a few, once I spread the word we found us a hot looker." Janella giggled.

Johnny grabbed his crotch, "I got plenty of what it takes." Threw his head back; laughed a gusto; let the good times roll some more. Janella straddled him, started playing and licking and tugging.

Several parties and days and videos later Purvis introduced Johnny to the man. "Be a one-time simple job. Easy money too good to pass up. Digging it out from a hole in the ground." "Public land," Purvis drawled. "Nobody owns it. You bring me anything you find. You'll get well paid for your trouble and keeping your mouth shut."

Johnny felt proud he had been picked over Emmett, but the minute Purvis tossed the army-green serial-numbered double-ended spike and trenching shovel on the kitchen table, Johnny knew straightaway the tool was likely stolen from the fort. He wondered if it came from an enlisted barracks supply locker, but wasn't about to ask. "I won't remember nothin'. Already done forgot it. But taking my car, license plates and VIN number an' all—might not be a good idea." He thought of his pockets full of money with more to come.

"I like the way you think ahead. I'll make sure you got a beat-up pick'em-up. Nobody pays attention to an old fishin'-huntin' truck."

* * *

The pickup growled smoke when Johnny started it. Sounded to him like a straight-four running on two cylinders. Johnny parked on the weeded-up logging road off the old Sand Bar Ferry dirt road and got out, let his eyes recon the area, then hurried in a half-run, trenching shovel clutched in his fist. He ducked through tangled corkscrews of honeysuckle and Virginia creeper. Blackberry brambles snatched a chunk of his t-shirt, gouged a bloody furrow across his shoulder. He stopped. Caught his breath. This was like field training. He scouted the layout he'd been told to follow, his heart beating slow with the thrill of the hunt. He hunkered and skidded down the embankment, tearing one knee hole bigger, and brushed aside healthy green-splayed leaves of poison ivy. Inside his scuffed running shoes, red-clay sand gritted between his toes as he yanked at the mat of weeds and nettles wrapping his worn jeans, knocking away a clump of last fall's moldy leaves.

One foot sank into the loose white sand beneath a pack of leaf-fall ooze. Johnny hoisted himself over the revetment bordering what didn't look much like nothing', certainly didn't look like no burial mound anyone would pay attention to or dig in.

Purvis had warned him, "Keep an eye out for fishing license uniforms on patrol. Haul you off in cuffs. We don't need no complications." Johnny could get tossed in jail. Couldn't forget the animal look he'd caught in Purvis's eyes. Nobody'd ever know what happened to him.

He spotted the landmarks. Purvis had described them, "Watch for a curved overgrown hillock of bleached oyster shells—will be on your left with whitish oyster shells across the face of the ditch." Private property or not, he could tell he wasn't the first to dig around here. The spot he was being paid to dig right in front of him didn't look like it'd been touched.

Johnny gave another furtive glance. He moved quick while nobody was in sight, hard muscles shoving the shovel and pick in fierce quick thrusts. It reminded him kind'a like digging foxholes. It was sweaty work as he chopped at tangled roots. He dug deeper. Spring water dribbled up in seeps of white sand. He figured this was some kooky wild-goose stunt. Grazed a knuckle on sharp oyster shells, but kept digging down a good foot deep when he struck something solid. It didn't grate or have the feel of rock or oyster gravel. He dropped the shovel and dug with his hands and arms strained hard. He ignored the scatter of pottery shards and the sharp edges of oyster shells, a couple of arrowheads. His fingers curled around the bulk of something that felt solid but soggy. He tugged and thrust a hand elbow-deep into the hole until his fingers felt underneath the wrapped bundle, almost-square with rounded edges. It was small enough to be carried unless it was part of something bigger. At first he couldn't budge it until it slurped free from the sandy loam with a watery suck. He lifted it out and squatted back on his knees to brush away at the faint braided bindings of hide and reedy grass. Small pieces of the rotted bindings fell away as he scooted over to where the sunlight peaked brighter through the overhead tree branches. He sat down and picked at the corner of some kind of rusted metal. The bindings were age-welded into hard clumpy knots. He gave it a brush with one hand but couldn't tell what it was. Straps of what looked like leather were molded tight with a slight curve to its boxy shape. Using his field knife from its sheath in one boot, he poked and flicked more sediment, wondering what was inside, pondering why someone wanted to pay someone to dig it up. He scraped some more until one leathery fold was visible.

He shook it. More water dribbled out, and nothing rattled inside. "Heavy to be so small." He picked at one narrow soggy leather binding and muttered, "Gotta be something valuable for anyone to go to all this trouble. Could be other stuff buried about. Folks hide things in crazy places."

He remembered Purvis's warning, "If you find it where it had ought to be, don't go fiddlin' with opening it."

He propped it against the tree, and went back to where he'd found it. On his knees, he thrust both hands to the bottom of the hole, clawing deeper in the soupy slurry. He felt the ground firming up along the bottom. His fingers struck the smooth round-odd shape. "Maybe more stuff?"

He dug faster and thought about those TV programs he'd seen. How highbrow types with more time and money than they knew what to do with dug up pieces of broken junk-stuff, little statues of practically nothin'. Dumb enough to give them to museums 'stead of getting on the internet and selling them on eBay. He glanced around at all the oyster shells, "Somebody sure was eatin' lots of oysters. Maybe this stuff was buried with somebody important."

He clutched the odd rounded shape and yanked. It hardly budged. He grunted, then yanked harder, its edge slurping free of the muck to expose a dull brownish off-white, pitted, stone-thing. He wiped the wet mud and rotted ground cover away, and found empty eye sockets glaring straight back at him. Bits of scalp and hair clung to the side of the skull just above the hole in the side of the head.

The snap of a twig jerked Johnny's head around, jolting him back on his butt with a muffled surprise, "Shit! You scared the hell out of me. Thought you was one of those fish and game uniforms."

He was holding the tightly-wrapped bundle Johnny had left against the tree. "I was watching you poke at the package."

"I wondered what it was," Johnny said. Glanced toward the skull with its rows of teeth, one tooth with a shiny gold rim and no jaw bone, "That thing surprised me."

The man grunted. Took a closer look, "Indian."

Johnny said, "Cain't be old like what I dug up. Not with that round hole that looks like it's made by a bullet."

"Interesting you'd find a skull," then turned his attention back to the small bundle.

"It was buried in the same hole," Johnny said. "Might be more."

The man whipped out his knife and pried at one edge of the strap. Pieces crumbled away exposing elegant swirls and curlicues beneath the wrapping. "Wrapped tight." He walked over to an old granite road marker where the packed ruts of Sand Bar Ferry Lane forked away from the once-upon-a-time trail to Fort Gordon. He teetered the bundle on top of the marker, "This had to be the last place it was buried." Like the face of some long lost love, he gazed at the moldy thing touched by the slip of centuries gone.

Johnny said, "What is it?" bent closer for another look.

"Doubt you'd understand if I explained."

It was more the way the man said it than what he said that Johnny didn't like. "Where's my money?"

"Right here." He reached inside his jacket.

In one swift move the man's hand came up, the knife firm-gripped, and plunged it to the hilt up and under Johnny's ribs. Johnny's shifty sea-blue eyes slammed open. His mouth gaped at the dull fuzzy buzz between his ears. The hand with the knife steadied. The other hand grabbed Johnny's shoulder as he levered the blade sidewise and deeper into Johnny's chest.

Johnny's chest felt heavy, and he got sick to his stomach, like he was gonna throw up. Pain like he'd never felt before ate through him. He struggled to catch his breath. Sunlight glinted off his gritted teeth. Lips froze in a contorted silent scream. He sputtered a short grunt, his wildly thudding heart fluttering against the blade. His fist twisted in the man's jacket—the tighter he could hold the more it wouldn't matter. His knees weak, all he could see was the thin dingy lips right in front of his eyes. Couldn't get his breath. Sagged against the knife probing deep with a final inescapable kill-thrust. Johnny's breath spurted in bubbly gurgles, his blue eyes locked faraway beyond nothing while crimson froth slicked on his lips. The flooding weakness loosened his grip, and his ragdoll body slid away. With a gurgle he plopped to the ground onto his stomach.

With his hand still holding the knife, the man hauled the body onto its back, and yanked the red slurried blade out. Muscles in the unseeing face twitched. He hurried to his pickup where he'd left it up on the logging road, unlocked the carbon steel tool locker bolted to the truck bed, and pulled out the ragged mud-stained blankets and a stack of plastic contractors bags. He carefully wrapped the knife in the blankets, then double-wrapped with the plastic bags before hurrying back to the body. He ripped away the t-shirt. The proficient gash two ribs below the left nipple was the only blemish. He made his way the few yards to the river's edge to make sure no boats were moving his way from either bank. Satisfied, he went back to the body. With the knife he slashed and cut until what had been a body was chunks of meat stacked in the flat-bottom skiff hidden the day before in the brush at water's edge. It wasn't the first time he had gotten rid of a body like this, never to be found. It wouldn't be the last.

* * *

Purvis came into the kitchen where Janella and Emmett were working on cups of cut-rate coffee. He said, "C'mon, we gotta go."

In his slow dull-eyed drawl shirtless Emmett said, "Whut?" He smelled of unwashed sweat.

"Your buddy Johnny's got something he wants us to do."

"Whut?" coffee cup empty. He grabbed someone's half empty beer from last night, and gulped it down.

"He said be sure to bring you."

"Gotta get my shirt." Emmett stumbled off to the bedroom where he scrambled through the bedclothes, Janella's panties, and the nightstand.

Janella yelled from the kitchen, "Your shirt's in here."

He looked under the bed, and rumpled through a pile of crumpled clothes, "Cain't find my underwear. May've not wore none. Gone commando."

Janella scratched an unshaved armpit. Called out to her husband, "Purvis, when y'all gonna be back?" Chugged another gulp of coffee.

Purvis said, "I got the red-eye shift tonight. Be morning before the next shift comes on duty."

Emmett clomped in, hopping on one foot as he pulled the second shoe onto a bare foot. "Where we going?"

"Pick up some stuff," Purvis said. "C'mon, we're wastin' daylight. We're takin' the SUV."

Out front Emmett said, "Why ain't we takin' the patrol car?"

"Carter needs it for later."

Emmett smirked, "I like turnin' on them fishbowl blue lights, goin' fast through the middle of town."

"You like any toys long as someone else buys 'em."

Emmett sucked at something caught in his teeth, then let his tongue play with what was left of a piece of pickle or something from the guacamole dip. As they headed across the Beech Island Bridge into Georgia, Emmett asked again, "Where we going?"

"Some bags to pick up," Purvis mumbled without giving Emmett a look.

"Whut?"

"Stuff," as Purvis turned onto the loop onto Dean's Bridge Road.

Emmett puzzled, "You going to Gate Five at the Fort?"

"Sort of but not to Gate Five."

"Whut?"

"I told you we had some stuff to pick up." Purvis's voice was edgy. "Buddy's got too much to load hisself. Needs some help."

"Buddy?"

13

"You met him at the trailer last weekend. That high school kid."

"Yeh," Emmett couldn't make a face come to mind. "High school kid."

"You ain't so dry behind the ears yourself."

Emmett bragged, "I'm way older than that stump-dumb football player."

"The kid ain't no football player. He just hangs around the gym so he can say he's part of the team. And I don't need no attitude from you about it." Purvis didn't care if Emmett liked Buddy or not. There was the job needed doing, and the extra hands would make it go better. "We can use snot-nose Buddy. He's a pipeline to his team buddies." He side-glanced at Emmett with a no-smile smirk, "It's like any business. Invest a little now, in a year we'll have high school teams in this whole area supplying through us." His smirk became a big grin, "Seniors graduate, and that'll feed us right into the college crowd across both states. Don't tell me you'd turn down that kind of money 'cause I'll tell you you're lying."

Emmett was silent as they drove past the Gate Five turnoff. Continued south until they crossed the Brier Creek county line dirt road toward the rugged bugs-and-varmints training areas of Fort Gordon. "Whut's down this way?"

"You always ask your top-kick sergeant so many questions?"

"Only way to make sure he could tell I was okay with pulling extra details."

"Gonna meet a buddy down this road. He needs help. He's waiting for us at a storage barn down this road."

They passed the empty house; drove till there was nothing except underbrush, scrub oaks, wild blackberries and scuppernong tangles. The red-clay road forked. The truck turned right.

Emmett glanced at Purvis, "Why we on the backside of the Fort? Nothin' out this way except scrub pine and pulp wood. 'Sides, I don't cotton to crossin' paths again with them MP patrols keeping their eyes on these fire-breaks." Emmett rubbed his jaw, remembering how long his back had ached that time they had to unload that convoy of supply trucks.

"Long as we're on this road, we're not on Fort Gordon. You ought'a learn not to mess with MPs and to keep your mouth shut.

Askin' dumb questions that ain't none of your business is never a good idea. Won't take us long in the barn." Purvis turned where there didn't look to be a road. Pulled the SUV up to a barn back off from the dirt trail. A new black sporty model, different from the one Buddy had been driving the week before, was parked hidden under the trees.

"That must be the new car Buddy's daddy give him. Wish I had a daddy buying me new cars," Emmett said.

"I'll bet you do," Purvis grunted.

In his hip-hugging designer jeans and cut-off sweatshirt, high school pretend-quarterback Buddy Raymond strutted out of the barn. Mister look-casual said, "What's he doing here?"

"Someone else Janella likes to party with," Purvis said. "And that's none'a your business. Where'd you get the idea you was the only one?"

Buddy looked Emmett up and down, "He gonna help us?"

Purvis didn't waste time. Asked Buddy, "Where's the load?"

Buddy said, "Nobody told me there was gonna be a delivery."

Buddy's attitude pissed off Purvis big time. "Cain't depend on nobody doin' the job right. If I left everything up to you hotshots, we'd be empty-handed and neck-deep in crap."

Purvis grabbed up a satchel from the backseat. Slung it over his shoulder, and stomped off into the barn. He heaved his gutty beer-belly up the ladder to the hay loft. "Why should anyone tell you? Your daddy always takes care of it for you." He swung himself into the loft; ducked to avoid the low-peaked rafters. Purvis called down to the two of them, "Come on up... you, too, Emmett."

Buddy scowled and followed Emmett up the ladder. In the loft Emmett looked around, "Ain't no packages delivered up here. Where is it?" He walked over to the wide square hole in the floor, leaning over and down into the empty hay manger below.

A matter-of-fact Purvis said, "Right here."

A startled Emmett frowned, "What's the gun for?" A dull sense of fear weaseled through Buddy's brain.

"Making sure you two do as I say," Purvis said with a sullen no-smile. He turned his cold-steel look on Emmett, "Shut up and do as I say, and throw that rope over the rafter."

15

A muddled Emmett, unsure about what all was going on, tossed the coil of rope like Purvis said do.

Purvis glanced at Buddy. "For a wannabe football player you sometimes talk too much, too."

Buddy swallowed, "I ain't said nothin'."

"Yeh... sure," Purvis mimicked Buddy's mousy attitude. He tested the rope, then tossed plastic wrist ties to Buddy, "Tie his wrists behind him."

His tongue dry, Buddy frowned; licked his lips, "What?"

"Goddammit! Do what I said do! And make sure it's done good." Buddy hurried with the ties. Yanked them tight around Emmett's crossed wrists.

Emmett looked at Purvis, "That hurts."

Purvis pulled the video camera out of the knapsack, "Have us a little fun. You know, fun? Sort'a the same kind like we have with Janella but different." Tossed Buddy the knife, "Cut his shirt off." When Buddy dawdled about doing it, Purvis yelled, "Cut it off! I have to tell you how to do everything?"

Purvis pushed nose-to-nose with Emmett, "You like playing at the big stud when the camera's on?" He ripped pieces of Emmett's shirt away, and said to Buddy, "Get rid of his pants. Cut 'em off."

Buddy shaking, "His pants?"

Purvis growled, "Pants and shoes... get him bare-ass. Janella don't like you young ones wearing shorts. She says it takes too long to get you ready to be stars." He sneered a cheerless grin and put the camera up to his eye; adjusted the focus.

As Buddy started slicing pockets and waistband, fear-shivers squirreled Emmett's chest, belly and wobbly knees. He tried to swallow sticky spit. Buddy saw Purvis was filming him cutting away Emmett's pants. "I never done nothing like this." He wasn't sure what Purvis was up to, but he sure didn't want to make him mad. He glanced at a naked bound Emmett.

Purvis prodded Emmett with his finger, "You ever tie up anybody?" Emmett whimpered; shook his head. Purvis threw a fevered look at Buddy, "Think what a star quarterback this could make you with the football team. Put this on the net. Make all kinds of money selling it."

Buddy freaked out a half-snivel, "You cain't tell my father," worried how his friends would for sure talk if they saw him doing this. Everybody looking at him. Could hear his dad yellin', "Ruining the family's reputation." Buddy never let on how he knew about his dad keeping a sweet young piece on the side.

Purvis jeered, "What's daddy gonna do? Not buy you another new sports car? Call the cops? More'n likely he'll get a private copy for hisself. You are one stupid shithead. Whole school knows what a kiss-ass you are."

Buddy paled. Except for a here-and-there muscle twitch Buddy didn't move.

For a big man Purvis moved quick. Rough fists grabbed Buddy, as Purvis yanked him right up into his face, "Don't turn gutless with me! Daddy cain't help you here. You do what I say, or I'll knock some punk-sense into that witless excuse you use for a brain."

Emmett uttered a spittled whimper, "Purvis, this is nuts."

Purvis pushed him away, re-focused the camera. "Ain't it fun?"

Buddy, bug-eyed, felt like he was about to shit. With a shaky breath he tried again, "Aw, man... " His gut ached and he knew he was about to piss his pants.

Purvis snarled a cuss-spit as his fist clenched fury-tight sprawled Buddy in a tangled heap in the corner of the loft, "I ain't havin' no snivelin'." He enjoyed seeing pain on Buddy's face. It was the same feeling he got locking up smartasses and bouncing them off the cell bars. In bed with Janella after times like that, he bored into her real good. Purvis hiked his crotch—after this workout he'd do her double good. From his throat came an animal sound somewhere between a blood-growl and a gut-deep howl.

Emmett groaned. His wrists were slick with blood dribbles; his shoulders ached from being twisted and crooked tight.

Purvis reached and grabbed Emmett by the hair, "Quit whining like some lowlife... that's all you're good at anyhow. We don't want our little party to end too soon."

Buddy's mouth gawked open and his eyes squinted for any easy getaway. "You ain't making no video," truly sure he didn't want to know nothin' more about none'a this. He huddled in a half-curl, half-sit against the wall. Buddy was afraid—like it was all happening in slow motion.

Purvis walked behind Emmett, "This'll make the best fuckin' snuff scene I ever done." Fist gripped harder. Choked Emmett. Until Emmett's neck bulged. Purvis felt the thick neck pipes of blood pulse against his fingers. Shoved himself away from Emmett like he was throwing away trash. Purvis picked up one end of the rope dangling over the rafter and looped one end into a noose, snugging the coil tight.

Buddy whimpered, "What you doing?" Crouched tighter into the corner.

"Have us some fun." Purvis stepped toward Emmett. Emmett arched his body away from the man. "Be still." Moved behind Emmett. "I told you to be still." Dropped the noose over Emmett's head and worked with it until he got the angle like he wanted it, snugged up against the side of Emmett's neck.

Emmett twisted and yanked harder, trying to breath.

"Taking care of unfinished business," said Purvis, and he shoved Emmett's feet off the board at the edge of the loft.

The body toppled. The length of rope snapped tight, but it wasn't a quick snap-kill. Emmett opened his mouth as his jaw jerked open, then closed, but no sound came out. His body lurched as his legs spasmed and his eyes bulged. His fingers clawed, then clenched, as his face contorted and his lips turned blue, then became darker.

Purvis stood at the edge of the loft looking down at the convulsing body-becoming-a-corpse. The body swung slowly back and forth, turning lazy circles at the end of the rope. The head canted at a funny angle from the neck while facial muscles twitched here and there on the frozen expression. Purvis yelled at Buddy, "Come watch this," always more sideline onlooker than doer.

Afraid not to do what Purvis wanted, Buddy's knees quivered as he inched forward, looked down; eyes frozen on the slow swing of Emmett's body. He couldn't make himself turn away while all around him dappled shadows of rippled sunlight stabbed through holes in the wind-torn roof shingles.

"He won't be givin' us no more trouble." Purvis put his arm around Buddy's shoulder, "Problem solved." He pulled some gloves from his pocket and slipped them on. "Powder makes good prints." Then he reached down and lifted a single kilo bag out of the camera's carrying case.

"What's that?"

"Emmett's favorite pastime."

Buddy choked, "That coke?" Glanced back and forth between Purvis and the bag.

"It ain't powdered sugar—uncut too." Purvis held up the bag to give Buddy a closer look. "Saving the good stuff back in the SUV. The kind you're into—crystal ice." He carefully kneaded the bag for any lumps. "Leave something for the MPs to find."

"MPs?" Buddy'd heard Emmett talk about gorilla-enforcer MPs and all kinds of fun they had back in the stockades.

"This is federal property. Place will be crawling with MPs. You want to deal with them?"

"You leaving Emmett hanging here? For them to find?"

Purvis tossed the shiny bag against the side of the barn, and watched it spatter into a white star burst on the worn floor boards below. He handed Buddy the knife, "Cut his wrists loose."

Buddy's trembling hand barely held the knife, "Skin bruises won't go away."

"This bein' federal property, feds'll be all over the place. He knocked his hands together to dust the gloves, "... stuff sticks ever'where," and pulled a crumpled paper from his vest pocket. "Leave them this suicide note right up here to find with all this white. Give them a ready-made motive of a drug buy gone bad and finding a two-bit piece of shit swinging at the end of a rope with his wrists showing bruises. They'll spend days tracking all manner of their own dead ends. All kind'a fingerprints around here—not mine. Even with this note you can bet they won't call it a suicide, but they sure as hell won't get no further than that. Lots of soldiers at the Fort into fun-stuff like this piece of shit hanging here. Why work up a sweat? Let them haul the garbage."

"Why you leavin' a note?"

Purvis uncrinkled the paper, pulling down two dirt daubers nests to hold it down so no breeze could blow it away. "Sometimes I think you're on stuff heavier than that piece at the end of the rope yonder. Leave 'em something to puzzle over. Go on, read it."

Buddy could barely make out the scribbled words. *Why go on? I've had fun. Nothing to live for.*

Purvis moved quicker than quick. He hit him hard, and Buddy dropped like a moss-covered rock. Buddy'd never seen it coming. Purvis pulled out a short leather cord from the camera bag and knotted each end around wooden handholds. Then he bent down and ripped a jagged tear in the sweatshirt, "Perfect finish to a sour deal; this package of shit over and done with." Buddy groaned. Purvis got behind him; pulled the leather cord around Buddy's neck. Crisscrossed the garrote and throttled it tight below the back of Buddy's ear till it buried into the flesh; then braced his knuckles at the base of Buddy's skull and twisted tighter until the tendons in his arms corded. For a moment Buddy's fingers fought to his throat; body convulsed; thighs arched, and heels dug across the boards. One shoe rolled to the side as bubbly spittle frothed the mouth. The body loosened slack, then slumped to a heap.

Purvis grit his jaw, his face tight next to Buddy's ear. He favored the rope. The knife wasn't bad, but it was messy; the gun too loud. Got a kick out of the personal touch. Felt the dying body relax. Doing this one turned him on even more. Was like hunting season. Snickered—Janella was gonna get it good. He'd take her to Mother's Bar early, or maybe one of their other places. Pick up some fresh meat. Make it a good 'un.

His heart thumped hard, "Messing in business, asking questions." Flexed his hands into fists, "Running your mouths. You two won't be doin' none'a that no more." He liked the thrill of power-of-life-and-death. He shoved Emmett's body away from him and looked at it. "You two'll make the usual official report. Soldier out for a weekend of fun and skin with all the nose-candy he could snort. Come back to Mother Army to end it." He spit on the floor, "You snot-nosed kids talk a lot... never say nothin' worth hearing," and wiped his mouth with the back of a sweaty hand.

Chapter 2

In the warm spring morning shade of the porch the cool breeze off the river made it seem cooler than it was. Humidity hadn't gotten to the coming summer's dog days, but the South Carolina river bottom was working on gettin' there. Stretched out, Craige Ingram straddled back onto the swing and ruffled fingers through russet brown curls still damp from his early sunrise skinny-dip off the dock. Idly, he gave a scratch to his German shepherd's ear. He should've known it was trouble the instant his German shepherd's ears perked with a muffled low growl warning. Lucky stood up, the gold-brown hair at the nape of his neck bristled straight. Lucky whined a glance at Craige, and gave another low growl.

Craige sat up. His pale-emerald Norman deWorthe eyes turned in the direction Lucky was fixed on while one finger held his place between the worn pages of a reference book on ancient Egyptian mythologies. He enjoyed his amateur archeologist hobby, but had backed into Egyptian mythologies while on another case. Even more so after he snapped up riverfront sections adjacent to Moccasin Hollow, Grannie Ingram's land grant home place that had become more than just a dogtrot remodeled home. Moccasin Hollow sheltered his heart and soul.

He'd found Lucky as a highway-abandoned pup. It didn't take him long to notice how quick the dog picked up hand signals and verbal commands, even to the point where Lucky seemed to anticipate what Craige wanted. Craige reached over; scratched the dog's ear, "Lucky, you hear something you don't like?"

Craige slid the opened book off his lap onto the swing, and stood. Lucky gave a low whine, and pulled away to the edge of the porch.

He glanced at Craige, then pinned his eyes through the trees toward the private drive that meandered a curve from Silver Bluff River Road toward the Moccasin Hollow main house. Lucky grew less agitated; stared a bit, and the ears came down as he nosed Craige's hand for more scratching. When he didn't get it, he laid his head back down onto the wide cypress plank flooring of the porch and rolled his eyes up at Craige.

"Bad dog... " Craige's you-dun-good. It was a bad-dog good thing between the two of them. Lucky thumped his tail twice; grunted contentedly.

Craige picked up the book. Ankles crossed, he propped his legs up on the split-rail bannister, one hand idling across his bare chest. His fishing pole was propped behind him next to the screen door. He caught the engine noise of the pickup, recognized it from the puttered sput of a cylinder out of timing, and watched it ease through one shallow rain-filled puddle. Same as last time, Crawforde had come to let him know he was on the hunt again.

First time the quiet-spoken Crawforde showed up, he had introduced himself right off, "Effington Crawforde." Stuck out his hand for a shake, "Friends call me Eff or Crawforde. I'm with the Archaeologia International, North American Division. One of too few, I might add."

In all of Craige's travels and plane-hopping, piloting his private jet, SpecOps Rest and Recuperation, or as an extra pair of hands at various digs from the upper Euphrates and Turkey or South America, before their first meet that day he'd never heard of Archaeologia International.

Craige asked, "And how does that involve Moccasin Hollow land?"

"I make my home in Newberry," Crawforde said. "Ostensibly my research involves the pre-colonial Indian cultures of what was upstate Georgia and Carolina territories."

"Ostensibly?" Craige's question was subdued while he held Crawforde with a steady-on studied look.

Crawforde added a dozy, "My research is serving a double purpose."

A penchant of the covert flooded through Craige. "Which implies your research is a cover." He'd been on his fair share of restricted assignments, but didn't cotton to how this was being laid out, or the fact that his question still hadn't been answered. "More important is exactly *how* your purposes involve Moccasin Hollow properties?"

"For a problem the US and Canada are trying to stop. Ongoing state surveys of Indian burial sites nationwide have focused particular emphasis in the gulf coast south and southeast Atlantic states."

"And this problem?"

Crawforde said, "Artifacts plundered from the sites of indigenous cultures. A problem that's gotten worse after floods undermined or washed open several of the sites."

It was the sort of hunt Craige heartily approved of, yet he didn't know anything about this individual. "There are some sites on my land," Craige said. "Some show signs of being dug in, but not if I know about it. I don't allow it."

"I was volunteered for the follow-up surveys, and to GPS-map the locations. It's the same old story... too few to police an increasing traffic in looted artifacts." He pulled the GPS scanner from his satchel, "Enter the locations; then download it to master files, mostly to state archives. These are the locations we've already marked from previous surveys."

Craige studied the GPS grid. "They're scattered in several clusters. No roads, but there are some old logging road shortcuts I can show you."

With the GPS grid it took Craige several hours through Moccasin Hollow backwoods and sloughs along uplands and the river where Crawforde's map showed some sites. Most were mounded heaps of oyster shell middens. Craige coasted his jeep to a stop, "This is one of the latest dig-holes I come upon."

"You trained in archeology?"

"I happen to have friends who are experienced archeologists, and very patient with my amateur digging. It's one of my hobbies." Craige looked around at the scattered bits and pieces, some not so small. It set his grit on edge all over again. He'd seen human bones before. Trespassing pissed him off—random vandalism tightened his attitude even more. He forced his annoyance into the shadows. "I can't say I haven't seen it before—in more than a few countries."

Crawforde said, "I wish I could say this was an isolated incident," fingers worrying in the fuzz of his stubby white goatee. "Some sites are worse upriver, totally destroyed. On private land before the lock and dam was built. Now they're islands. Owners tried to protect the mounds. Swore out warrants; pressed charges. Grave sites were still looted; provenance lost with little hope of salvaging any archeological etymos."

"Etymos... etumon... from Greek. Truth, true, actual." A trace of the ironic crossed Craige's face, "It's been years since I've heard anyone from the states use a word in its ancient meaning. From times before Imperial Rome... history has its place." Craige's thoughts drifted to some faraway nice place away from the savage and the callous indifference of heritage. His Cherokee blood coursed hot through Grannie's kin and more than a few creek-cousin kith. "It comes down to money. Not about what they are... just their price. "I catch anyone messing around where they're not supposed to be, I'll handle the situation. Gunny-sack 'em for the local constabulary." He glowered at several recent holes, "Money's no excuse for this sort of destruction."

Crawforde said, "Big money in artifacts—the older the better."

"It's been going on long before the pharaohs," Craige choked down his kneejerk-disgust. "The tomb trade is very lucrative with more than a few serious confrontations... Egypt, Turkey, the Middle East, looting in South America, around the Mediterranean."

Crawforde said, "No respect for the dead and even less for whose land they're on." He gave a nod at the burial sites, "Artifacts go into private collections—collectors pay big bucks. It's a profitable market."

"Money drives a lot of things with plenty dirt to go around, and will never be different." Craige refused to let it make him cynical, left him with an icy loathing, "Specially when those doing the selling or buying hide behind a fat payoff destroy an Indian burials the lands of their ancestors." His words trailed as he tried to soothe his Cherokee stirrings. "Our colonial migrations and land-grabs that went with it share major responsibilities for what took place. For the most part good folks try to live peaceful lives; pay their taxes and their traffic tickets. But ask them if they'd give up their homes and farms so Indians could get back some of what was theirs—the situation right quick can jump to hostile." He reflected on Ingram lands—Grannie's South Carolina land grant and their kin's Ingram holdings in Georgia and their Norman French and Scandia *nordmann* forebearers. The blood and sweat-soaked lives and hard work it took. "Same thing we did to Japanese Americans after Pearl Harbor." His words sounded brittle as they tromped along more old logging roads and flooded backwaters to more sites Craige knew about. "Destroyed whole ways of culture. About finished the job conquistadors started with the diseases they introduced."

"We don't have enough field agents," Crawforde sighed. "Not nearly the numbers to oversee the whole of the Carolinas and Georgia sites that we know about. Not to mention the ones that go unreported."

Craige said, "I don't like thinking about sites we don't know about or haven't been cataloged."

Crawforde said, "Be more useful if you got deputized and watched your own land. With eyes-on you'll spot a problem a lot sooner. Watch your backside, though. Treasure hunters outside the law can be dangerous."

Craige knew that only too well. By the next day he'd made a sectioned diagram of Ingram properties and added rotating times for regular checks. Found two new digs in less than a week. It would be simple to put sections with Indian mounds into a trust to the University Institute of Archaeology and Anthropology in Columbia. But, he knew it would be a scrap of pointless paper without the warm bodies to oversee enforcement.

* * *

Crawforde's visit had left Craige ill-at-ease. He recalled tales of his Georgia ancestors from decades long gone and that first Moccasin Hollow. His eyes threaded aimless. Imagined virgin Spanish moss-swathed bald cypress standing guard along the shores and back in the wetlands amid century-old hundred-fifty-foot longleaf pines, sprawled swamp magnolias and great Southron live oaks, all from the good fortune of having acquired the undeveloped sections adjoining Grannie's original grant, one section holding her gravesite. He couldn't deny the unfading Southron in him—land was everything. This land gave him refuge—a place called home with deep roots for Grannie and her orphaned young gran'son. It was Moccasin Hollow that provided a safe harbor after the murder that took his parents. Grannie was his family. With Craige, family roots went way deep.

Long-ago after-supper times in the evening summer-cool, him and Grannie on the porch swing and Grannie telling him, "Was maybe one'a your great-aunts that lived somewhere down around Louisville, Georgia. Some place down the dirt road that run by a creek. Was a place near Galphin's Mill near Queensborough Town. Married a Greer. Leastwise I think it was a Greer. Never could be sure about some of that fiddle-faddle 'twixt a man an' his sweetie. Git the urge, things jus' happen."

Good memories were worth having, but looking back one could see twenty-twenty hindsight plainer than when it was happening. Craige had come by a bloodline that was full-charged bullheaded and obstinate. His parents' death probably saved him from being one more arrogant wasted street fighter or a bronzed surf-an'-sex beach bum. California had promised a fun life without mentioning dangerous undertow rip currents. Moccasin Hollow and Grannie promised something else. The growing-up years with a loving Grannie sometimes left piecemeal glimpses of what could've been wasted. Grannie intended otherwise. He could see the years with iron-SEAL BUD School being the beginnings of icing on the cake. He grew into the slow move of life of Grannie's Carolina upcountry, and became part of the huntin', fishin', running in Grannie's world. It would never leave him.

Through kitchen windows, out on the porch, in the yard, or him fishing at the yard-edge of the deceptively lazy slosh of the Savanno River's ebb and flow, Grannie'd often watch her *Peadinger* gran'son. Her yonder-river had baptized him, and seeped into the flesh and blood of him the makings of a can-do man. It gave his soul a good soaking, but didn't get rid of an Ingram sureness most folks read as arrogance. It wasn't. Granny had a ramrod backbone that buckled down on her strong-willed *Peadinger*. She'd send him to his corner if he didn't get his schoolwork done like she knew he could. Whup his skinny butt when he sassed or wasn't polite with respect.

After a switchin' across his legs she'd pull him onto her lap, and rock him gentle-like, "Grannie don't like what you done, but Grannie stills loves her Peadinger." Rock him some more. He loved his Grannie.

As he got into his teens, Grannie kept her eye on this special gangly chil' of her South. She taught him practical figures and writing before the first grade. When he took up math courses in high school and two college level courses in the eleventh grade, she knew what she needed to get done. One of her best friends she'd growed up with was the gran'ma of one South Carolina senator. Went to church with their whole fambly.

After one Sunday sermon Grannie cornered him in his pew and asked his opinion. "His grades be good. Don't hardly take no proddin' to git at 'em. He's good with figures and that high-level math."

The senator put his arm around Grannie Ingram's shoulder, "Wish all kids had a grandmother who looked out for them. I'm more'n glad to help."

"If'n it'll help some, his father was a veteran," Grannie made sure to mention.

The senator said, "That'll give him a leg up when he applies to any of the military academies."

When they got home from the Sunday dinner on the ground, she said, "Got somethin' serious I been thinkin' on. You done good with your studies. After you finish high school I ain't havin' you sittin' on your hind end on the river bank fishin' away your life."

Peadinger said, "I like fishin'."

"Goin' fishin' is a good way to stay close and keep the calm about you, but you got a good brain in that thick head of yours. Might cost a tad bit of money, but if it comes to a have-to, I'll sell some pieces of land for your tuition." She told him about her talk with the senator. "He gimme some papers I want you to think on."

Craige read the papers and thought serious and hard on it for a goodly number of days until he made up his mind. He wasn't about to let Grannie sell her sweat-and-work land. He filled out two applications; got a Presidential nomination, and one day a letter arrived in the mail—an appointment to Annapolis. It wasn't his only letter. The senator had egged young Craige to apply to the all the academies. He also got accepted to the Air Force Academy in Colorado Springs. He chose the Naval Academy. Big engines or fast airplanes had never held much interest for him.

Grannie once watched him doin' homework, "All them figures an' scribbles sure don't make sense to me."

"It's just another kind of language," he'd said.

Craige knew he had a lot to learn; he could get lost in some of the advance math theories. Then he got interested in computer programming and computer science and engineering during his senior high school year. He took some college equivalency courses, and was exempted from a few required courses at the Academy. For Craige, Annapolis became a whole other world—a sort-of shock. It wasn't laid-back Moccasin Hollow except for some of the hard-work stuff. And it wasn't just Plebe Summer or the isolation; he'd grown up solitary. More like, it was the mindless regimen for the sake of regimen. *Tear 'em down to build 'em up* didn't quite make sense, but one lesson he did learn his Plebe Summer... regimen and gold stripes sure 'nough mattered to the gold-sheathed icons that marshaled midshipmen attitudes. Craige made sure Grannie got copies of his grades so she'd know he was keeping up his scores. He knew how proud it would make her. It did.

The last time he saw Grannie, she didn't mention she'd been feelin' poorly. His having her grave dug and readied at exactly where she once said she wanted, and the awfulness of seeing her coffin sink into the ground covered with the earth of Moccasin Hollow jolted Craige's world into jagged shards. That day became a crinkled calendar he never got rid of. In the upheaval betwixt his ears, he couldn't sleep. Grannie's Peadinger made a cronk-side decision. His grades tumbled.

Grannie's caution would echo over the what-ifs he stumbled through—"Never do any decidin' if'n a body's upset."

It wasn't the first or the last time Ingram doggedness snatched his backside from a bad choice and a considerable more growing up to teach him to straighten up. It was a twilight beginning of a good learn, but it was slow and dogged to come.

Right before Plebe year Christmas break he made an appointment. Wearing a crease-perfect uniform, carrying a certified copy of his top-ten transcript, he arrived on the marked time in the Commandant's office, fresh shorn and spit-shined. He withdrew from the U.S. Naval Academy.

"This is a step that will affect the rest of your life," the Commandant said. "You sure you want to do this?" he asked, as he read the steel behind green Ingram eyes.

"The Midshipman is sure, sir."

"You're not obligated to volunteer for active duty till the end of this year."

At rigid attention, "Yes—sir."

"At ease, Midshipman."

"Yes, sir," Craige snapped to a sharp-practiced parade rest.

"And you want to volunteer anyway?"

"Yes—sir. Active duty, sir," eyes locked to a spot on the wall behind the Commandant's head.

"Why?" The Commandant scanned the midshipman's academics, extracurricular sports, instructor evals.

"Because... sir," Craige faltered.

"An outstanding record. Family problems?" He'd seen it before.

Craige screwed down on the upwell of emotion. The hurt fresh all over again with an unnamable ache worse than her funeral. "Sort of, sir."

"Anything we might help you with?" He read the emotions across this Midshipman's face.

"Nothing, sir."

"You haven't answered why you want to withdraw," the Commandant stated with a puzzled frown. "It will be my recommendation whether your request is approved."

Craige blinked several times—prying at feelings buried innards deep. He took a deep breath, "Education, sir. My grades aren't what I want them to be... sir."

With a slight frown, "Midshipman, you're in one of the best universities... with opportunities that can change your future."

"Yes, sir."

"Opportunities you aren't yet aware of or know about."

"Sir, the US Naval Academy is one of the best," words right off a recruiting poster. "But it isn't for me, sir." His straight honest words were from an eighteen-year-old heart full of jumbles.

"You have the rest of this week to think about it. Tell my secretary to set you up an appointment with me next Monday... fourteen hundred hours."

"Yes, sir."

Craige didn't change his mind. The Commandant signed the request. Midshipman Ingram was issued temporary orders until five weeks later when he reported aboard Recruit Training Command, Naval Station Great Lakes. Seaman Ingram made top squad leader in boot camp. On Pass-in-Review Recruit graduation he got his pick of schools for the advanced training and took extra credit courses for his bachelor's program. After he finished his master's in satellite surveillance programming, he received his officer's commission and promotion from ensign to lieutenant junior grade.

Craige's grown-up-with-like-a-brother from first-grade-through-high-school teammate Graysen *Graystone* MacGerald had enlisted about the same time Craige left the Naval Academy. "Can't let you hog all the fun. Strut around in your white uniform, and get all the attention from the lookers in the ports we visit."

It wasn't quite like that. The two of them joined the SEALs, Special Warfare Combatant. Craige could see Grannie smile from way back in Moccasin Hollow... Peadinger done it again and done it his own unyielding way. Backed into something he really come to like.

Lieutenant Ingram didn't know it, but his academy records and college degree programs got spotlight-attention of the Office of Naval Intelligence—as well as several other spook-setups keeping track of his progress—ONI wasn't Uncle Sam's only sniff-and-lurk gang.

In meetings with endless pots of coffee and conference tables of brass and bigger brass, the message was the same: "He's got a mind of his own. Don't give him a job unless you want him to run with it."

Naval Special Warfare Preparatory School Great Lakes came next. Somebody was watching INGRAM, Craige H. G. R., making sure South Carolina Ingram was serious enough to not pull another US Naval Academy dropout. He and Gray soon became known as an indestructible resilient navy twosome. They received their orders along with a one-way ticket on a commercial flight to California—Naval Special Warfare Training Center Coronado, the training phases of BUD/S, and the Navy SEAL Trident insignia.

Craige thought his next set of orders looked lean, and to him they seemed vague. No port or naval facility, only a name and address of a never-heard-of mining barge company. He asked Gray, "Where's your orders for?"

Gray did a quick glance at the unofficial looking header on Craige's originals, "Sure not the same place. Guess this is where we part. We gotta keep in touch... take our leave at the same time so we can do some fishing back home."

The address on Craige's orders was simple, no letterhead. A number on a dilapidated street with a warehouse-looking exterior that needed scraping and lots of paint. No flag, no signs—no street name—one of Craige's initial experiences with no-paper-trails, hush-hush covert moves well underway. He tried the door. It was locked. He knocked. It surprised Craige when it immediately opened.

A hand reached forward, and a curt voice ordered, "Originals." The man took Craige's paperwork. "Been expecting you, and your security clearances are revised to date." He slammed-locked the thick steel-reinforced door behind Craige, "Your plane was late. Skewed our schedules; we're behind our jump-off time." He quickly eyeballed the pertinent part of the orders before shoving the papers into a wrist-locked worn briefcase; snapped it smartly shut—all-business no-insignia no-expression, "Welcome to the SWATH unit. Follow me."

The two made their way down a long derelict ramshackle corridor. To Craige it was the most broken-down excuse for a warehouse he'd ever been in, including abandoned river-docks he and Gray had poked through. It was—from the outside. US Navy newbie-Ingram was face-to-face with a taste of the covert. Intro to SpecOps would come later, and be buried a whole lot deeper. One of Grannie's *sure 'noughs* flashed his thoughts—laid-back Moccasin Hollow turkey stalkin' done been shoved on the back burner. One slip of a snapped branch and the gobbler faded into the scrub. Derelict as it looked, the corridor deck was swept clear. Craige was hooked on thoughts of cleaning away a few SOB conspiracies and leaving the world a better place.

There were weeks of more one-on-one encounter exercises, unceasing surveillance twists and double-blind encryption. His in-house hole-and-corner honed with the latest tools of the trade and a buds-only no-hoopla recognition, Craige was ordered to put his CTUnit together. Gray was the first one he got on the wire.

* * *

Active duty days ended. Gray and Craige hotfooted home to river-town turfs, making sure they could keep in touch with their spook-buds. Grayson joined the local constabulary across the river with his usual hard-fair approach, by-the-book beat cop. Ever'body on the streets knew no-nonsense Graysen MacGerald.

Days became weeks. The edge of muggy heat fell some. Craige kept busy doing fix-ups and trash-prune clean-ups; reroofed the woodshed; finished chopping and stacking the last of the fireplace logs.

One early all-night morning, Craige took a long slow-sip of his sunrise steamy bilge-oil coffee, his arm snug around Terri. Their bare bodies entwined; quilt-wrapped on the porch swing in the chill river-fog nip of near-sunup.

Craige slowed another swallow, "You wore me plum tuckered out."

Terri's hand lay on his, "You're just recharging." Patted his stomach; played at the hairs around his bellybutton.

Craige said, "You keep up your home-cookin', it won't be long before it leaves me a gut from all this layin'-around good lovin'," licked the fresh dampness behind her ear.

Terri nuzzled her head against his shoulder. Soft raven curls trailed easy tickles across his shoulder and hairless chest; murmured, "Mmm... not a bad way to go."

Later in the afternoon-hot of the day they grabbed fishing poles which stayed in his flat-bottom skiff while they skinny-dipped. After more skin than dip they lazy fished; had fresh-baked blue gills for supper.

As they idled away the rest of summer's languid days, leaves of the sweet gum trees tinged with faint reds spattered with yellowish edges. Indian summer teased with near hot days that turned brisk at night.

Terri's hair glistened in the gold-greens of a coming sundown as she stuck her head out the back mudroom screen door, "You have a call; asked for you by name. He's on hold—wouldn't give me a name."

In the kitchen Craige grabbed a cold pale lager from the fridge and reached for the phone, "Ingram."

"Howie?"

Hearing his SEAL panhandle he'd borrowed from the Howelle branch of the Ingram family tree, his mind shuffled faces. Knuckles white on the phone, Craige was more than wary-curious about the distant-familiar voice. Nobody called him that except passing unfamiliar familiars who couldn't take a hint. "Speaking." Had learned straight from Grannie to hold back when he had only bits and pieces of the unexpected. The familiar voice snapped a name to the face. *Elbow-licker* was Craige's cleaned-up understatement for what he knew about this one.

"Alpsworth Bailey... the Third."

Craige's attitude was lock-step stark, "... Bailey." Bailey's self-centered denseness grated at Craige the first time he met him. Whether it was Alpsworth Bailey the Second or Third or Fourth didn't matter to Craige. He was a lieutenant the last time Craige had seen him. Odds were he'd been promoted, middle management usually was. The sour taste of Washington City and backroom shenanigans stung Craige's memories. Covered their ass; made sure one another and their offspring raked in the *crème de la crème* plumbs. Never tried to bury uniforms and bureaucrats who didn't give a shit about those in their command or the taxpayer money they tossed around in bundles. Fragging incidents had more behind them than the personal.

With your SEAL buds, those at your elbow had your back. If death harvested among them, they grieved; packed their feelings deep-down and got on with it. Craige took one of his slow-down breaths. Sidled on his PI mantle. Hair-triggers weren't going to change the world—or Alpsworth the Third. He had worked with Bailey only twice, the last time for a Joint Chiefs' Pentagon Think Tank on high-resolution surveillance for the offshore islands and coastlines.

The Third said, "Figured you'd recognize my voice."

"How'd you find me?" Craige never told Bailey his SEAL panhandle.

"It wasn't easy."

"But you know someone, and they owed you a favor." Craige let the silence get uncomfortable. Bailey wanted something.

Bailey sputtered, "You still there?" Ingram had hung up on him before.

Craige meant to make Mister Pretentious uneasy; put him on the defensive. "Still here."

"Well... " Bailey cleared his throat. "I gather you know this isn't a social call."

"You were never one for social calls unless you wanted someone to do something without anyone knowing your face was behind it."

Bailey tried to hide his discomfort, glad he was on the phone and not face-to-face. He'd witnessed the unpredictable, when Ingram didn't like the way things were played. "I need serious help."

Craige wanted to say how Bailey always needed serious help. "You always bite onto half-truths when your butt's in a tight spot." He couldn't help being curious about what kind of shit Bailey wanted to hide from."

"Can we meet?"

Craige said, "What's this about?" He wasn't inclined to help, and certainly not with Bailey's hem-and-haw.

"AWOL."

"Army?" Craige glanced at his caller ID. Warning flags flapped all over Craige's common-sense impulse to end this. "At the local fort?"

"Yes."

"I'm no longer active duty," didn't care about Third's problems. "Never dealt much with army green when I was."

Bailey needled, "Living the good life of a country squire?" He had always been jealous of Ingram's well-heeled pockets.

Craige surprised himself with a tinge akin to pity, "Something like that."

Bailey said, "So the two of us have had our misunderstandings."

Craige said, "Our *situations* were considerably more than any misunderstanding." Grannie's stiff-neck disapproval welled up inside his attitude.

"I'm into something the army doesn't want blown out of proportion."

Craige knew where that fit, "Which means something they don't want on the news. Preferably buried deep... way deep." He could tell Bailey was an inchworm away from his snivel-mode.

You've always had a sixth sense of the how and what ways to get things done."

"And your ways are reliably not *good ways*. Let's cut right to the bilge water. We've both worked with the desk jockeys and their minions on the Potomac. Their first choice is always the cover-up. Nothing new about that." Craige let the rawness blister through the phone lines. "What you're saying is, your boss—or more likely bosses—ordered you to take care of a complication and you don't know how to do it and cover your ass at the same time. Your bosses are sticking your butt in a hard place. Must be something outside Mother Army—involving civilians."

"Something like that," the voice quavered.

Craige cut right to the snag, "Civilians don't fall under the Uniform Code of Military Justice; that is, unless we're dealing with a felony on federal property. If that's not the case, what's this AWOL crap involving a civilian?" Craige felt discomforted about the real reason Bailey would go to the trouble of finding him. The Third must've had his or someone's staff, probably FBI, rustle through telephone companies to locate him. "My guess is you're prying around on some sneak assignment through channels restricted outside CONUS, and ones not legal inside the continental US." Craige's suspicions sprouted all manner of weeds. With CIA, FBI, blacker SpecOps stirring his thoughts, "You're worried you can't come up with solutions quick enough to suit your chain of command. Give me the facts—and don't assume I'm volunteering."

"Meet me in my office at the Fort. I'll fill you in on the details. It's a special assignment."

"Who'd you intimidate into giving you a special assignment?" Craige's suspicions were now in warp speed overdrive. "You involved? Covering some general whose son decided he didn't like scrubbing enlisted barracks floors. Figured daddy could get him out of it? Didn't work so went AWOL?"

"I can see country living hasn't dulled your tongue."

"You're dancing around the details and not saying anything." Craige wasn't about to let Bailey squirrel off the hook. "And while we're at it, we're not meeting in your bugged office."

"I don't have all the details," Bailey answered. "If I did, I wouldn't talk about it over the phone. Where can we meet?"

"Duke's... half past five tomorrow morning."

"What's the address?"

"Anyone in Augusta knows where it is. Do you good to get out of your gold-braid world and mix with the common folk. That is, if you're up to it." He put the phone down, his glance locking with Terri's gold-flecked mahogany eyes. "If he calls back, I'm out. Take Bailey a month to figure out anything simple," a low grating behind his words.

Chapter 3

Terri rolled onto her side, her face so close to his their noses whisper-touched. The bottomless yellow-flecked mahogany of her eyes caught the fierce emerald-swirl of his lidded half-asleep eyes. In their still, shaded-times between dusk and dawn, the set of his face said it all. Terri was at ease with the day-to-day quiet reserve of him. The ferocious unbridled temper that swam deep beneath seldom broke loose except for Ingram-reasons. When wound tight, the hairspring trigger could be quiet one moment, and a flash explosion the next.

He laid one arm across his eyes. Yawned. "I'm taking my voicemail off-line. Otherwise it'll be full of Bailey."

They lazed through early twilight flickers, their bodies interwoven to near daybreak. His whole body relaxed. Several interludes before the sun's clean orb peeked through the thick grey-green lavender-aroma wisteria to brush away the ground-misted bayous, he drifted off into a slaked slumber. Craige finally stretched his six two frame from an early morning toasty body-heat bed and eased his feet to the floor. Terri liked to snuggle—easing away from her arm across his belly didn't work. Chest and thighs goose bumped in the shock of chill.

She opened sleepy eyes in a hair-strewn face. "You going out so early... " her hand quietly stroked along his naked thigh. She relaxed her head back on the pillow, "Can't talk you into staying a bit longer?" Throaty enticement to the heat she knew he liked. She nuzzled down into the sheet; sniffed at the faint traces of his Sandalwood cologne and Vinolia shaving soap.

He reached over; gave a quick peck to her ear, "Staying around you could get a man in trouble."

"The kind of trouble you enjoy," stirring the smoldering gentleness of his eyes.

"Ingram men aim to please."

"Which you do so well." Like a temptress svelte leopardess she snuggled deeper into his aroma of the pillow.

He ran his fingers through her splayed tresses where his head had been on the pillow. The back of his fingers made the lightest of strokes along her neck, and nestled along its curve. He had often wondered what it was about this one that was different... about the way she held the core of his heart. Dressed in her guileless elegance but knockout stylishness or bare skin next to him in the flickers of the crackling fireplace—it didn't matter. No matter where they were, whether a quick glance or studied gaze, when Terri looked at him, an excitement seeped into his soul.

Wood-on wild shore leave raw beach rituals, twosomes or group gropes... Craige had been part of but never quite fit into hit-and-run; whip it out; whip it in; wipe it off, and grab his money clip and boxer briefs—if he'd worn any or couldn't find them. High school visceral-jockster postgame locker-room revelries of whichever naked-ready body was the closest, *not-who-but-who's-next* never baited him. Some bleary-eyed teammate's, "I'm gonna fuck this one's eyeballs out." He never understood the intrigue beyond "felt good" of barnyard hump-hump-and-wipe quickies with no warmness, and no connection with the other body.

Terri Wofford Stanley was from a faraway other universe. A widow with one son, he realized just how much she meant to him when they were almost killed in that hidden chamber—an old bank vault. The deepness she gave him swam through Craige's secluded core. It had from the first moment he saw her. Waking up next to her, or knowing it was her stirring the good smells out of the kitchen, left him with a tranquility eager to stretch and cozy back under the covers. Waiting for her to come for him was a tantalizing eagerness. Each of them was secure in the other, an unspoken commitment that suited them both, wallowing in this something that scoured away the troubled world. Early before-dawn breakfast or mid-dark picnics were often shared or grew cold on the plates.

He lightly touched her lips with his. If he did more they'd be in bed the rest of the whole lazy long day. Their tongues barely brushed. Her hand softly trailed behind his ear to hold his head, while the plump ripeness of a bare nipple peeping just above the sheet puckered between his lips. He could still feel where they'd hardened into his chest.

He whispered, "You taste good."

He loved playing with them, always with the wonder of them since the trucker's wife working the late shift at the Kwickie-9 Shop & Gas on the Charleston-Beaufort Road had shown fifteen-year-old paperboy Craige the delight of after-school afternooners. He didn't waste much time starting afternoon paper routes after that. Teachers in several classes caught him not paying attention. He wasn't about to tell them how his endless daydreams were real. He told Gray.

"You hookin' up with her!" Gray bug-eyed. "... oooweeee. Grannie ever finds out... "

"Promise not to tell," Craige spoke with a fierce glare at Gray.

But Gray told some of their soccer buds. Locker-room talk wanted him to tell more. Some sneaked their dads' girlie mags; gathered around with furtive glances at centerfolds or video grab shots of their dads' homemade XXX CDs. CDs got copied to ready-flash drives and really got passed around. Made-up stories about how much they knew, what they did in the backseats or on the tailgate of their pickups—on their backs or doggie or whatever. Craige never forgot that afternoon he was collecting for his paper route. Her car in the drive, the front door open. He punched the doorbell, waited, pushed the button again, knocked, hollered, knocked louder. The screen door was unlocked.

He stuck his head in, "Hello in the house, anybody home?" Wondered if she was sick or hurt; couldn't move. He didn't like being in someone's house if they weren't there. Grannie would tan his hide for sure. Just wasn't done. Hollered again, "Hello."

"I'm back here. Come on back."

She didn't sound hurt. She wasn't. She was in bed, and she was all-naked-all-under, not even a sheet covering her. He gawked; didn't turn; scared, curious, "Mam?" licked his lips. "I rang the doorbell."

"I heard you, but I didn't have any clothes on." Coy. "I jumped in bed."

Youngster Craige couldn't swallow, "I'm collecting for the paper."

"Is it that time again?"

"Yes, mam."

"Hand me my purse. There, on the chest of drawers."

"Yes, mam," dutiful, polite with the curious impulse to run out of the house—but didn't." As he handed her the purse, her hand grazed his. Lingered to slide along the front of his jeans.

The touch went straight deep down inside his belly. Her lipstick was the reddest he'd ever seen.

"Sit down." Patted the bed, "You're quiet a fine young man."

Gulped. "Yes, mam," hardly took a breath.

Fixed her look right at what she wanted. "... real nice." Rubbed his shoulder, "You play football?"

"Soccer," tongue sticky. Licked at his dry lips.

"You look like it," her scalding touch hotter than he ever knew skin could be.

Craige stammered, "Mam... "

She peeled him naked. Her touch was marvelous, different from any touch he'd ever felt. Coaxed him onto the sheet with her. Sidled against him; straddled him. Her large ponderous body loomed above his round wonderment eyes. Boyhood blistered gone, pinning him to her till she was ready to quit. It began his whole new life, hurrying each afternoon after school to spend the time in her bed, or wherever her notions took them.

"Your grandma ever ask where you're spending all your afternoons?" hands playing over all the places of his body.

"No... yeh... sometimes. Told her I'm helping my friends on their paper routes."

"I love young ones," her tongue started at his neck. Went everywhere. "Train 'em like I want 'em."

Teenster Craige reveled in his new-found body. Liked doing it more'n more.

* * *

The sky lighter, Craige stepped into the rolling steam of the shower, turning on the hot sprays while he shaved. He patted his stomach; muttered, "Gotta get more regular with the exercises," and glanced down at a little-to-no belly, "Gotta get with the workouts before I sprout love handles." No way was he allowing that to happen. Water jets pulsed his skull and shoulders.

Going commando, he slipped on broke-in corduroys, a denim shirt and his over-washed jogging sneakers and crumpled white athletic socks, then brushed at the damp curls of dark brown hair. The keys were where he'd left them in the kitchen. Outside he swung into his rebuilt Jeep—Lucky waiting to leap into the passenger seat. "You bad dog... " Dog was on the seat in a heartbeat. Craige scratched the ears. Got a big wet tongue nuzzle across his face as though Lucky understood each word.

With hardly any breaking-dawn traffic except for the early shift at SRP, Craige took his time on the road. Less than half an hour later, with Lucky waiting in the open jeep, Craige was in his usual booth at Duke's. He made a point of being early. It gave him time to reconnoiter faces that were out of place. As usual it was already filled with the old money, the wizened, the experienced, and the usual *nouveau* hangers-on huddled at the counters and in booths—politics and taxes always the given agenda. His watch told him it was twenty minutes before Bailey was due. He ordered coffee. Duke's Eatery was one of the few places where select locals could count on finding yesterday's reboiled coffee with a jaw-clenching kick—exactly the way Craige liked. The wrinkled scrawny owner swore by it and made sure the last of the day's coffee wasn't poured down the sink. Poured it up; started a fresh filter and water for an urn of fresh-made so it'd be ready for those what wanted coffee-colored water. During many a night-dawn recon, Craige had acquired the sucking bitter yank of reboiled he'd come to enjoy.

The dark-haired waitress almost managed to squeeze into a dress barely holding at the seams; fit like body-molded skin, but failed to shave off her accumulated birthdays. She managed to serve his table anytime she was on her shift and he came in. Her stage-best smile through thick eye-liner and clumpy mascara was intended for an unmistakable *whatever you want*.

"Morning." She leaned over with a perky, "Been a while since I seen you in here. Got your special brew all special and waitin'." Poured his cup extra slow with her usual bad-tooth big grin. Wasn't just coffee she was offering, but every townie in town knew not everything offered in the diner was on the menu. Duke's wasn't just an eatery.

Craige said, "That coffee ought to hit the spot." He didn't want to even figure how any man would be able to pry her out of that dress with those braless puppies almost already over the top without ripping zippers. As she walked away, he wondered if she wore panties. Recalled his high school paper route days and some of the locker-room rough-an'-ready girls. They never wore anything either.

"Brazen hussies," Grannie would say with her churchified blazing look. "Brazen hussies is all they is. Brazen Jezebels set to tumble any man what gives them a second look."

"Well, you haven't changed much," Bailey stood next to the booth and gave the waitress a tandem lingering look before sitting down.

Cup in midair, Craige stared up at the pinched nose and squirmy eyes. He hadn't seen Bailey come in. "What's this? No uniform? Rank with its usual privileges?" His dislike-distrust of this man ratcheted up a notch. Knew his waitress hadn't taken eyes off either of them.

"As I said, it's a special assignment. Uniform would draw attention."

"Nobody would bat an eye whether you were in uniform or not... not in this town. No matter what you were wearing you fit in like a whale in the middle of an Atlanta freeway during rush hour—which in Atlanta is all the time. Your being here without your uniform is the closest I've ever see you come to passing up a chance to wear your bling and glitter. You love the gold, the attention, and the rows of fancy ribbons."

Bailey said, "You've got a fair number of stuff for your chest yourself."

"That I do, probably more than you," Craige gave a nod. "In a box somewhere."

The waitress hurried over, "You two decide what you want?" Her eyes barely above her order pad, back and forth between the two men. Gave a double-quick more-than-a-passing glance at Craige.

Craige said, "My usual." Drained his cup. The bitter aftertaste a pleasant distraction, as he gave Alpsworth the Third a short nod, "Go ahead. Order. My treat. She knows what I want." Reached for the grape jelly-smudged menu next to the napkin holder and handed it to him. "Anything on there is good."

Alpsworth glanced up at the waitress, "I'll have what he's having."

Craige waited until she walked away. "What did you want to talk about?"

"What's the hurry?" He replaced the menu.

"It's not a matter of hurry. Ever since your phone call, it's the way you're dancing around cutting straight to the meat of it. By the time you tell me what's on your mind, I figure we'll be long finished with breakfast and ready for lunch. Duke's closes about three in the afternoon."

"You haven't changed."

"No point in changing. It's like the time you told me I needed to get a new attitude. It was your sidling-way of saying I wasn't doing what you wanted the way you wanted. That hasn't changed. Never will." The waitress came back over with two plates heaped with eggs, grits, sausage, biscuits and gravy. After refilling Craige's cup and checking to see if they needed anything else, she left. "Now what's so important that you went to the trouble to get my unlisted number but couldn't tell me over the phone?"

"I need help."

"You needed help before you were out of diapers."

Bailey paled along his neck and under his ears as he tried to ignore the remark. "We got a problem I'm not quite sure how it needs handling."

Craige read his reaction, "And you want me to handle it for you?"

"You still have your PI license?"

Craige's eyebrows raised slightly, the Third conniving without even trying, "Which means you know I do, or you wouldn't have asked."

"Cut the shit, Ingram," the needling getting to him. "We got a situation on our hands, maybe a killing, and a group of upstanding pillars of society on both sides of the river are pushing all the buttons—demanding action."

"Unhuh... politics and payback," Craige cut direct, "Who?"

"Morton Raymond for one."

Craige gave a rough chuckle, "Whoever sold you Morton Raymond as a community pillar is leading you down the primrose country path." Took a big swig of coffee. His words flat, "All Mort Raymond cares about is anything that affects his real estate holdings, 'specially a negative cash flow. Who's the maybe-victim of this maybe-murder? And what's an army investigator doing messing in local police business?"

"That's part of the problem. Seems Mort Raymond is a major supporter of some of the big lobbyists in the state legislature. Throwing his weight around, calling in political favors, screaming for answers."

Craige was even more direct, "And you're caught between the brass up your chain of command and the political heat that's coming down."

Bailey said, "His son was found dead on federal property."

"Buddy Raymond?" All manner warp-and-woof deceptions tumbled Craige's thoughts.

Bailey gave a soft snort, "I figured you'd pick up on the name." Bailey's face tightened, as though talking about it made it worse, "South end of Fort Gordon near the Brier Creek County line. Strangled. If not professional—it was certainly planned. Done from behind with a garrote, pants around his ankles."

"Assaulted?"

"Autopsy said no. There were no bruises on the body except for the neck and postmortem abrasions."

Craige said, "In an investigation still underway and a lot of questions hanging in the air, smoke and shadow conjecture can create more problems. Holding off releasing unsubstantiated details might be a good face-down wild card to keep facedown and held wild-card tight."

"Except Daddy and his political pals are squeezing for a quick wrap of the case. Been getting scuttlebutt from the Beech Island police. You have any unofficial contacts on either side of the river that could quietly look into what's behind this?"

Bailey the Third was fishing, and Craige got a distinct dislike of the fishin' hole Third was fishing in. Bailey had to know about him and Gray being in the same SEAL unit. Not about to mention Gray or Buckingham Metro Law Enforcement or Gray's IST, Investigative Support Division Homicide—and for sure not Gray's Investigative Support Team. SEAL-bud Thadeus Graysen MacGerald wouldn't sit still for any sort of loose scuttlebutt in an ongoing investigation in the Buckingham Metro Law Enforcement or the Homicide Division of IST. Aside from Gray, Craige could imagine the butt-ripping Gibson girl hairdo Mabel Struthars would turn loose on Bailey and the hot seat she'd light under Bailey's whole chain of command if she got wind of Bailey trying to harm her boss.

Mabel had been working for Gray ever since he first joined Metro Law Enforcement. No one was more loyal to him. Mabel sniff out anyone poking around behind Gray's back, he'd seen Mabel get meaner than mean in an ugly squabble. Craige and Mabel were tighter than tight when it came to covering Gray's backside. Wouldn't take Craige long to get a fix on exactly what shenanigans Bailey the Third was mixed into.

He said, "Daddy Raymond has his hands in lots of pies. State boundaries in the middle of a river never stopped him." With all of Daddy Raymond's under-the-table open-secrets arrangements, Craige wondered what else was at the money-funnel bottom of the Raymond cesspits. Perkins Used Cars and Jenkins Construction came to mind. Raymond Sales Brokerage made a perfect front for money laundering dirty cash.

"If Raymond is deliberately muddying the waters, he's either hunting for something or covering up something he wanted to keep buried. The dangerous angle comes into play if those secrets are already loose." Craige razored a glance at Bailey, "Scared can be a whole lot dangerous."

Third asked, "Scared of what?"

"For the obvious—covering the money trail," Craige spit the word *money* like it was a proven. Most of his PI cases spun around the variations of either hide-the-money or follow-the-money. Other cases spun around run-amok emotions that blazed and consumed and tripped up the best of plots. "Daddy may be trying to keep the stink from whatever escapade his son got tangled in. If it was messing in his business arrangements, it was something Mort wouldn't tolerate. Answer that, you'll have a hook on the motive... and maybe a lead to the killer or killers. A caveat you might want to keep in mind... it could get unpleasant for the brass, 'specially those responsible for base security."

"Dammit Ingram," Third's voice uneven and loud.

At Bailey's outburst Craige noticed the stares from the wizened white hairs and shiny bald spots of the fathers and grandfathers of the old line founding bloodlines who gathered at Duke's on predawn weekdays to settle daily accounts. Bailey didn't have a clue.

He cautioned, "I'd lower your voice. You're getting an audience your boss won't like hearing from, and he will hear about it. They'll make sure of that."

"I don't give a shit what these rednecks don't like," Bailey snapped.

"You'd better give a shit. The faces you see in here right now could buy and sell your whole family out of one afternoon's petty cash. Old money hereabouts don't like loud or crass. They don't like Johnny-come-latelies or outsiders either. No matter who you think you are." Craige couldn't believe what a blind ass Bailey truly was. "You want answers, you're going to have to work with these good ole boys. And another thing you better keep on that chalkboard of a brain you don't use—and keep it right up front: No matter what Morton J. Raymond is, bottom line... he's homegrown and you're an outsider. Outsiders screwing around with homefolks won't fly. Whatever crap Daddy Raymond is stirring will cover you so deep no one will ever know you were in these parts, and nobody in these parts, including your chain of command, will lift their little pinky finger to pull your butt out of the fire." Craige leaned forward, green eyes in a squint, "You're the lackey sent out to keep dirt from splashing on your boss or up the chain to the top dog." Bailey squirmed as Craige bluntly explained the way it was. "Outsiders stirring when they don't know what or who they're dealing with ought not stir. It don't matter who they are, how much money they got or who they know, they'll get the kind of attention they don't want." Craige lowered his voice, making Bailey strain to hear, "Generations of families born and reared here accept it as a birthright. In many ways it is, and you better recognize the rules." A slight quick nod toward the next booth, "Newspaper editor. Next to him, a bank president. Across from them a U.S. Senator. These golf shirts and overalls that look to you like a bunch of dumb no-nothings sit on more old money than Wall Street could count."

Bailey didn't gawk, but he stared, his covetousness in full bloom, "And you're one of them. With more money than you'll ever spend."

"Damn right. You're a topnotch example of what people call the *ugly American*. You judge everything by its dollar sign, including yourself. Your attitude and the greenback is worthless, and we let it get that way. This is my home-turf. My roots are deep here, and I'll do pretty much anything to protect it."

"You enjoy putting me down," Bailey's attitude bordered on rancorous.

"Let's not get personal. If I wanted to be bothered putting you down the notches, which I don't, it wouldn't take much doing. You put yourself down more than anyone else could." Took a swallow of coffee. "I've worked with more efficient SOBs than you'll ever be. We don't have to like each other to work together," an admission he hadn't made to himself before. Puzzles intrigued him, especially those driving the beast side of man—even more when they could involve a buddy like Gray. He wasn't about to sit still without trying to buffalo that into a full stop.

"Then you'll help?" Bailey breathed a little easier.

Craige said, "I didn't say that."

"Yes you did. Otherwise you'd let these wolves have at me like you've done a time or two in the past."

"I may let you squirm in their feed trough anyway. Your boss can finish off what's left," Craige drained his cup. Fixed Bailey with a Grannie Ingram look, "Why you think the killing was professional?"

"Drugs and what you said... money."

"One successful drug run can triple its investment." Craige leaned back, "That's a big temptation for high flashy living that kind of money can buy. Wrecked lives, killings, addiction, ruined families, disease don't matter in that world.

"I don't understand why people don't look, which sometimes that includes me." Looking through instead of paying attention to each moving body in the humdrum every-day crowd was a blind spot that had slipped up on Craige more times than he liked. On the surface the devious and the warped could appear straightforward. It was what was on the inside that sometimes got Craige into trouble. "Street dealers are little fish, raw meat, they come and go, and are quickly forgotten. Always a hungry someone waiting too step-up, take their place."

"There was at least a kilo of coke splattered around the bodies."

"Bodies?" Craige's attention was once again brought to the forefront.

"A second body and in the loft a suicide note, a soldier discharged about two months ago. Body was strung up in the barn where Raymond's kid was found. It looked like he'd killed the kid, then ended it for himself," handed the fold of paper to Craige.

"Or made to look that way. Any tire tracks? Anything?"

Bailey heaved a long sigh, "Several vehicles had been there with only traces of tread marks in the heavy leaf-fall and pine straw. The barn had been there a long time."

"Likely from when the government bought up the sections of land between the county line and Gate Five." Craige read the note; handed it back to Bailey. "You have a problem with how the crime scene was staged?" sensing Bailey had reservations.

"Over the last six months MPs have been watching the names and faces of soldiers buddy-buddy with Raymond's son. The group was into some kinky stuff, all of it with drugs thrown in as a bonus."

"Or as bait." Craige was trying to convince himself Bailey hadn't overlooked anything that hadn't been obvious. He'd seen how easy it could happen. "Kinky is the norm in the drug world. You know that," not satisfied Bailey did.

"Whoever killed the kid tried to make it look like murder-suicide."

Craige said, "Any idea how Buddy Raymond fits into this theory of yours?"

"We're not sure," Bailey grimaced. "You talk like you knew him."

"If drugs were involved, I'm not surprised the Raymond kid was mixed up in it. He's been in several scrapes that his daddy hushed up. Hushed up or fooled himself into believing he'd hushed up. Everybody knew Raymond's kid was flaky."

Remembered Grannie's, "I never hold to washin' dirt in public. Though sometimes the dirt got to be washed."

Craige said, "Big town murder can get real personal, but add in the metropolitan areas plus the bedroom communities on both sides of the river and you've covered a lot of real estate to what is no small town."

"Small towns and communities straddling the river have grown, spread out. A killing in a small town or community can leave a bitterness that lasts longer than calendars have numbers. One like this puts you right in the middle of local politics. From the git-go you start throwing your weight around and you're dead in the water. Morton Raymond can't handle money worth a damn. He likes the reputation of being Mister Big. He's not, but plenty cash flows through his hands. Which means it's flowing through other hands as well." Craige took a deep breath. "Buddy was an only son." Wasn't wasting time trying to make Bailey understand. It made him too cocky and he was cocksure enough already. "I got to ask... what's your rank?"

"Why you want to know?" He gave Craige a surly glower over the top of his cup.

"You wouldn't stick with the army unless there was something in it for you."

"Major."

Ever the ass-kisser flashed Craige's thoughts, then Ingram lightning-quick, he switched thoughts, a quirk that never failed to rattle Bailey, "I want a copy of the official autopsies."

Bailey pulled the folded papers out of his jacket and grinned, for once anticipating Craige, "Figured you'd ask for them."

Craige caught Bailey's self-satisfied glance as he folded the copies and stuck them in his pocket. "How detailed was the army's investigation?"

"Figured you'd want that as well." Reached Craige the folder.

Its thickness surprised Craige. As his coffee cooled, Craige skimmed the bulk of dog-eared pages, "Some of this dates from before the murders. Who's this Crockett?" He held up several sheets. "Army's looked into him right thorough."

"Investigation involves a lot more than two murders."

Craige asked without looking up, "How much more?"

Bailey said, "Enough to know that there's a lot we don't know."

The admission surprised Craige. "Gawd... I've never heard you be so flat honest before." He laid the file down; looked straight at Bailey, "Why's the army looking outside its own investigation, such as you contacting me?"

"Prelim investigation is getting into jurisdictions outside the army not covered by the UCMJ."

A nasty caution flag fluttered between Craige's ears; caught the dark emptiness in Bailey's Machiavellian eyes that right away told Craige he'd struck close to someone's target zero. "Beyond army jurisdiction—or are you doing this outside official channels?" He wondered if Bailey was up to something more personal. Craige got up, "I'll be touching base with you." He tossed down a generous tip, and grabbed both checks.

An edgy Bailey quickly followed Craige outside and across the parking lot, only to stand stupefied as Craige climbed into his jeep and pulled into the morning traffic with a German shepherd sitting next to him. As Craige drove he turned this meet topside to bottom and back again. The tenuous factor about it jangled at him more than a simple troubled dislike of the man. It had a country-distrust taste about it that Craige tried to dismiss as personal. Still, it wormed a gut feeling at him that had saved his life more than once. Old scabs that had nothing to do with Bailey brought a low-pitched discontent snarl at an outside world inserting itself into the sanctity of Moccasin Hollow.

Clean-cut in middle school, on the surface Mort's son had been outgoing. How did Buddy Raymond turn into a drugged loser? Craige didn't buy it being peer pressure, but he didn't discount it either.

Craige had always been immune to that. That's what Grannie taught him. More than a few times she'd said, "Believes in yourself. Don't never turn loose'a that."

There was more behind young Raymond's all-American act or he wouldn't have ended up part of Bailey's worries. What if Buddy was part of a stage-set cleanup snuff—a ready dead body to what really happened? The money Morton Raymond liked to flash only made Daddy Raymond more of what he was—run of the mill ever'day vulgar with an ostentatious grandiose vulgar rococo house in Silver Bluff Bayou Estates. Might pay to have a quiet chat with Agatha Hutchers and Sallie Mae Drutherferde, Craige's two bag lady friends, always on the move, always with their ears wide open for where the dirt could be found. Since they'd gotten to know him, they'd never steered him wrong. Word was Raymond's employees were afraid of him. Knotty doubts clouded Craige's thoughts—family problems? How and where had young Raymond sidetracked to a dead-end in a barn, a political-muck with the feds and Daddy's circle dancing the blame-game tango. With what little Craige knew, mistrust and skepticism scrambled the patterns. This could entail a lot of footwork and digging around barnyard muck.

He turned off the highway onto his gravel drive. Craige thought of the first rule of any knotty investigation—pick a place, any place. If there's rot, the stink will tell. Lucky broke his thoughts as he parked when he bounded out, loping toward the house, tongue drooling, tail wagging. Craige got out of the jeep, "Yeh, I'm glad I'm home, too." Ruffled the ears; got a wet lick.

Craige stripped off his street clothes; put on his kick-about fishin' cords. A few minutes later, he shoved off from his dock in his flat-bottom Cajun pirogue. No bait, no lures, no fly fishing tackle, no fish to clean, poled nice and easy along the shallows. As early dusk eased across the waters, he laid his pole in the bottom, and let the pirogue drift among the moccasin-draped overhangs. Snakes didn't bother him nor he them. Hands propped behind his head, he laid back; let his mind stir the files Bailey had provided. The vermilion isolation of a cloud-fringed sunset melted softer as the underbellies of the white cotton-puff clouds turned from gray to a deeper purple. The sluggish river became an undulating mercury-hued comforter. The whine of a mosquito broke his contemplations in silhouettes of shadowed colorless obscurities.

He poled slowly back to the dock. As he picked up his cell to call the Raymond house, he spotted Terri's note. He put down the phone, punched the keyboard off standby, and saw in the you-got-mail window in the upper left of the screen something from Terri.

She'd texted, "See you later this week. Sleep tight."

He could almost smell her perfume, the smell of her hair, a nice warm hug right now would feel good. Instead he dialed the Raymond number.

A mellow female voice answered, "Hello."

"Mrs. Raymond?"

"This is Mary Bernice Raymond. Are you the teacher that wanted to speak with my daughter?"

"No, mam," Craige introduced himself. "I need to speak with your husband, Mort."

The voice hesitated, "Craige Ingram?"

"Yes, mam."

"Was Corinthia Ingram your kin?"

Craige caught the faint trace of Gullah, Sea Island Geechee any Southron would pick up in a heartbeat. "She was my grannie." Taken slightly off-guard.

"My goodness gracious, what a small world," the vowels dragging slower. "You were that barefoot little boy in Oshkosh overalls running around her house, hollerin' about a frog you'd caught."

"Yes, mam." He had intended on moving quick to question Mort Raymond about his son's death, but could tell his quick intentions and surprising Raymond might come to an unexpected something less. She was either ditzy or this was a smokescreen diversion; give husband time to bury evidence. If it was an attempt to distract, she was good.

Her smooth talk might work on some—but Craige wasn't letting it happen. Direct was best, "Mam, is your husband there?"

"Gracious sakes," Bernice Raymond pondered, "I gather this isn't a social call."

"No, mam. It isn't." Craige caught an ever-so-short hesitancy from her with an uncanny sense that Bernice Raymond was subtly trying a smooth diversion. A good wife shielding a crass husband could be a problem—unless she had another reason, like maybe she was involved. As Mort Raymond's wife talked, the tone of her voice became a grating Silver Bluff Trace horse-trader finagle in his ear. Slight changes in the timbre of her voice told him more than she was ready to admit. He wasn't going to learn much from this one. When she paused a moment, Craige repeated, "Is your husband there?"

Her change was like the flick of a light switch, "He isn't here right now. May I take a message?" Social chitchat was over.

"I'll try later. When's a good time to call?"

"I'm not sure. He had to go to the courthouse in Aiken."

"Thank you." He could tell she was lying.

Craige was pissed after he hung up. He'd let his hunch put her bait on him. He wouldn't tell Bailey, but he'd keep his eye on Mary Bernice Raymond. Later that evening under the spatter of the shower, the thought hit him. He chuckled as it seeped through his stubbornness that it wasn't Bailey's doing that got him into this. Just maybe he was bored. Craige didn't sleep well that night. As he tossed and turned, befuddled images of Sallie Mae and Agatha buzzed his dreariness.

* * *

They were clearing foundation sites for the new bridge, readying them for the pour when the backhoe hit it.

"Damn." The operator, nimble on the controls, danced the hydraulics; jittered the scoop to spill the load loose then pulled it free. He brought the shovel arm up, made sure the hydraulics weren't jammed, lowered it to rest on the ground, and climbed down to examine the repair-weld. It hadn't split again.

As the roar of the diesel died down, the foreman yelled, "Keep it on the ground!" He scrambled along one side of the dig to look at the bricks lodged in the bottom of the bucket. "That's all we need," he mumbled as he jumped down.

The operator leaned over, "What'd we hit? Not no water or gas main. Wadn't no sparks; couldn't be an unmarked power conduit."

The foreman was on the phone; the operator waited. The foreman's bulldog red face said it all; punched OFF. Yanked his soggy cigar butt out of his mouth and flung it to the ground. "Fill it up, goddammit. We ain't paying a crew to sit around and wait. Fill in the goddamn hole. It's in the wrong place."

The gruff pudgy operator glanced toward the river where the concrete pylons marched in a curved arch from the Georgia side. "Sitting in his air-conditioned office, how'd he know it's in the wrong place?"

He couldn't afford to lose this job. Had a grandchil' on the way; certain it would be a girl; wanted to put some money back for her college. Throttled up, and dug into the pile of heavy yellowish kaolin clay, the arch of home-fired bricks soon buried.

Chapter 4

Billy's squeeze-of-the-week timorous girlfriend looked all around. "We shouldn't be here." She looked behind her, up at the stucco side of the house, and its shuttered windows reflecting the moonlight. "My mother would have a fit if she ever found out we'd sneaked onto this place."

He knelt; tugged at a draggy raveled shoestring, "Who's gonna tell?"

"What if we get caught?"

"Who's gonna catch us? Nobody ever comes down into these tunnels."

"All these spooky night-critters that sting and bite," swatted at a web. "And it's full of spiders. I don't know why I even let you talk me into this."

He grinned; teeth glistened in the bright full moon, "You can't resist my sweet-talk or when we have sex."

"Maybe it's your varsity jacket."

Billy squeezed her hand, "Maybe it's what's under my jacket."

"Don't you ever think of anything else?"

The single dim cone of his flashlight bounced ahead of them, "Who you think you're kiddin'. You like sex as much as I do. Quit girly-whiny. You hang around Mary Beth so much, you're beginning to sound like her."

"I am not whiny." She tried pouty, which never worked with Billy. "I don't like these creepy places. Sometimes you're creepy—I'm scared." She swatted at more cobwebs.

"It was about here." He pushed at the stones.

55

"You're weird. Nobody explores places like this. How you know about this?"

He said, "Found it one day." He pushed harder. The damp stone made a dull grating noise, and a small section of the sidewall moved inward.

"You mean you were trespassin', like we're doin' now." She grabbed his arm, "The caretaker'll hear for sure."

"Nobody's going to hear. Redcliffe is up the hill a ways. Once that grumpy old man goes to his cabin, he stays there. Don't come out."

"Billy, we're gonna get caught." A bunch jittery, she threw more glances all around.

He whispered, "You kept bitchin' at me to bring you with me. You didn't have to come."

"Billy Martel!" snuggled tighter to him. "You knew I wasn't about to stay in that car by myself."

"You never did like being in a car by yourself. Always liked me in there with you."

"Quit teasing me," half mad at him, half scared at the drippy dark all around them. "I can't see nothin'. How'd you find these tunnels? How many times you come down here?"

"I told you."

"You never told me how many times."

"You'll be alright." He grabbed her sweaty hand tight.

"It's so dark in here. And stuff is drippin' all over me."

"What'd you expect?"

"You don't like my mother." She shivered; brushed at something crawling on her arm and clutched tight to him. "Snakes like cellars and places like this."

"Your mother is all the time buttin' in."

"My mother says don't never crawl under houses when you can't see what's under there."

"You do a lot of things your mama says not do." Snickered. Baited her, "You want to stay here while I go on?"

"Don't you dare even think about leaving me alone down here."

He flicked his light farther, "Come on," moved ahead of her.

She stumbled to catch up, "It's so spooky. Are we under the house?"

"Far as I know." One careful step after another, "There's a cellar opening from outside. All these passageways end down on the river."

"By the river!" voice jerky. "Billy—I want to go back. There's cottonmouth moccasins on the river. I don't want to be where they are in the middle of the night!" Fear drove her whisper louder, "They been out since before Easter. They're stirring for sure."

"They come in here sometimes." Billy smiled, couldn't resist, bragged, "Seen two the last time I was here."

Flapping her hands in fear, tippy-toed her feet as far off the muddy as tiptoes could get. Couldn't see nothing. Near about to wet her panties 'cept she hadn't wore none. No panties made it easier in the back seat with Billy. He hated panties. She got tickled once when he got her blouse tangled with her jeans. He didn't like her laughing when he couldn't get buttons and zippers undone. He liked Velcro.

"Down near the river the tunnels been blocked up with trash and mud by floods. Not open that far anymore, least not the ones I've followed. Snakes all over. Friend of mine with that construction company working on the new bridge said they uncovered some old bricks, same like these. Their boss made 'em cover the bricks up. Said it looked like a tunnel or a sewer drain to him."

"Oh, god... don't tell me we're wading through stuff flushed down toilets."

"I figure they'll cover any tunnels before they finish the new bridge. That's why I wanted to come now. Won't be long before ever'body forgets about there being any tunnels. I wanted to come down one last time." Put his arm around her, "We won't go down where the snakes are." Comfort her now; easier to get her naked later.

Still skittish, "I remember once when you promised me you wouldn't do something and you went ahead and did it anyhow."

He snickered, "But after we did it you told me you liked it."

She said, "Not then."

"That's not what you said last night when your folks were at church and we fucked in their bed."

"How old is this place?"

"One of my teachers said they were built back before the revolution."

"What revolution? What are you talking about?"

"When the Redcoats were here."

She said, "Now I know you're bulling me. Nobody wears red coats. Well... maybe those stuffed shirts at that golf place across the river."

Bill snickered, "They don't wear red ones; they wear green ones. Tunnels were built in case the Redcoats garrisoned the old house for a fort. Colonials used the tunnels so they could get at the soldiers in the house from underneath."

"You're talkin' about a long time ago."

"Main tunnel once branched off along the river. There's tunnels across on the Georgia side, too. Most'a them are blocked full-up."

"Anything down here besides this awful mud?" Water dribbles spattered her cheek. She flinched. "I don't like this place—I'm never going explorin' with you again. You explore in some of the awfulest places."

"Found some rusty metal stuff, couldn't tell what it was. Found an old rotted boot."

"This tunnel go to the main house?"

Billy said, "Passages off it once lead from the house."

"Anything up there?"

"Don't know. Never been up there."

She said, "Those Redcoats just leave?"

"Had to. Or we Rebs would've killed 'em. Or gators would've got 'em."

She said, "The tunnels were never filled in?"

"Some were when the new Redcliffe was built. I don't know if the old woman that lived here did anything about the tunnels under the house."

She said, "Drapes stayed pulled shut all the time. Windows never open. Wonder what it's like inside?"

"Folks say she lived in Ardochy." Billy stopped so quick, she bumped into him. He stared down, "Shit!"

She caught her breath; cold shiverins went all over her, "Billy!" Started flapping her hands all nervous again. Titties bobbled against sore nipples teeth-raw from last night, but she didn't pay her titties no mind. His light made a small dull circle around the wooden box half full of arrowheads, broken pottery and one skull with the jawbone missing.

Billy said, "That sure wasn't here a week ago." Shifted the beam to the toe of his boot where two blood-red glitters caught his attention. He leaned down and picked one up.

"Don't you dare touch that nasty thing!" She gawped at the skull, fingers clenched hard into Billy's arm.

Billy rolled the shiny bit in his palm. He couldn't see much. It looked like glass; reminded him of busted marble taws, the big ones that could really scatter, only redder, no zigzag marbled colors.

"Billy?" He ignored her. "Billy!"

Called back, "What!"

"I thought I heard something." She searched into the dim nothingness.

"You're always hearing something." He flicked the beam down to the jawless skull, one eye socket cracked at one corner.

"Billy!" jiggling again, "I told you I heard something," this time flapping her hands.

"Whatever it was," aimed the beam back on the skull, "it sure wasn't that one. I don't hear nothin'." He listened hard to every drip and gurgle—still wasn't sure. There was something gritty sounding that wasn't there before. Sounded like it was above them or in the long tunnels. Was there, then stopped. He swung the beam into the blackness.

Her half-whisper moan became a scared plea, "Billy, let's get out of here." Really sure enough, she couldn't hold it any longer. Needed to pee somethin' awful.

Without thinking, his fingers made a fist around the dark red glassy pebble; shoved the broken piece inside his jeans. The skull melted back into the dark as the bobbling wobble of his flashlight turned back the way they came.

* * *

The buzz of the alarm roused Craige from his drowsy catnap. His hand fumbled and slapped at the switch to stop the buzz. The sky was too daylight bright for it to be anywhere near sun-up. Slack-jawed yawn, stretched, he didn't want to convince himself it was time to roll out of the sack. Usually he didn't sleep this late except on occasional dawn-cool mornings. It wasn't one of those mornings. Lucky padded into the bedroom; gave him a big wet tongue morning-slurp across his face.

Craige scruffled the dog's ears, "Best wake-up lick I've had this morning." Plopped his head back into the pillow and sprawled naked across the damp-cool of the sheets. He liked the sluggish smells of the late wisteria and Confederate jasmine mixed with the heavy bayou smells floating in a river-mist off the river. Fat water droplets hung heavy on the screens. He had napped and tossed through a goodly portion of the cool night. Lucky gave him a nose-nudge.

"Enough of this bein' lazy," and tumbled out'a bed. The muted buzz came again. It wasn't the alarm. His unlisted cell gave another repetitious buzz in the stillness of the sleeping porch. He reached for it; the display showed TERRI. "Hey sweet thing," flopped spread-eagle back on the bed, pillow under his head.

"Figured after you'd had your first cup and before you were out the door this was the best time to catch you."

Her enticing voice gave him all sorts of ideas. "Haven't had my first cup yet," squeezed his eyes; wasn't sleepy any longer.

She said, "For you this is late."

"You're not the only thing that makes me late," he said. "Gotta spoil myself ever now an' then.

"Every now and then is a good thing."

"You are talking about sleeping?" Followed it with a throaty growl in her ear.

Terri said, "Wish I were there. We could spoil each other."

"You got me used to your kind of spoiling."

"I sort of got that idea." Then added, "You'll have to miss me this weekend."

"Office IN-box catch up with you?"

"Paperwork on two trust accounts," she sounded disappointed. "Successor trustees changed. One died after a long hospital stay, the other has some legal snags. A couple of the spendthrift heirs want to quibble over the details."

"They want a bigger cut of the pie, and a few lawyers we could name want to increase their percentages."

"I'd like to say that wasn't the case, but that could be one of the worms in this merry-go-round," Terri said "And I want to make sure the bank's on top of it should a family haggle get stirred among the heirs."

"Job is never done till the paperwork's finished," he chuckled.

She said, "I was looking forward to the weekend."

"Me, too."

Terri's breath made a baited sound in his ear, "We'll make up for it with an interrupted weekend."

He gave her another growl, "You're lucky you aren't here right now."

She said, "Aren't you being the lusty one. You always were a morning person. Maybe I ought to start calling you more often early in the mornings."

"Was sort of fun what you did with those silk scarfs."

"Imagination can be a fun thing." For Terri his solid sense of self was always an enticement. She was comfortable with men who were comfortable around strong women.

Craige said, "These trust settlements going to tie you up next week?"

"I hope not, but in this case the buck stops with me. Depends on whether we hit any bumps I don't anticipate," she said. "If probate or the appointment of successor trustees drags out, I'll need a midweek break." Paused, "Guess I better get with it. Morning's slipping away—I've got to get my hair ready for the office. Catch you later this week."

"Remember to be gentle with me."

She snuffled softly in his ear as the connection ended. He came off the bed, the chilly sleeping-porch mist wash-boarded goose bumps across his stomach and belly. The hot shower felt good. Towel-wrapped, he went into the kitchen and fixed a steamy cup of coffee; smeared homemade yogurt on burnt-around-the-edges English muffins, singing his fingers. In his bedroom he hit the lights to his walk-in closet. From the underwear drawer, he pulled out a pair of cotton boxers; tossed them aside. He felt like going commando. Instead, he reached for his old pair of suspenders, cotton stonewashed jeans and an all-cotton mexi-colored shirt with three quarter sleeves. After adjusting the suspenders, he felt the caress of soft cotton rubbing smooth against arms, chest, thighs. He liked the feel of cotton—thought back how many time Grannie soaked and washboard-scrubbed their clothes. His school clothes got kind'a ragged, but they were lye-soap clean and softer than soft.

He slipped on high-top white cotton socks; boots, his favorite leather vest; finished his coffee and grabbed the keys. Dawn was well into morning by the time Craige parked in the far back corner of the lot across from Mort Raymond's office—and waited. Coming up on an hour later Raymond drove in. Craige got out; walked toward Raymond. Had his PI ID out.

Raymond was disconcerted, "I know who you are. You been followin' me?" His cast iron face blustered, "You've been harassing my wife." Turned his back, swaggered toward his office. On the way he pulled out a long cigar, bit off the end, spit. Over his shoulder, he groused, "Leave my family alone." He was used to being obeyed, no questions asked.

Craige's icy expression didn't budge; he didn't move, "I wouldn't have to talk with your family if you'd man-up and quit hiding behind a woman's skirts."

Mort Raymond jerked to a stop like an invisible tight rein had heaved taut. Turned, "What?"

"You heard what I said." Craige tensed; shoulders hunched, battle-ready if it came to that. "You have a habit of making yourself scarce. When it's convenient."

"Ingrams always had a reputation for being smart-mouthed."

"I wouldn't bad-mouth someone else's family when your own son couldn't stay alive." If boy-dog friction was the button to rattle Raymond, Craige figured he might as well light the fuse sooner rather than later.

"You sonofabitch—Buddy was my son," said Raymond, moving closer but not too close. "Coming here, slandering a man's son when my son can't defend hisself."

Craige reckoned Raymond was about to swing. A public parking lot, a busy intersection, was a good place to twist a bastard's short hairs. Let him swing first—be Raymond's last punch. "What makes you think our little visit here has anything to do with your son? I'd make a calculated guess you know more about his death than you've told the police."

Mort Raymond went ash-pale, "What the fuck makes a white-trash bastard like you think you can barge in! Butt into my business like you got some kind'a privileges to pry into anybody's private affairs?"

Craige moved lightning fast. He goaded with fingers of one hand shutting off the blood, squeezing Raymond's jugular till the man's vision blurred. His other hand at the base of Raymond's neck applied incredible pressure; bent Raymond's head back, putting his lips so close to Mort Raymond's ear they almost touched. "Listen to me you greasy bloated pig," lips hardly moving, "I'm saying this once. You can talk with me or you can talk with the feds. Personally, I'd prefer it stayed between the two of us—law doesn't require me to read you your rights. Suit yourself, but you'll like me a lot better than the feds. So will your friends." He tightened his grip, "And while we're at it, keep a civil tongue in your head when you talk about my Grannie Ingram, or I'll put a real hurt to your face," shoved Raymond away.

Raymond coughed; stumbled backwards, clutched his throat, "I just buried my son. Can't you give the dead no respect? Besides, Buddy was killed in Georgia. That's for the state boys to handle and you're not a cop."

"My licenses straddle either side of the river. Besides, if it was a kidnapping, which I doubt, that's crossing state lines—which makes it federal."

"You're no fed neither. You're nothing but a lousy cheap PI gumshoe."

Craige would've laughed at Raymond's movie-lingo if his gut-deep disgust of the man wasn't so deep. He bristled, and his eyelids dropped. Mort Raymond took a step backward. "He died on federal land," said Craige. "You want to argue? I can arrange it real quick. On second thought, it might be fun if I went ahead and let them have a go at you. Watch you squirm. Knowing your so-called pals will be wondering what you're telling the feds."

"Alright!" Raymond wanted to cuss this troublemaker to damnation and hell—but didn't. "What you want to talk to me about anyhow?"

"What was your son doing sneaking onto the southern end of Fort Gordon?"

"I don't know," he said, rubbing his throat.

"How long had he known the other one that was killed with him?"

"I don't know anything about the other one."

"Dammit, Raymond... " Craige acted like he was pissed. "You telling me you have no idea who your son was running around with?"

"We didn't talk much."

Craige said, "Sounds like you didn't talk at all."

Raymond shouted, "Some goddamn worthless soldier killed my son!" spittle sprayed the air; drooled his chin. "Probably some drug degenerate—I don't know what it was about. They ought to round up the lot of 'em. Stuff all kind of drug-runnin' perverts in ovens like Hitler did. That's what's wrong with this country, too many weirdoes running things. Law takes their side. Hard working honest citizens got no rights. Something ought to be done; ought to clean 'em out."

Craige capped a tight lid on his base disgust with this ignorant bigot running his mouth how others ought to be cleaned up and cleaned out, all the while behind the scenes running his own kind of arrangements. He didn't believe a word Mort Raymond was saying.

"For your information most of your so-called perverts are beer and liquor drinking, tax paying, married, next door neighbor pillars of the church. You want to get into that? I can make sure everyone knows you're taking a good look at some of the arrest reports." Stepped a threat toward Raymond, "One of the men on my Navy SEAL team—big strapping farm boy. Mean bastard in a fight, could take any four men without working up a sweat. Any of us could depend on him to protect our backs; rip your head off if he thought you mistreated kids." Craige's eyes smoldered, "He was killed on a recon mission getting information for a beach landing, fighting a dirty little war to protect this country so chicken-shit garbage like you who want to build ovens can keep your precious money-pot fiefdoms. The likes of you might whisper your hate behind Darrell's back, but I never once saw a bastard with balls big enough to walk right up and spit their hate in his face. Freedom you'd hog for yourself and deny to anyone else." For flickering blinks of time, Craige wanted Mort Raymond to be the one dead instead of Darrell. "Now you want to make this easy or you still want to shovel shit?"

Raymond wanted to be somewhere else, anywhere away from this man. His voice dropped, "I don't know how long they knew each other."

"You know Emmett Whitfield?"

"I never met the dirty drug-pushing has-been of a soldier."

"I didn't ask if you met him." From somewhere inside, Craige's inner voice told him Raymond couldn't stop lying if he tried. "How do you know he was a pusher?" He hadn't mentioned Whitfield was a soldier and Bailey supposedly hadn't released any details. His first impulse was to shove Raymond's mouthy lies preferably up his ass. Instead, the same inner voice said to fish for as much as Raymond did know, "What about your son's friends? They know Whitfield?"

"I doubt it."

"But you're not sure?"

"No, why would any of them know Whitfield?"

"Somebody somewhere knew both of them well enough to kill them at the same time. Who were they?"

"What?"

"Your son's friends? I want names." Craige more convinced the man was hiding something. "And I'll be wanting to talk with you some more," walked back to his Jeep.

Raymond gave him an assassin's look, shaking and sweating harder by the time he got inside his office; slammed the door. Smelly sweat streaked along his blotchy jowls, skin pale, bluish splotches; pulled out a handkerchief. Wiped his lips, mopped his face, and reached for the phone. He listened to the rings on the other end, jumpy, watching through the window as Craige pulled into traffic; drove away.

The ringing stopped, replaced by a voice on the other end, "... yes?"

The abrasive tone in his ear made Raymond jump. Raymond said, "We got a problem."

"Raymond?"

Wheezed a half-cough, "... yeh."

"I told you never to call me at this number."

"We got a problem," he repeated.

"What sort of problem?"

"A people problem," Mort's handkerchief busier across his face.

"There isn't any other kind. What about?"

Raymond said, "A nosey private cop."

"Who?"

"Ingram just came by here."

"Ingram's nosey. He has a reputation for that. So what! The cops aren't going to bother us. That's taken care of."

"Not with this one. You don't know Ingram." Raymond couldn't shake the wiggle of fear that was twisting his stomach.

"Take care of it."

Mort about choked, "What you mean?"

"I have to spell it out?"

"I didn't agree to no killing!" renewed panic.

"Who you think you're bulling?" came the harsh reply. "You're in this up to your neck. You never cared what had to be done long as you got your cut. What you mean is you don't want to get your hands dirty. Don't want to know stuff that has to be taken care of. What goes around, comes around. Take care of it."

"What should I do?"

"If he keeps causing problems, take him out."

"I never killed nobody."

"It isn't hard," then added, "Let him keep digging and your squeaky clean ass will end up where nobody'll ever find you. Don't think for a moment I'll let some PI with more money than god take me down." The threat was followed by silence. "I wouldn't break a heavy sweat. A little planning and it wouldn't take more than five minutes."

Stammered, "What?" It was happening all over again. No matter how much money was in his bank account, he was second fiddle in the world.

"Take care of it or I'll take care of you. Ingram ain't using you to get to me," slammed the phone down.

Mort Raymond sagged into his overstuffed chair. His heart was hammering and he couldn't get his breath. His hand was still on the phone when it rang again, the light winking above his private number. Only a few had it, his wife not one of them. A call back? He didn't want to talk to the bastard again. It kept winking at him. Raymond fought the wave of stomach cramps. He hated the damn phone, hated the whole rotten goddamn fucking situation gone downside up. It was gonna be so easy. More money than he had ever had. Never be poor again. Could forget those times in that awful shack where he grew up. Things get too hot, he'd change his name; disappear without his harpy social climbing wife and daughter. The ringing drummed louder the longer he stared at it.

His hand reached, trembled, almost dropping the mouthpiece, "Raymond."

"Where the fuck you been?" Purvis demanded.

Raymond relieved it was Dalugosh. "With a customer. Secretary ain't here."

"Come Friday, don't forget the game."

"What?"

"Goddamn, Mort, you drunk or got a hangover? You tie on a wimpy mid-week big one or something? You know Friday is poker night. You losing it in your old age?"

"Got a lot on my mind." Beady pig eyes squinting; it'd be perfect. They'd all be there. They'd never be suspicious with everyone around. Cunning hitting high gear—if the bastard was going to twist his arm to do the dirty work, he would. His way. His lips sweaty but not for the reason Purvis would have suspected.

"Janella and Winona'll be there. Got a new video they made. Ought'a make some real money off this one. Fresh-picked young stuff."

Mort said, "So what's new? Janella and Winona are always after fresh meat."

"Make for a good party," gut-laugh. "See you there."

Raymond said, "Yeh. See you there," sweating harder by the time he hung up.

Chapter 5

Craige pulled around to the back of the house; parked next to the kitchen mud-room door and unloaded groceries. Made sure he hadn't left any freezer and fridge-stuff out, then headed into his master bedroom. Triggered the remote to what looked to be a solid wall in the bedroom. The concealed panel slid open into the hidden rooms that had been built into the hill behind the dogtrot original Moccasin Hollow. The row of green indicators a steady green, the stand-alone generators were at optimum operation; voltage steady, climate control holding ambient on the mark. He powered his network off standby, brought up the backed-up database, and punched up the file he'd updated yesterday. Appended to the second page were the stats he'd entered on Buddy Raymond. He reached for the phone with its scrambled line and dialed the scrambled secure line Bailey had given him.

"Bailey," answered immediately.

"Ingram here—you get the info?"

"Yes."

Craige said, "You at your desk?"

"Yes."

"Enter this code into the URL field," Craige slowly spelled out the alphanumeric string as he punched in his override-feedback command.

Bailey, hesitant, "That's no web address."

Craige gritted his teeth, determined to be patient at least for a bit, "It is once I encode your terminal."

Bailey caught his breath, "These servers are encrypted."

"How 'bout that," Craige said. "Just enter what I gave you. This cross-connect is time sensitive. Pussyfoot and do nothing and it won't work. You'll see an encrypted field open. Attach the file. It'll ask for name. Enter your last name. And Bailey... "

"Yeh?"

"It's a one-time connect. Don't use the string-code again on any system. It'll tag your system as an illegal unauthorized user. Any attempt to access or tack will be identified to me. I don't know what damage it might do to your system, but scrambling hardwired memory chips, and whatever motherboards or servers you think are secure is a given. I get a notification like that I'll deny I even know you. Cut you loose; let you sink or swim on your own."

"I'd heard rumors your spook pals fed you a lot of R-and-D prototypes for field testing."

Craige said, "I have no idea what you're referring to."

Bailey was eager, knowing Craige would do exactly what he said. "You find something?"

"Nothing specific, but there's a helluva rotten stink to it."

"Dammit, Ingram!" Bailey gruffed. "I don't have time for your games."

Craige said, "If you think I'm playing games, I'll toss the ball back in your court. Either send me the file, or don't send it. Handle this yourself. You must have someone breathing down your neck." He knew it couldn't hurt to do a bit of his own trolling. "There's someone I want to talk to." Byte-count popup flashed Craige's screen followed by DOWNLOAD COMPLETE. "I'll get back to you."

He snapped the connection. With the stink Raymond had left him, Craige didn't much care what Bailey would do. Knowing which of Bailey's buttons to push, he could always count on Bailey rising to the baited carrot. He punched in the macro to connect the URL temp-code, and the download window popped up. Craige felt a touch sad for Bailey. The man was too eager to belong, too arrogant to fit with the crowd. Maybe they were more alike than Craige wanted to admit. Squashed the thought; didn't like it one bit. He headed down the hallway. The bedroom panel silently closed behind him.

* * *

Tall, slender, sixteen-year-old Carson Hamsworth stood inside the Dalugosh trailer. Blue-black eyes gawked darting between Janella and the freckled, crow's-footed Blondie, halter-top and shorts slouched at the kitchen table. "My stepdad said for me to come over here. See if you needed help with the yard work this afternoon." Beyond the cracked, never-washed kitchen window a litter of assorted junk cluttered the weeded yard—hardly a yard much less a lawn.

Janella smacked her gum with a crooked grin; garish shade of vampire-purple lipstick smeared lopsided a tad higher than her lips. "That was sure nice of your new stepdad." She eased off the grungy sofa, "You and him get along okay?"

"I guess. Pretty much."

Janella said, "When your mom an' him get married?"

Carson stammered, "I don't know."

Janella smacked her gum; giggled, "I ain't seen nothin' about it in the paper."

Denim and Dimples Blondie looked at Janella, "Is this the one Purvis was talking about?"

"Could be," Janella said. "Your stepdad tell you what I needed?"

"He said you wanted me to help you with something," Carson still gawking back and forth between the two women. "Said for me to help with whatever it was."

Janella grinned at Blondie, "And pay off some'a his poker IOUs." The two giggled. She moved up close, smelled the day-fresh sweat of the youth. He would be sweatier by the time they were through with him this afternoon.

"Mam?" Carson knew enough to know yard work never had been what he was told to get done. Knew it when stepdad told him where he was to go. His school pals talked all kind'a tales about the Dalugosh place. Knew some of the yarns were true.

Janella patted his shoulder; her hand slipping along his back and shoulder, "Don't you worry none. We're gonna show you a good time, and you'll be giving serious thought to comin' over more often."

"Yes, mam," queasy goose bumps. Sure what they wanted wadn't somethin' he'd ever done.

Dimples said, "Where your stepdad live?"

"Over in the valley." He swiped the drop of sweat trickled down his armpit.

"Thirsty?" It was her ready-trick to ease the kid's through any nervous naked.

"No, mam," blinked at Dimples, then to Janella, "I'm not thirsty."

Big grin, "You will be before we're finished."

Janella said, "Ever been to a party like this?"

"Like what?" sticky tongue licked dry lips.

Janella said, "Spend an afternoon keeping a couple of friendly older women company." Dimples twirled a peroxide curl at Janella's crack about older women. Her put-on smile looked put-on. It was.

"No, mam, not really. In my stepdad's trailer him and mom sometimes take showers together. We only have one bathroom and not much hot water."

Dimples was impatient. She liked shy green meat, but she was way more impatient for her share of the video money. "Your step-daddy told Purvis what a fine big man you were growing up to be," her hand played through the holes in his faded sport shirt.

"Soon turnin' seventeen."

Dimples rubbed her under-sized over-stuffed halter-top up against him, unbuttoning two more buttons on the threadbare shirt. Helped him slide it off. Both women caught one another's look at the gangly blemish-free uneventful chest. Janella's finger idled at the waist, working to loosen the worn jeans. Played with his belly. Carson took quick short breathes as she zippered down the jeans in a quick effortless whisper. He didn't have on no shorts. Janella figured he likely didn't have none or didn't have a clean pair.

Her hand swiftly slipped inside; eyes widened, "Purvis was right. You sure are growing up into a fine man."

Dimples' tongue slipped busy across her lips. Pushed against Carson. She had to be at work early. "Lordy mercy and he's not even full-growed. He'd sure enough win this month's award." In a faster hurry, "Get him out'a those jeans."

Janella reached for the tape measure. Was her job to get the newbies' stats in case Purvis wanted to set up a rematch, or better, a

71

special request. "We know a few in these parts we can set him up with. No wonder Purvis wanted us to break him in."

Dimples undid her top, ready to get the video rolling. "You and your buddies ever show off to one another?"

Carson blushed, "Sometimes in the showers after practice some of the guys tease me."

Dimples said, "We work this right he could be in with the high school crowd and his buddies. Run us a for-pay size contest. Make a whole series of videos and DVDs. Put 'em on the internet."

Janella said, "All Purvis wants is to get this show on camera. Purvis done talked with Carson's stepdad about settin' up Carson's younger sister."

Dimples said, "Purvis pay step-daddy for this?"

"You ever know Purvis to pay anyone?" Janella chuckled. "He's too cheap for that. Far as he's concerned he done enough by writin' off their IOUs. Purvis told me step-daddy haggled about how he ought'a get a percentage of the sales. Purvis didn't let that go no further. Wadn't about to put up with no one buttin' into his business deals, even if it is a nickel and penny sideshow."

"What you mean?" Dimples surprised. "They's lots of quick cash come into the cash box at the bar. You cain't tell me this is a sideshow."

"Don't matter. Let's get this done with."

Dimples eyed Carson, "I'd pay for this one."

Janella gave a rasping guffaw, "You'd pay any good hook-up young one." Took Carson by the hand, "Why don't we go to the back and get comfortable."

At the sight of the room, Carson couldn't believe the soft haze off the crushed red velvet bedspread and studio lights, "This is some fancy setup you got."

Janella caressed the velvet like she was touching his skin, "You just lay back right here." Patted a spot. Gently pushed him back, "Stretch right on your back." Made sure the camera was set and plugged in. Once she got this one tamed down a bit, might could do some even better retakes.

Dimples moved in on the other side of Carson, "We ain't gonna need no KY."

Carson never felt anything so good as what these two was doin'. Didn't want it to stop, and it didn't before two whole scenes got shot. He was going for more until Janella told him Purvis would soon be home. Carson wasn't sure what more these two wanted, but somehow he didn't want'a be watched by no husband. He hurried up and put his clothes on; beat a quick exit.

Janella watched him run to his oil-burnin' truck, "That one's gonna be a lot of fun."

"Take some trainin'," Dimples said.

"That'll be fun."

Later that evening Purvis edited the videos. "With some more coaching the kid can make us some big money," another swig of beer. "Got some repeat buyers at the bar up an' ready to add to their collections." Desk chair creaked as Purvis leaned back. Grinned at Janella, "Wonder what it'll take to get the sister in one. Customers like new faces."

She gave him a sour look, "I ain't so sure 'bout the sister. She's awful young."

"Now Sweetmeat, don't go gettin' no attitude on me. It's business and you know it. We cain't change what the customer wants. Always been that way... always gonna be. You had a real good idea about pick-ups at the bus stops," pecked her on the cheek.

Janella, all warm and gushy, "We might have to hold back on that a bit. Kind'a risky. Too easy for the competition to set us up."

Purvis said, "We find out who's behind that, won't take no time to put an end to anyone buttin' in."

She said, "We did get some good footage out'a some of them." She snuggled up against him. Her Purvis was such a big strong man and he was her big strong man.

* * *

When he finished reading the downloads from Bailey, Craige engaged his quantum-encrypt, entered the hieroglyph alphanumeric encodes tagged under PerBast, and connected the random cipher subroutine. Then he made copies of Bailey's downloads, renamed the file and backed-up the original and the copies to a removable bio-prototype chip before he closed the encrypt program and returned the systems to standby. He'd make a deposit box run; switch this bio-prototype with the older one. He'd watched a fire aboard Norfolk Naval Station destroy years of mainframe programming and never understood not updating backups.

Any aggressive hackers or unauthorized pings phishing his systems would kick in battery power and critical backup with an overwrite-wipe of all hard drives. In case firefighters were onsite and he wasn't, the system would kill all power to make sure no firefighters came in contact with hot wires. His computer rooms were fireproof. He had too much SpecOps and backdoor SEALteam contacts and phone numbers to take chances with his master files and programming data.

He glanced at his watch and rolled his chair to the other keyboard where he opened his encrypted file. It had been a year or two since he had talked with Kur. Leaning back in desk chair; fingers locked behind his head, he soaked in the odds stacked against his idea being outside the box and the off-chance idea would work. Purvis was too cagey—yet, maybe not. "Nothing to lose. Might as well see what happens." Opened his PerBast encodes, and brought up his DoD files with the lists of scrambled phone numbers. Dialed the number.

It surprised him when the pleasant voice answered before the third ring, "Fort Gordon, Office of the Director. How may I direct your call?"

"Is Kur Rohmer available?"

"There in no one in this division by that name. Shall I transfer you to the base operator?"

"Eiríkur Rohmer. If he isn't in a meeting or with someone, tell him Peadinger's on the line."

"One moment please." Craige heard the transfer.

Rohmer came on the line, "Craige Ingram. I thought you fell off the edge of the world."

"Nothing more drastic than retreating into my cave on Mars."

"I'm assuming this isn't a social call. I've got a strategy meeting in a few minutes."

"I'll keep it short. PI business." Craige said, "I need to track a vehicle."

"You have a plate number?"

Craige said, "Along with make and model of a law officer cruiser."

"I should've known," Rohmer chuckled. "How detailed you want it?"

"Facial recognition of the driver if possible."

"Won't be a problem," Rohmer said.

"That new satellite launched this week or the latest 37D upgrade?"

"I hope you're on a secure line," Kur said.

"We are. My system verified that the moment my call was answered."

"We're not using the 37 upgrade. We did away with PLCs."

"Good idea," Craige said. "In the electronic battle of mean versus meanest those Programmable Logic boards were problems waiting to happen."

"There's been some nasty incidents already. Gotta go. Will get back to you once we have the data. Don't be such a stranger. Let's get together for lunch soon."

"Will do. And thanks." Craige hung up. Least it would give him some idea where Purvis was leaving tracks.

Couldn't use Kur's satellite photos in open court, but the high resolution shots could show when and where to look. If he was lucky, he would take his own photos that could be used. He glanced at his watch again as he headed out the door and into his Jeep. There would be just enough time to get to football practice as the team was finishing after-school scrimmages.

A few minutes later, he nosed his jeep up to the chain link fence on the far side of the student parking lot. There was no need to draw unnecessary attention. Out on the field he spotted Billy Martel scrimmaging with one of the teams. He'd timed it about on the dot because it wasn't long before they broke into bunches, back-slapping camaraderie; headed toward the showers. He took the sidewalk toward the gym's freight entrance, the back entrance to the locker rooms and showers, and waited.

He recognized the auburn curls and Billy's stocky frame, and quickly moved in step behind him, "William Martel."

Billy's head came around, helmet in hand, and said something to his teammates. "Yes, sir?"

"Craige Ingram."

"Yes, sir, I know who you are. Your grandma used to babysit for me and my sister. Would bring us homemade chocolate fudge." A sweaty forearm wiped from brows and eyes, "She was a nice old lady."

Craige hadn't been ready for that. The kid was outgoing, moved like an athlete, and so far was minus the arrogance. Old warnings clanked his gut. Flipped a coin between his ears whether or not to tell Billy that he was investigating a murder. "You know what I do?"

Billy shrugged, "No, except the last few weeks you been asking a lot of questions about Buddy's death."

Billy's upfront honesty didn't surprise Craige, but he hadn't been quite ready for that either. Wondered how much Martel knew. Was the *friendly* an act? "I'm a Private Investigator."

Eyes lit, "You're a private eye? Not a cop like they said?"

"Like who said?"

Billy shrugged, "Beer and pizza, Saturday football talk."

"You buy beer?"

"Come on, Mister Ingram, you were in high school once."

"Yeh." High school seemed a long time ago—years that had passed way too quick.

"You not fixing to ask me where I bought it, are you?" And as quick, "This official about Buddy?"

"Should it be?"

"You gonna bug me about the beer?"

Craige said, "Forget the beer."

Billy relaxed some, "What's it like being a private eye?"

"Being a PI has its advantages for someone, like we're talking now." Craige was serious but not stern. "For starters the private eye handle went out a long time before you were born."

"Not in the books I read."

"You read lots?" This one wasn't your run of the mill teen.

"Sure, but don't tell my football buddies. Most never pick up a book. They find out how much I read, I'd never hear the end of it. I think most of 'em can't read, or can't read very good."

Craige said, "You and Buddy Raymond friends?"

"Not close. We hung around some, mainly at Friday rallies or after the games."

"He into drugs?" Craige's lips tightened, "I'll take that for a yes."

"No."

"Which is it?" Craige asked. "Yes or no."

Billy hesitant, "You can't take it as a *yes*. If I meant that, I'd say so." Held Craige's look, "I don't like to spill stuff on other folks' business."

Again Martel's openness came unexpected. Craige looked at Billy. This one was different. Craige found himself liking what he was seeing-hearing, "Even those that break the law?"

"I don't like gossip," Billy glanced away, then back. "We all break the law one way or another. That's what rules are for... see what we can get away with."

"You're real young to be such a philosopher."

Billy said, "You telling me you never broke any rules in those faraway places your grandma was so proud of you working at?"

"Yeh, I broke rules." The surprises kept coming from this one.

"Guess that makes us even," Billy said. "You didn't answer my question."

"PI's are supposed to do the asking," then, "What question?"

"What's it like doing a PI job?"

"It's okay. Now, what about my question?"

"Yeh, Buddy experimented with grass and some of the hard stuff. Never did understand why he thought he ought to be doing that."

"About what I thought." Craige said it real low. "I don't understand drugs either."

Billy said, "Buddy and his dad didn't get along."

"That's what I hear."

"Started running with a rough crowd." Shoulders slumped; hung his head, "Mister Raymond gave Buddy anything money could buy, but never did things with him. Never gave Buddy what he wanted most. Never was around to do things with him. Buddy once told me that over at my house. Said he wished he had a dad like mine, even asked my dad if he could go fishing with us. He liked going fishing with me'n dad." His eyes dropped to the ground, then back up to meet Craige's. "I tried to be his friend. Buddy would do dumb things to get his dad's attention. Anytime he got caught he'd brag how his dad would fix it. Most time his dad did. I couldn't go along with the drugs."

Craige felt an emptiness of missing things he might've done with his dad. At least one bit of the ugly Raymond riddle made sense. A lost wasted young life had cried out for someone to care. Felt useless and abandoned when no answer came back. No telling how much Buddy Raymond's life could have meant with a little different turn here or a kind word there. Remembrances surfaced of those who'd cared enough to make a difference in his own life. "You like to fish?"

Billy said, "Dad and me used to go a lot before he died."

"Sorry about that."

"He got awful sick. Dad worked hard all his life, made sure there was food on the table and a roof over our heads. He loved Mom. I'm not getting married till I know I can love my wife like he and Mama loved one another."

Craige said, "That's a good way to look at it, plus it's good you could see that with your parents."

"Dad never took hardly any vacation." Eyes down, "Before he had the heart attack he'd been getting awful tired during the day. Found him in his car off the Beaufort highway. Been dead about six hours but he managed to get the car off the road, out of traffic. It rolled down into a ditch. Nobody found it till morning." Billy's words tumbled into some faraway place. "Sure do miss him."

"Plenty fish at my place, and you're welcome. Introduce you to my German shepherd. Once he knows you, there's no problem. Will take a chunk out of anybody up to mischief. Nobody to bother you."

"That would be nice."

"You do any hunting?"

"Sort of interested in getting better at bow hunting. Think maybe I might try some at your place?"

"Let me know when you're coming." Craige smiled at the kid's eagerness. "German shepherd's real picky about who comes near the house. Once he's introduced, you're safe."

Billy smiled, "I might like to be a PI."

Craige felt somewhat winsome as he shook the young man's hand, "Nice meeting you."

"You, too. I'll take you up on the huntin' and fishing," Billy said. "Coach is waiting." Gave Craige a high-five, and loosed a hurried sprint toward the gym.

* * *

Craige ducked out of his shirt and T. Wiped under his pits with his T; tossed shirt and T toward the mudroom laundry hamper. Missed. He reached for a clean glass from the drain board and splashed a shot of Glenfiddich scotch onto two square cubes of ice. He didn't like curved cubes. They bunched under his nose; got in the way of sipping his scotch slow. After kicking off his shoes he turned on the garden hose to slow trickle a clump of Grannie's favorite roses in her bed around the old black walnut stump and wiggled his toes in the grass. The wild Georgia azalea cuttings he'd set to sprouting nearby were already showing new rootlets. They'd be ready to transplant before long. By soaking them slow overnight for a week, they'd bloom next spring. He didn't care for the hothouse hybrids. They were too picayune for his liking, always needing looking after. The wild azalea backwoods honeysuckle cousins that grew pale pink petals with near red centers would look good around the partial-shade side of the house. Those and Grannie's wild Georgia roses never bothered with aphids. He added water to the cuttings in the stone jar, then reached up; tested the fern for dampness. Give it some water. Took a slow sip of cool scotch.

He pulled up a ladder-back porch chair and propped his feet up on the porch railing. Another long slow sip of scotch hit the spot. One hand slowly rubbed across his chest as a tried and true rule augured at him—*never get personally involved with an investigation.* The fishing-hunting invite wasn't personal, but it was edging the rule. It was a good rule—except when it didn't work. Lots of kids took a bad turn at some fork in their decisions. All it took was a little caring and the other fork would've been the one walked. Billy Martel didn't strike him as any ordinary kid. Was he one of those rarities that lived by simple proven rules... like honesty? Or was he even more savvy-extraordinary and was cunning enough to be hiding something? Craige tried to shake the eerie feeling that it was his own suspicious nature tinting specters that weren't there. Yet the feeling wouldn't go away that Billy had nothing to do with Buddy's death. What if Billy was involved? Or—more deadly—knew something without knowing it was behind what got Buddy killed. Billy sized up people quick, strong streak of street-smart for a kid not yet out of his teens.

Grannie's rule. "Well-mannered young'uns and pets reflect good parents and owners."

He'd checked Billy's background but missed the part about Billy's dad. Doubt refused to settle. Another sip, "What could he need to hide?" He needed to check deeper. See if anything floated to the top.

Lucky nuzzled his hand wanting an ear-scratch. Craige glanced down, "Always wanting attention," slow-knuckled the ear. Dog's head went lopsided, grunting contentedly. "Wouldn't mind a little ear nuzzling myself." Hiked his balls; sipped more, "That woman is sure making it comfortable to get in the habit of not liking to sleep alone." Lucky gazed up as though understanding every word; licked his hand for more scratchin'. "Something ain't right," mimicking Grannie's tone when she had a nameless itch that couldn't be reached. He emptied the glass; jiggled the cubes, enjoying the shift of daylight turning yellow a darker gold and greens greener as daylight faded. His mind idled as he stood, stretched.

Lucky nuzzled and licked more. Big golden eyes speaking better than words, fixed up at Craige, tail wagging a wide thump. It probably saved Craige's life. Craige bent to rub the furry head just as the silenced hiss of the shot shattered the fern basket behind Craige's head and ricocheted to splinter part of the post. Dirt and bits of green spattered in a burst. With a drilled reflex Craige dropped to a crouch; rolled off the porch at the corner. Lucky yelped a warning low snarl just as Craige hand-cupped a muzzle over the dog's mouth. The shepherd would attack if he didn't stop him.

Craige gave a short definite command in his Cherokee dialect, "Wa-ya."

Lucky's head snapped toward the direction of the shot. Ears up. Heeled to Craige's right. Craige did a quick line-of-sight from post and pot, then off toward the highway and back across the yard, the dense foliage and tree cover beyond. Lucky had zeroed direct toward the wall of green and the only direction the shot could've come from.

Craige saw no movements in the foliage. Birds were silent. Lucky gave a low muffled growl, neck hair fuzzed. The dog's whole body quivered, and Craige's neck hairs prickled stiff. He recalled starless black moonless beaches, bellied behind trees or convenient lumps of ground on some illicit border crossing when unexpected patrols showed up. The fear never varied, bored marrow deep, chilling hot blood and icy-sweat heat. He listened hard, half expecting another shot or the sound of the shooter coming to make sure of the kill. Nothing. With arms and legs spread flat against the lower edge of the house, he felt naked. At least he wasn't in plain sight of anyone up on the hill. Dog's focus never wavered.

He wasn't about to lay there, a target waiting for the shooter to get a cleaner aim. One quick snap of his shoulders, Craige tumble-rolled through the kitchen door. His weight ricocheted against the doorjamb; split a hinge loose. In the den he reached into the drawer next to the sofa; grasped the snub-nosed 9mm special he'd picked up in Petrograd—refused the Leningrad name for the sewer-greed mass killer Ulyanov. Up on one knee he seated the clip, and flattened against the wall. Carefully, he scrutinized through the kitchen windows; nothing out back towards the river or the picture window beyond the dining table. With a quick glimpse along the porch, Lucky was still heeled where he left him, ears fixed in the same direction. Statue-still, Craige had good views across the yard, the dock and driveway from where he was.

The birds were still silent, convincing Craige that whoever it was, had slipped away while the slipping was possible. The possibilities came down to the same bottom line—he'd gotten someone's attention and for sure upset them. Who? When? He went over the last few days. Mort Raymond? Was his suspicion of Raymond personal—clouding his judgment? The personal bias could mislead. Adrenaline tensed his thighs and shoulders. Letting his eyes sweep back and forth, Craige took cautious steps back out onto the porch. He felt a sudden sting in his big toe; pulled a sliver of his scotch glass out of the bright bloody speck. Lucky sniffed, licked it.

He started to strip as he made his way through his exercise room and realized he still had a firm grip on the 9mm. He laid it on the shelf behind the weight bench, undressed, and hit the shower. After drying off, he pulled out a U.S. jock brief. Flung it aside and began rummaging through the dryer till he found the contour jock he liked, slipped it on. He enjoyed the snug fit of full cover over his butt. Adjusted the fit; did reps till sweat was dripping; muscles burning. His shoulder hurt where he'd smacked the doorframe. He sat at his desk with all the notes he'd made spread out in consecutive dates and created a flowchart of those he knew about, any connections they might be twisted in with one another. An aggravated growl rumbled his throat—too many disconnected maybes. To one side he pegged the faceless shooter along with possible others he didn't know about.

Early the next morning he pushed off from the dock. Just as quick, Lucky was off to chase chattering squirrels, shuffling possums or whatever critter. With strong steady strokes Craige rowed the flat bottom out onto the river and against the current. The quiet syrupy boil of the river matched Craige's thoughts. After a good workout upriver to the bridge he drifted back downstream into eddies along the bank where he plopped his homemade shellacked cane pole in the water—did little to no fishing. Nearby, he heard Lucky rustling along the bank and the overhangs where he had seen more than a few water moccasins plop off their sunny branches into the eddies.

He never liked being bested, when he had the sinking feeling he'd overlooked something and let it happen. The skiff drifted slowly downstream. By the time he noticed, he was way below his dock. He cut in the electric trolling motor, added a stroke now and then, and soon gently bumped dockside. Of one thing he was certain: his asking questions had stirred a shooter's cover-up that had an explicit touch of the desperate. Nosing about had juggled someone's applecart. It wasn't the time for playing his hold cards. Instead, he would ratchet up the heat a notch or two or three, see what could just float to the top—and not get shot in the doing. He knew he was raveling frayed concoctions that weren't hanging together. A Grannie gut-feeling and funeral parlor dead-ends, Craige was convinced he was dealing with more than one perp. Firing from ambush wasn't Purvis's way. Still, Purvis had the rep of being impulsive. Money was never far from his mind and backed up with brute animal muscle to get his way. It wouldn't be the first time Craige had seen money go out of control and lethal. Purvis had either done the barn job, watched it done, or had it done, and was a likely candidate for making the shot.

He had no proof, and what few facts he had made it easy to check alibis Purvis could easily concoct. Anyone could pay a dozen flunkies to lie. The two in the barn were warnings; examples intended to be found; intended to intimidate. It smelled like Purvis; let threats do the intimidating. But Raymond was different. He'd kill to keep things quiet and be sneaky in the doing of it. Craige couldn't see Raymond with the guts to try the kill-shot. Couldn't see Mort Raymond with enough guts to plan a kill, much less go through with it unless he was cornered. A dark caveat bubbled his thoughts—cornered animals were dangerous and unpredictable. Craige knew he could be wrong. And it wouldn't be the first time. A first-kill was the hardest unless it was spur of the moment. No matter the motive—fear drove the wildest of motives. After Kill-One it got easier. In mid-thought Craige stopped—what if Bailey didn't know about a first one? With a cottony tongue to the roof of his mouth Craige considered that he might've always been one of the targets. Couldn't make that fit. Anyone in these parts knew threatening him was the worst of bad ideas. If the shot wasn't to scare, then someone wanted him out of the way. Whoever was next on some list could be real easy—just look for the next body. He didn't want to wait for that. Ending up dead was easy.

Chapter 6

Mort Raymond paced some more back and forth in his den, then paused, eyed the silent phone one more time. He dreaded it would ring; afraid it wouldn't. During last night's long unsettled sleepless night that stretched into longer hours, he kept coming up against there being only one way. For never-killed-nobody Mort, his doing the killing wasn't even on his list, much less at the bottom of it. Purvis had a reason for wanting him to do it; Purvis wanted him on the hot seat; wanted him cornered. He didn't trust Purvis. Who Raymond could trust was even more of a problem. The thought of pointing a gun or pulling a trigger made his hands shake, and pointing it at a Navy SEAL made his hands shake worse. He never made no deal with Purvis to kill nobody; never made no deal with nobody to kill nobody. His heart raced. He never planned nothing like this. Tried to make himself think about how to do it clean—didn't want no shot-up body in no morgue. Purvis would blackmail him, and enjoy making him sweat. He could sneak dynamite from Carl Jenkins Construction Company; wouldn't be difficult. The foreman most times never locked the shed. He could take an old clunker from the used car lot. That way they'd be no paper trail for nobody to follow, not even if the VIN number was found; traced back to his car lot. Cars got took from lots all the time. It was his car lot so it wouldn't matter if his prints was found. Just be sure his prints weren't on none of the wraps of the dynamite. Dump in the body; take care there was no blood trails nowhere. Be sure and use plenty dynamite to bring down half the mountain on the site. Wouldn't be no body left to identify or no truck neither. No body for Purvis to shove in a cooler. Not knowing nothin' about body parts and teeth and bones and DNA gave Mort a chance to feel good about how it could be done. Out-fox Purvis at the same time. Thought it up all on his own. Mort felt good—for a little bit.

Sweating heavy, mouth dry, another gulp of raw coffee only made his pounding headache pound harder. He opened the gun cabinet, took out his favorite engraved 30-06; caressed along the special blued sleekness of the barrel. Raymond liked hefty profits, quick real estate deals, over and done with, cash in the bank. Preferred a customer over a barrel; hooked on a sale's contract; pay up or forfeit the earnest money. That was the best kind of kick on any day. Placed its blue sleekness back in the rack. The 30-06 made too much noise. He disliked face-to-face showdowns unless he held a royal flush with no wild cards—and Ingram was a wild card Mort Raymond had no control over. Mort didn't like that. Using a gun was a bad idea.

Buddy's crossbow was next to the shotgun. Quiet, no sound, perfect. He lifted the bow, took three arrows into the back yard. Fired all the bolts. Didn't know where the first one went. Second one missed the big oak. Third one glanced a nick in the tree trunk.

"Can't be too hard to work if my doped-head kid could use it." Tossed crossbow and bolts in the front seat of the car, and backed out of the drive.

It was getting on toward dusk as he crossed the Beech Island Bridge; passed the condominiums and what was left of the Goodale Inn. After taking the ramp onto Gordon Highway he headed south. He had to find someone—a target alone. Practice doing it quick. Between the Old Atlanta Highway and Gate One there was nobody. No nameless hitching drunk soldier that could easily disappear. He dumped the idea; another soldier dead would have Ingram asking more questions. At the next off-ramp he did the cloverleaf and headed back the way he came. He considered scouting the bus station, but remembered schedules had been cut—not enough of a crowd for the picking. Considered the airport—too many witnesses. He was getting anxious. Frog Hollow or Pinch Gut? Witnesses again, knowing the old harpies were always watching from behind their genuine plastic lace curtains. If the mill crowd caught him, they'd put the hurt to him without bothering to call the law. Up ahead he spotted the last off-ramp before South Carolina. Thinking this had been a bad idea, he made a right at the bottom of the ramp. He just didn't want to stir anything that would get him attention. Heart pounding; sweaty circles under his arm stinking; he felt cornered between Purvis not giving a damn about legal and Ingram poking around, stirring what Mort wanted left unstirred. He turned onto East Boundary and the road home, when the levee cut-through caught his attention.

He swung a hard left and eased off the accelerator with a rubberneck gut-ache at all the plush rich-folk's houseboats. Hung a turn at the second cut to head on home. He didn't feel like poker tonight no how. The *For Sale* sign on the big blue-job houseboat grabbed his eye and his billfold. Another one moored astern of the *Lady Inn* just up from where the restaurant's lighted veranda thrust an eerie jut out over the river. On impulse he swung in and parked. He never could pass up checking out a deal. Weather was nice, walking might help. It felt safe over here, no one around who knew him. He went aboard, "Hello on the houseboat." Waited.

He tapped on the sliding door; cupped his hands around his eyes for a look inside. Could see no movement; then tried the door— locked. No realtor's key box. He walked along the dockside of the boat, across the bow with its propane grill, and continued along the narrow outboard walkway to the stern. Boat looked in good condition. A telephone number to call for anyone interested was written on a rain-spattered piece of butcher paper. The dockside hull rubbed and bumped against the oversized dock bumpers as he jotted down the number. He stuck the small note pad in his pocket and looked over the side. A small outboard runabout tied alongside nudged lazily against the low riding gunnels; painted the same blue and white.

Unexpected, "Can I help you?" the stranger's blue eyes squinted.

A startled Raymond found himself facing a man, mid to late thirties. The parking lot had been empty. Mediterranean looking, lots of Greeks lived in Augusta. Close cropped ebony curly hair, tank top and tight spandex black workout pants. Mort wondered how anyone squeezed everything into something so tight with no ball-room. Tall, slight, but evenly muscled, he carried the longest goddamn oar Mort had ever seen. Reached plumb over his head by a good four feet.

The man repeated, "Can I help you?"

"Didn't see anyone around. I was just lookin' at this one," force of habit reached for his business card. "Mort Raymond, Real Estate and Land Sales."

"Interested in buying?" the rugged face somewhere between remnants of adolescent cragged with episodes of high living.

It was a look of fast-living Mort Raymond understood quick enough. "Hadn't thought about it till I drove by and saw the sign. Your boat?"

"No. I'm with one of the rowing clubs here." Gave a nod toward the open gates of the boathouse, "Just finished a set of warm-up reps on the ergometer. Was about to get my shell ready to take out. River traffic has eased off. Ski wakes quiet down late in the day, good time to row, early morning right after sunup is good, too. Makes for calm water, maybe a fishing boat or two. Saw you over here. Owners of this one are getting divorced. They left me with the key so I could show it for them in case anyone wanted to look."

"Sure," Mort grinned, never one to pass up the unexpected. "You work around here?"

"Graduate school at the college up on the hill, that locals still call Augusta College."

Mort hadn't thought about the campus. Better than Fort Gordon. Nobody paid much attention to the college crowd, anything for a quickie-hookup. Not a matter of who. Only who's next? Salesman Raymond caught the not-so-harsh nasal clip that definitely was not Southron, "You're not from around here."

"Connecticut."

Raymond asked the usual, "How'd you get way down here to Georgia?" laying on the accent.

"Engineer at Plant Vogel and got to liking it here. Decided to stay, attend graduate school. Want to see this one inside?"

"Sure."

Rower squeezed two fingers inside his waistband; fished the hidden pocket of the skin-smooth rowing shorts. Pulled out a key, unlocked the door on the rear barbecue deck and slid it open. Flipped the switch next to the patio-type door. Table lamps at each end of the long blue brocade sofa came on.

Mort followed behind, "Engines work?" Raymond, intent on something different than the man thought, needed a few minutes, eyes skirting about the room.

"They did at the end of March. They used this one at the starting line for the regatta."

Raymond asked, "Has it been away from the dock since then?"

"Not that I know of. They split after that. It's pretty big, hard to miss on the river, but I'm not down here all the time. If either one of them took it out they didn't tell me."

"What's back there?"

"Galley, bedroom and double baths. Last time I was inside was after that heavy rain last week. Wanted to make sure there were no roof leaks."

Mort asked, "What about the bilge pumps?"

"I check the engine compartment each time I come down. Oil sump is right like it's supposed to be. No water getting in. Boat is plugged into dock power with pumps on auto. Bilge level start to rise, the pumps come on, but I check to make sure."

"What's above?"

Rower said, "Equipped with sun deck and upper deck controls."

"Lights back yonder work?"

"They should. They're on a different circuit. Let me see," heading toward the bow.

Mort knew he'd have to be quick, fear pumping his heart faster. The man was in better shape than he was. At the far end of the bar Mort spotted what would work real good. The small bookends easy to grip, looked marble or a good plastic imitation. Either way, heavy. He snugged one tight in his fist, backed against the bookshelf.

"Found the light switch," rower called from up forward.

Mort called, "What's this?" Waited.

Footsteps came toward him, "What?"

When the rower came through the door, Raymond raised the bookend and smashed it against the back of the head. The body hit the floor like a gunnysack of coffee beans. Didn't move; eyelids fluttered. Mort moved quick; dragged the lamp off the bar. Shade went one way, base smashed against the bar. Mort wrapped the cord around the man's neck with double twists around his fists. Shoved one knee between the man's shoulder blades and tightened. Rower groaned, eyes flew open, legs and thighs bending, up on his elbows, fingers clawing at his neck, battling for air, one hand outstretched, grasping at nothing, skin bulging blue, neck vessels ballooned, mouth working. Mort pulled tighter.

For a moment Mort thought he wasn't going to hold him down; hadn't hit him hard enough; couldn't let him get up. He grabbed the bookend smeared with hair and a little blood, and smashed it down hard. Again and again. Blood coated his hand. The moans stopped. He grabbed the cord, tightened it tight as he could until the pupils gaped wide and black; chest quit gulping. Bloody spittle drooled onto the mottled tan brown carpet. Urine ran through the rower's shorts. Mort glanced around. He had to find towels or rags, clean the rug, pick up the pieces of the broken lamp. Who'd miss one lamp in the squabble of a divorce? He tugged at the ring until he got it off then yanked off the watch. He jerked down the tight stretch of the shorts to get at the inside pocket where he found a driver's license and another ring of keys. Just to be sure he hadn't overlooked any personal items, he stripped the body naked. There were personals stuffed inside the shorts, along with Nike shoes, jock strap, cropped tank top, and a gold neck chain he'd not seen. He would get rid of everything. In the kitchen he found the roll of garbage bags; stuffed in clothes, pieces of the lamp. He pocketed the key to the sliding door.

He hurried to the bathroom, grabbed towels, and stuck one under the gaping mouth to soak the reddish spittle. He knew from cleaning up after guttin' and prepping deer, blood was the hardest to get out. Thinking ahead, he might want to use this location to get rid of the body, when he did Ingram. He went to the door; checked the parking lot. He wanted no surprises. He hurried to his car and opened the trunk where he kept old quilts and blankets. Before anyone saw him, he'd load the body and get out of there. Didn't like all the street lights. Smart move would be to never come around this place again. He never realized how easy it was to take a life. It was the same as hunting, was like spotlightin' deer. He wiped the sweat off his face— could get hooked on the high sport of it. He hadn't been comfortable with the crossbow, but the bookend had worked fine. He'd take a hammer for Ingram. The unplanned spur-of-the-moment dry run turned out better than he'd expected. Except *Murphy's Law* wasn't finished with Morton Raymond.

"What'cha doin', mister?" A kid, seven, maybe eight stood behind Mort holding his big bicycle, "You gonna go do some fishin'?"

Mort about shit. His world tumbled bottomless in a chokehold gawk, "Where'd you come from?"

"Rode my bike," kind'a puzzled by this pudgy grownup man who sure ought'a know what you did with a bike. "Mama said I could go ridin' if I finished my homework before dark. So I come down here to skip rocks on the water. Lots'a good gravel up by the curbs. Make good skippers."

Mort's gaze stabbed back and forth between the kid and the trunk of the car, "What?"

"You come down to fish?"

"Thought about it." Panic stomped Mort's chest. Couldn't think of anything to say. Wheezed. Hurt to breathe; headache pounded harder.

"Ought to be good fishin'. Gonna rain tonight though. Mess up fishin' tomorrow."

Mort glanced at a cloudless sky, "How you know it's going to rain?"

"Mama told me." Shoved the bike; hopped one leg over; caught the peddles, "Gotta go check the river. See ya after a while, mister." He sped off in a wheelie flurry, spatter of gravel.

Fear paralyzed Mort. One yellowish sodium street lamp fizzed into the dusk light. The fizzling hiss startled him as the streetlight sputtered brighter; blotched his face. He didn't know what to do. Couldn't undo what he was in the middle of. Getting caught with the body would ruin everything. Getting throwed in jail would be worse. The bastards who got him in this mess would pretend they knew nothing, let him rot. He would be laid out for the whole country club to see. Jail would make him an easy target. Purvis would see him put with convicts who'd do anything to make a deal. Getting caught was Mort Raymond's biggest nightmare, and thinking about it put him in a body-soaked smelly sweat.

He hurried back inside before the kid came back. He locked the slidding door; turned out the lights. It would be better not to move the corpse with his car—no telling when somebody else might show up. But he couldn't think of where he could dump the body where it wouldn't be found. Ingram had an in with one of the best forensic examiners around. He put the body in the trunk, that damn forensic sleuth that worked with MacGerald would find out it had been in a car. Ingram was already eyeing him. Ingram would make sure his car would be the first place they'd look.

He rummaged through the bedroom closets until he pulled down a bundle of blankets. Back in the galley, he grabbed a meat cleaver and a big carving knife out of the knife block and returned to the body with an armful of towels. He hurried to the shower-bath tub, yanked down the shower curtain, and laid it on the floor next to the body where he spread garbage bags on top of the pad of blankets. Making sure to roll the body on one of the bags, he heaved and grunted as he dragged the body to the tub and tumbled it in. With the meat cleaver on the floor next to him, he rolled the head to one side to stretch the skin at the base of the neck barber-shave taut. Swallowing several times before he could touch it, he gripped the thick-bladed knife and leaned over.

He'd get rid of the head, hands, no finger or palm prints, and no dental records. He turned the cold water on to wash away the blood before it clotted; stained the grout. The skin tight, he sliced deep. Once he cleaned up, there'd be no trace. Wasn't nothing he could do about the blood type—unless there was no body. He'd handle that later. Deals gone wrong for Mort Raymond was nothing new. He lived by the motto—*Bastards are out to get me*.

Murphy's Law still wasn't finished with Mort. The shower leaked. Bloody ooze crept across the floor; soaked the knees of Mort's pants—red all over the floor and carpet. He made a mad dash to the kitchen; cracked his shin on a bar stool and scattered a holder of cocktail napkins across the bar and floor. Scrambling to find a bucket, pan, rags, mop, anything to scoop and sop with, he remembered seeing the pegboard with a bunch of keys. He hurried around the bar; found one that looked like it might be an ignition key. If he could get the engines started, maybe it'd pressurize the sump to the disposable water holding tank. Suck away the leak. He ran through the den toward the lower steering console. His hand trembled as he aimed the key. It fit. Holding his breathe, he turned the key. Gauges giggled, panel lights flickered. Beneath his feet a rhythmic growl settled into a steady throb. RPMs steadied, a single red flash above the key, warning about the anchor. He did a quick check of the fuel gauges—near a full tank. He would let the engines run; charge up the batteries. He stared at the throttle; had never had something this big out on the water. For sure didn't want more of a screwup; pull away from the dock and the engine quit. He could take it downriver and get rid of the big pieces.

From down the hallway came the steady gush and gurgle of the water tap he'd forgotten and left running. With the engines still running, he returned to the gory task. He finished the headless torso but stopped with the hands; it was taking too much time. Shiny joints and tendons gleamed at the neck where he'd chopped with the cleaver. The shower was a mess. He wrapped the bags and blankets around the body parts. Making sure the door key was still in his pocket, he stood by the main console, his thoughts jumbled. He toyed with easing the houseboat down river and into one of the bayous. Houseboat props could be stern-mounted or mid-hull, but he wasn't sure on this one. Nixed taking something this big into shallow-draft bayous. He could wrap the head real good. Stuff it in the trunk. Get rid of it separate. Taking this hulk out on the river was sure to get someone's attention. If he dumped the pieces over the side, he was afraid they'd float. Damn fisherman would spot a body floating by. He could cut it up. Turtles and gators would handle the smaller chunks.

Damn kid come by at just the wrong time, "Should'a had the body out'a here by now."

It didn't bother Mort to waste one life figuring out how to do Ingram. He started to grab another blanket when the idea hit. "Don't mess up the car."

Problem would be if someone found the body—one of the owners or one of their lawyers. His poker-caution decided. He cut up the torso; dumped the chunks into the skiff; poked holes in the bottom of the minnow-well and sealed float sections. Then he cut away the bumpers, threw them aboard the skiff. White bumpers would flash along the riverbank like the underside of a deer's tail, begging someone to take a look. He sliced through the lines holding the small boat alongside. Rain would hurry the current, and the safety cable at the lock and dam had been busted for a long time. The skiff would go right over the top. He shoved the skiff out into the current and watched it swirl, drag and bump along the low launch docks, then gently curve out into the current in swirling pirouettes. Mort stared for the longest until it was just a speck at the bend of the river and out of sight.

He'd show up at the Friday night poker game, nobody the wiser. Act like nothing was wrong. Be home about the usual time.

* * *

Mort holed up in his home den-office. He couldn't shake the dread that somebody would find out. Smelled exactly like he hadn't taken a bath in days. He hadn't. Hadn't dared sneak out of the house to his office in town to snitch money from his pigeonholed hidey-hole. He had his credit cards but was afraid to use them. He'd seen Purvis use the state internet-connects with credit card numbers to locate any ATM on about anybody. If he used the cards to buy a fresh set of clothes; any of Purvis's eyes might spot him. If Purvis was looking for him he'd be on the lookout for Mort's car; put out an APB. Getting his tag number would be no problem for Purvis. Mort left his car down the road. Out of sight inside the old barn behind the rundown filling station; bushes grown up all around both. Clumps of wisteria, swamp magnolias, and chinaberry trees matted with honeysuckle and scuppernon' vines were a made-for curtain between vehicle and the busy highway. He had used the outside door to his home-office and snuck in. Wife on the far end of the upstairs never came into his office.

He would let her know if he needed an alibi, "'Bout all she was worth for."

The other night Mort had spotted Purvis parked near Perkin's Used Cars. Couldn't be for no other reason than Purvis was watching him. He'd thought about switching his car with one from the lot, but all the keys were in the front office on the lot so decided against that. Purvis might spot him, or some seedy bastard workin' late in the service shops would see him and give Purvis a call. He considered going to his own car, drive off, drive anywhere. Never come back. Quickest road out was across the river, head south, Florida, New Orleans, catch a boat or plane to anywhere as long as it was a long way. Some place where nobody knew him or Purvis. Purvis was a bulldog; he could call in favors. Raymond shivered.

He hated the stink of being cooped up in a house that was like a jail with nothing in it he cared about. Raymond knew running was the worst thing to do. He didn't trust Purvis and hadn't for a long time. He didn't care about the drug paybacks or rake-offs from the skin videos. Quick and easy and safe was the kind of money he liked. Even if he took out Ingram, Purvis would kill him to shut him up, and get rid of anybody who knew anything about it. He heard the clump-clump of his wife coming down the front stairs into the foyer. Clump-clump grew faint. She was likely on the way into the kitchen. She lived in the fridge. He tried to think of any other place he could be alone, a place Purvis wouldn't find him. Any place to hide—the poker game sure wasn't it.

He thought of the old filing station. Right there in front of him to see all the time and close to his car. He wouldn't have to risk his wife askin' dumb questions, running her mouth. He couldn't wait till morning to slip away because the housekeeper came early; she would come in where he was to empty the wastebasket. Then his wife sure enough would start harpin' at him.

He listened. The clump-clump footsteps receded back up the stairs, then he slipped out the side door and hurried down the road. The side door of the old station was ajar. His shoes crunched broken glass scattered across the floor as he edged to the slatted front window. He tried to get a better look between the boards nailed over the windows. Beyond the curtain of vines there was no traffic, no headlights on the highway. The rest of the night he stood ramrod fearful at the tight little window as roaches rustled the leaves and old newspapers, mosquitos buzzed, and rats squeaked in the damp piles of matted, rain-soaked plaster and fallen ceiling tiles. He wasn't about to stretch out. He needed to keep an eye out for anything unusual.

As daylight approached, he retreated into the mildewed storage room with its stink of motor oil and gasoline. His back hurt; legs ached. Instead of getting into his car and heading out of town, he thought about driving to the public docks across the river. He still had the keys to the houseboat. It would be the last place anyone would look. He could cruise by on the levee road above the dock and see if he could spot any yellow police tape. If there were no cops he could sneak aboard; take the houseboat all the way to Savannah. He didn't like the idea of going through the locks, but there wasn't any other way to get downriver.

Nixed that. "Take a day or two to get downriver. Once they notice the houseboat gone, they'd have choppers in the air. Purvis'd know in no time. He'd have to leave the boat or ride it out with Purvis using choppers, waiting."

He had to decide before sun-up because he sure wasn't spending no more nights in this place. He didn't like running, leaving it all to the bastards that got him in this mess. It wasn't his fault. Maybe there was still a way to make this work. He could pull off his dead-man disappearance and fuck Purvis in the process. By not breaking his usual routine, he'd have the edge.

His squinted eyes took a quick look through the boarded slats. Sweat beaded his face and neck. Early traffic wasn't bad; mix in with them. Sweaty fingers twisted the car keys—if he was going to use his car it had to be now. He eased out the side door, and hurried into his car; locked the doors. Hands trembled; cheek muscles quivered. Fear battled greed, and greed won.

He backed the car out and pulled in behind two eighteen wheelers. Half an hour later he was parked down the back side road from Redcliffe where the car couldn't be seen from the main road. He snuck through the weeded field to hunker inside the latticed gazebo of the once formal garden. Once there, he crouched and waited. Nobody was in sight, and only a dim light reflected in the second floor window of the caretaker's cottage. He watched for the light to go dark with back and forth glances in case the caretaker-keeper was making his rounds and forgot to turn off the light.

* * *

The next day Mort waited. When it got close to poker-time, he left his hiding place and drove to the location, parking his car between two trucks, a pickup on one side, a dually on the other. He gulped a breath of air when he spotted Purvis's patrol car parked right up front. The cigar-smoking bourbon-and-beer poker game at the slapped-together wooden houseboat was already in a full swing. It usually started before noon, and went on all day and all night. The rickety houseboat tilted at its usual off-level angle. Any time John Law planned a bible-toters' clean-up-sin sweep for the media, Purvis made sure the poker boat got moored on the other side of the river. The state line in the middle of the river was a flimsy cain't-touch-me-now gambit. It made for a good excuse and would this time. And Ingram wouldn't know about it.

Mort turned off the motor and fixed on the weak flicker of the bulb at the end of the ramp down from the bank to the lopsided fallin'-off screen door and narrow rotten walkway of a porch. Somehow the bulky outline of the two story ramshackle barn, balanced on empty oil drum-floats, reminded him of Purvis and the trailer mess he called home. Mort was jumpy. Every headlight that winked through the trees along the old levee dirt road made his heart skip a beat until the lights moved on. He'd watched Purvis beat drunks when they sour-mouthed him or didn't do like they was told. A spotlight swept along the river beyond the houseboat. Somebody was frog giggin' on the river, likely headed home after a night of it. Their empty boats were always tied along the docks or on riverbank trails. He wandered down to the riverside of the houseboat; craned a look up and down the river. Its surface was a calm undulating silvery-white. Nobody was in sight.

He checked his watch; there was still time to change his mind. It wouldn't be a problem to find a boat—take it, be gone and to hell with the car, "Wife can buy her own."

Purvis wouldn't send a shooter after him, like he done to take out Ingram. Trying a stunt like that was the worst thing Purvis could'a done. Didn't want to think what Purvis would do if he found out Mort hadn't even tried to get Ingram. Purvis wanted Mort's neck in the wringer. Purvis would sit back and enjoy turning the screw. Take no risk. Likely take him somewhere; make him beg.

In his whole life it seemed like nothing ever went easy like he planned. He never should've gotten wrapped up in this, but he'd make sure this time was different. He crossed the shaky plank stretching between the soggy bank and rotten deck; shoved the door open.

Purvis barely raised his eyes from his cards, "Where the hell you been?" Reached for the bottle; filled his glass. "We was wonderin' where you was."

Raymond said, "Had a customer."

"Never seen you worked up about a buyer. What happened? Deal go sour, or did you get stiffed on a sale's contract?" Laughed like it was a good joke.

Raymond knew the bunch of them talked about him behind his back. "Nobody stiffs me." He'd show them before he was finished. He'd have the last laugh. Nobody outsmarted a horse trader like him.

Along the dirt road, a vehicle pulled to one side and stopped. Driver got out; didn't slam the door. The floating-shack eyesore houseboat was a local landmark. So was what went on there. Taking care not to be seen, he had been waiting for Raymond ever since the poker crowd began to show up and was puzzled why Raymond was a no-show. He had about decided to leave before someone spotted the strange car when Mort showed. The driver slapped at the whine of a mosquito; he would give a regular like Mort a little more party-time. The faint din of wild hoots and guffaws drifted toward him. He checked the snug grip of the Beretta; released the clip with its meticulous hand-loaded copper-coated hollow points. It was a favorite weapon but repeating MOs was a sure way to let a good cop finger out a trail. Making sure the screen door didn't squeak, he quietly moved with careful footsteps one after another along the pine floor of the walkway.

Mort took his usual seat at the table, tried acting casual, his mind not on the game, "Runnin' the car business ain't easy. I need a break." He grabbed the bourbon; downed a double shot.

Purvis across from him, "You're sure puttin' it away."

Mort said, "Been a rough day," poured another shot.

"Settle down, Mort," Purvis said. "Ease off the juice. Janella and Winona are upstairs. Maybe you ought to take a little trip up to visit them. They'll help you get rid of some of that tension." Gave a mouth-only leer, "Hamlis kids are up there." Spit. "That Hamlis kid's gonna do real good for us. Be good for business. Even better once we get him and his sister together. Girls have the camera ready to go." Face quick-changed to a dead chicken look, "Sure enjoying themselves when I last looked in. You get too liquored-up you can't take advantage of the entertainment."

Mort snapped, "I ain't in the mood."

"Kick back... we're among friends here. No need to throw your attitude."

Friends. Hell of that—Purvis would back-stick his own grandmother. Images of the shower-mess flashed Mort's thoughts. Swirled the liquor in the bottom of his glass; sloshed it down in one swallow. "Gotta piss." He stumbled toward the makeshift screened-in porch hanging off the rear of the houseboat. The bulb on the porch had been burned out long as he could remember; fan didn't work neither. Leaned forward on one hand. Eyes roamed out into the half shades and murky outlines along the river; listened to his pee spatter in the water. The silenced hiss of the shot almost slipped past without any sound.

"What the fuck!" Purvis recognized what it was. The sound was followed by a heavy bump and scrape and thud of metal against the side of the houseboat. Any card game was forgotten.

Purvis jumped up. Glasses and bottles tumbled.

Someone squawked, "Reckon it's the cops?"

Purvis said. "I'd know if it was cops."

By the time they scrambled up the shaky boards of the ramp onto the bank, there was no trace of Mort anywhere.

One said, "Sounded to me like it came from back yonder on the porch."

They crowded down the ramp and onto the porch. Nothing was out of place, not even the big hole in the screen.

Mort Raymond no longer had nightmare problems.

Chapter 7

For the second time in a week Craige waited in the parking lot outside Raymond's office. Something wasn't right. He had cruised by Raymond's gated house a few times and seen the wife's car there but no sign of Raymond. He didn't believe Raymond had the nerve to take a shot at him, but the man wouldn't flinch at calling in favors and having it done. He had called Raymond's office several times, each time getting the same answer.

Ditzy gum-smacking private secretary repeated, "Mister Raymond ain't here."

Craige figured it was about time to play another wild card and use the direct approach. Didn't call, make an appointment, or let on to anyone. He entered the front door of Raymond's office and faced Ms. Ditzy with his Mister Casual mode and a slight nod.

She stopped in mid-chew, "I ain't heard nothing from him since last Friday."

Craige kept walking straight toward the closed door to Raymond's office. Her startled reaction told him exactly what he wanted to know.

Flustered when he didn't stop at her desk, she clambered out of her chair to get between Craige and Raymond's office door. She didn't quite make it in time. "I told you he ain't here," tried to shove between him and the door. She didn't make that work either. Up against him, "You cain't go in there."

Craige liked the heated mash of her tits, but the overdose of her cheap perfume turned him off. He kept one knee strategically placed. Wasn't giving her a chance at groin-mashing. It might feel good if she was doing it different, but he never trusted a female in heat trying to put on a bull elephant charge. Even the attempt was way out of her league.

She twisted against him, "He ain't here."

"That the only line you know?" He gripped the door handle.

"You cain't go in there."

"And exactly how are you going to stop me?" Dead-faced, he did a fixed appraisal of her tits slinked in a silky Blue Lite Special something.

"I'll call the cops."

"That's about the best idea I've ever heard you come up with. Why don't you do that," using enough of a muscled shove against her to push the door open and her with it.

She hurried to the phone on her desk, and gave Craige enough of a moment's disruption to do what he needed done. He doubted her phone call was to the police, and couldn't help wondering what other nonexclusive duties she performed. They couldn't be much. Cunning maybe, but smarts were one of her less developed attributes.

From the outer office he heard her squeaky panic, "Purvis—you get down here right now! That Ingram creep is in Mort's office." Voice loud, "Don't yell at me! I tried to stop him."

Craige knew Purvis fit into this, and he wanted to know how. Purvis wasn't local law. Was he bypassing the locals when they wouldn't go along with his deals? He wished he knew the exact lay of the land. The obvious was that Purvis didn't want anyone knowing, which meant neither did Raymond. He chuckled at the thought of one of Grannie's stern looks. She would've understood what a mistake it was to lay that puzzle in front of this gran'son.

He slipped the padded holder of the ion-etched nano-chip transmitter out of his pocket. Making sure the contacts were seated, and he hadn't over-tightened them to place, Craige quickly pressed it snug high up under the brass foot of the floor lamp. It was sensitive enough to pick up anything even if they moved the lamp. He would have preferred the phone but he was already running the risk of getting caught. He gave a quick looksee around the room, doubted the shooter's weapon would've been stashed there. There was no time to do more, least not right now. Maybe later if forensics became an issue. He spotted the two locked cabinets, one as big as a wardrobe armoire and tall enough to hold rifles and handguns.

From the outside office, he heard her voice rise, "You can just shut the fuck up! You ain't chewin' my ass 'cause some big bully shoves his way in with nobody here to stop him."

He casually walked out of the Raymond's office.

"You're in trouble, buster," she said.

Over his shoulder, "Story of my life," as he pushed open the front door and was out and gone.

Purvis's patrol car screeched up to the front ten minutes later.

She said, "You took too long. He done left."

"He know you called me?"

"Course not." Ditzy gave him a look, "You think I'm stupid?"

"What'd he want?"

"How would I know? By the time you got finished yellin', he was out the door."

Purvis was red-faced pissed; hated stupid idiots that made more trouble than they were worth. Muttered, "Sonofabitch fuckin' around where it's none'a his damn business." He headed toward his car.

She yelled from the door, "Want me to try and call Mort? He ain't been answerin' his phone."

"Hell no! He'll just make things worse."

She went back to her desk and wadded up her gum; threw it in the trash. Then she unwrapped a fresh piece of spearmint.

* * *

Craige pulled around behind the kitchen; had the driver's door open before he saw Billy Martel sitting on the kitchen steps sharing his chili-dog with Lucky. "So much for a watch dog." Gave a nod, "Billy, you've made a friend. Lucky's a big moocher when it comes to being hand-fed."

"Mister Ingram," tossed what was left of his chili-dog to Lucky.

Craige leaned; scratched Lucky's ear, "What got into you?" Dog's tail thudded, wet tongue licked Craige's hand. "You don't usually get so friendly with strangers."

"Me and him ain't strangers. He wasn't sure at first. Fur hackled on his back, but he never growled." Billy patted the dog's back, "Not no more." Lucky swiped a wet slurp along Billy's face. "If a body's been around dogs and weaned wolf pups, you can tell whether dogs are mean. Dog's got a sense about people. I could tell this one was well trained."

"You been around wolves?"

"A few times. Raised some from pups. I found a dead wolf on the highway. Saw her tits were swollen. She'd been suckin' her pups. Couple'a days later I was looking where she might'a had a den. Heard 'em whinin'. They were hungry, barely had their eyes open. Folks claim there's no wolves in these parts." Quick grin, "Nobody told the wolves. They're here all right."

Craige said, "Wolves are good for keeping deer populations under control."

Billy said, "Your dog was skittish till I licked the back of my hand and let him sniff. Sat down on the steps here with him. Me'n him been getting to know one another. He sure likes having his head rubbed."

"He likes having anything done as long as you're paying him attention."

Billy with a big grin, "Me an' him both."

"Guess the three of us are a lot alike. There's lemonade in the 'frigerator. Made it last night. It's good and cold."

"That'd taste real good. Gonna get right warm today."

Craige said, "How'd you get here?" Spotted no bike.

"I walked."

"From where?"

"Over from Johnstown.

Craige said, "That's quite a walk."

"Hollings and me went fishing early. Weren't getting no bites, and Hollings had to go to work. We're gonna try later this afternoon. Rains upriver muddied the creeks. Water's clearin' right good. Be good for bass and bream. You told me I could drop by any time."

"Long as the dog gives you the okay... it's good by me." There was something about Billy Martel, maybe the younger brother he never had. "I'll get the lemonade." He crossed the front porch and unlocked the kitchen door, habit-instinct taking inventory of anything moved while he was gone. He didn't expect Lucky would've let a stranger in no matter how friendly they were.

Billy heard the car before he saw it. So did the dog. Lucky stood, tail didn't wag; growled low, fuzzed-up. Billy recognized the patrol car—Purvis Dalugosh. He didn't like the man. His dad had warned him about the Dalugosh bunch, "Stay clear of Purvis and his crowd."

His dad never said why, but didn't have to. Billy had a good idea; locker room scuttlebutt was never much off the mark, 'specially when the locker room was part of the meat and bedroom games played between students and a few teachers. Billy wondered if he ought to tell his friend Craige. Purvis for certain wasn't here to see him. Decided he'd just listen. Figured Mister Ingram already knew about the Dalugosh.

Patrol car pulled to a stop as Craige came out with two glasses. Billy could tell by the look on Craige's face, this was no neighborly. Likely not gonna be pleasant neither. Glass in each hand, Craige stopped at the top step; screen banged shut behind him. He stayed on the top step. Wanted to look down at Purvis, make Purvis look up.

A red-faced, Purvis got out, near yelled, "Ingram!"

Billy's eyes widened like big silver dollars. "What you want, Dalugosh?" Craige's voice was low, attitude cocked and ready. Lucky growled a low warning.

"You been harassing Mort Raymond's secretary!" strode toward Craige.

Craige read the body language. He'd seen it too many times. The man using size to intimidate, that worked often enough. When it hadn't, the badge had. Craige handed both glasses of lemonade to Billy. Craige took one step down and got straight in Purvis's face, "That what she claim?" His eyes didn't flicker.

"Don't smart-talk me!" slowing as he got to the bottom step. Physical intimidation wasn't working, and Purvis knew it. He strutted out the badge, "You know goddamn well you was in the office!"

"Never said I wasn't," muscles tensed for the strike if Purvis was stupid enough to move into him.

Purvis hesitated then blustered, "I catch you bothering her again, I'll throw your ass in my jail."

Purvis's hesitant bluster told Craige that his visit to Raymond's office had rattled the playpen of whatever it was. "You don't have a jail," face like a stone.

It took Purvis by surprise. "What!"

"This isn't your jurisdiction, and you're trespassing. This property is inside county lines. State Patrol's got no jurisdiction unless local law enforcement calls them in and Raymond's secretary called you. No one else," his planted bug already active. "You're breaking the law and there's a witness," let Purvis think he meant Billy. The surprise would come in open court that his `witness' was Raymond's secretary, and at least part of hers and Purvis's little chat. He hadn't done any illegal entering to plant it and he hadn't tapped the phone, so the feds were on the outside. At least so far. "And a few other surprises you don't know about." Might as well plant a few more weeds to rustle Purvis's sleep.

"What?" more flustered. Nobody had bucked Purvis Dalugosh in so long he'd forgotten what it felt like. Billy glanced back and forth between the two. Purvis sneered, "Gonna act smart-alecky?" Threw a glance at Billy, "Kid's underage. Who's gonna believe a kid?" Devilish grimace at Billy—get him in front of a camera—sweat his whole family with sleazy smut. "What you doing here anyhow?" Glanced back and forth from Billy to Ingram.

Something in the callous way Purvis looked right through instead of at Billy jangled a warning klaxon through Craige. He'd heard the now-and-then rumors of the Dalugosh business breaking in young stuff. Had seen enough in the military and sports to know it happened.

Craige said, "He has permission to be on this private property. You don't. You're not out here on official business." Craige twisted a different tangle to his thoughts—maybe Purvis wasn't all about drugs. Felt dimwitted for letting the simple part of a possible motive skirt past him. The drug angle in Bailey's reports could be a red flag to a whole lot more. Craige had seen how sewer-dealings floated right under the surface, payoffs and scams covering the stink. Purvis might be the muscle, but he also might also be the ugly greed tip of the iceberg. Neck deep in business on the side with underage being a money-plus. It wouldn't matter to Purvis or Mort Raymond. Had

Buddy Raymond and Emmett Whitfield been killed to send a message—but not about drugs?

To misjudge Purvis Dalugosh was kissin' cousins to ignoring a hungry *T-rex*. Uncompromising greed was readymade dangerous. Purvis believed he was untouchable, the kind of dangerous who'd trigger spur-of-the-moment solutions and not even blink at killing. Craige recognized the same thing in his own dark shadows and clandestine plots-and-plans. Whether his son's suicide note was genuine or a plant, Mort Raymond wasn't uptight about a damn note. Raymond was afraid 'cause he knew too much, and that kept Purvis uneasy.

Craige figured prying at secrets was playing a lethal roulette. Offense was still the best defense—it was also the best chess strategy, "Your coming way out here, flashing your badge about why I was at Raymond's office, makes me real interested in what business you and Raymond have going on."

Purvis about shit. "You snoopin' son of a bitch!" His hand moved to his weapon.

Craige was faster. He never liked wild gun play, and wasn't about to let shooting get started; give big bad Purvis a legal reason. Rammed chest-to-gut with Purvis, his hand gripping Purvis around the gun butt and trigger guard. Pinned Purvis's wrist, "There won't be any bullets flying loose today on my property without my say-so and no probable cause. For sure not by threats from anyone acting outside the law," eyeball to eyeball. In the frozen moment Craige didn't flinch; could smell stale garlic. "Being familiar with the law, we both know you're way beyond it. Don't come on my land and threaten me and don't send your sniper friends to take another shot at me. Least they have more guts than you." Shoved Purvis away; wanted distance between them—but not too much. "Now get off my property before I have you arrested for violating the law and harassment," never raised his voice. "Push that issue and you face losing your badge. You're not the only one with contacts. You'll end up having to pay for your gas and whatever vehicle you might end up with." Craige hadn't missed Purvis's surprise by his crack about being shot at.

Purvis stumbled backward. He had been caught off-guard by Craige's cougar-quick move. He was accustomed to acquiescence, and was dumbstruck his bluster hadn't worked. Backed toward his car, muttered, "I'd watch my back at night if I was you."

"I always do," Craige snapped. "Better men than you know have learned that the hard way," gaze frozen. "They never got a second chance."

Purvis floor-boarded. Wheels pitched gravel as he roared away.

Billy said, "Man, I never seen nobody stand up to Purvis Dalugosh before. You talk with me 'stead of at me. Like I'm a grownup."

"You almost are."

In Billy's eyes Craige was a real John all-American Wayne hero. "I got to go."

"I'll put your lemonade in a go-cup. Take it with you."

"That'd taste good."

Craige cautioned, "I'd keep what happened here between the two of us."

"I will." For sure he wanted to ask him about all the places and things Billy had heard tell Navy SEAL Ingram had done. "Can I come back sometime?"

"Sure. If I'm not here Lucky will make sure you're alright. Probably stay with you while you fish. Sometimes I take the dog with me. Anytime you're by yourself fishing, you keep an eye out for Dalugosh."

"I'll make sure."

"The man's not above poking around when he thinks no one's about."

* * *

The two boys hefted the lightweight battered two-man skimmer of a red canoe above their heads. The cricket bucket flopped at Billy's waist as he and Hollings slid the canoe out half way into the water. Hollings climbed in; wobbled till it steadied; grabbed one oar and settled in the stern.

"Cricket bucket's right here." Billy set the chock-full bucket behind his seat and Hollings.

Hollings brushed his black hair out of his face, "Lard can of wigglers is right next to it." He was wearing his favorite blue sun-faded t-shirt almost white, its skateboard monogram hardly recognizable.

Billy's toes squished in the soggy bank as he gave a hard shove; hopped in the front. The canoe silently glided out onto the water. He grabbed the other old wooden oar. "Make sure our fishing poles don't stick out over the sides. Branches'll knock 'em out."

"They're here in the bottom with the stringers." Didn't bump the oars against the canoe; scare the fish, as they kept to the riverbank shallows.

Billy and Hollings had been on their way to partner-up; do a big yard; spotted the canoe at a PTA sponsored yard sale. Both looked at one another; didn't say nothin'. Billy hurried to one of the women, "Mam, if you'll hold that canoe from nobody else buyin' it till we finish our yard-work job, we'll come back with the money." They pooled their money and bought it.

Billy all grins, "Got us a for-real fishin' rig."

Hollings said, "I know a good spot in Mama's garden where she won't mind me digging. Dig up some good wigglers." Outgoing Hollings with a ready smile, his face not as slender as Billy's, tended toward husky as adolescence chubby filled out.

Rustles scurried along the jumbled undergrowth creeping down to the water, the dense foliage occasionally brushing their shoulders. They stayed out of the strong current to the South Carolina side. A mellow Southron accent back-and-forth between the two in the cloistered hush of their private easy-living carefree times.

A sleek bass boat, its glittered fiberglass hull speckling in the sunshine, swung slowly out of the scrub toward them. The high-powered outboard prop was raised clear of the water, while the electric motor trolled silent. Beer-swizzler was working his way through his double twelve-pack with a fancier rod than he knew what to do with. He pinched his eyes in a neutral squint toward the two boys. Billy and Hollings nodded as the big and shiny passed. Raised to be polite, both could spot trouble, and this one was trouble. Billy thought of Purvis; would never forget how Mister Ingram had quick-handled that. Hollings looked at the boat, imagining the day he'd have enough money to get him a bass boat. Both watched the polished vision slide away downriver.

Hollings said, "Sure is a nice boat."

Billy said, "Sure is, but it's hard to fish from one'a them ski jobs."

As they eyed the vanishing ski boat, their canoe drifted across an underwater snag that slid along the bow turning the point of the canoe into the overhang of bushes that dragged around their shoulders.

Both ducked. "Crap... " Hollings tried pushing the limbs up and loose.

"Keep an eye out for moccasins sunning in the bushes."

"They drop in. Use the oars; flip 'em over the side."

"They like these overhangs," Billy shoved them loose from another tangle of twisted leafy limbs. Slowly back-paddled. Neither were afraid of snakes. "Don't want a scared moccasin dropping in the boat. Scared snakes bite quicker. Most just want to hide."

"There's a bigger limb underwater back here," Hollings poked at it. "Back straight out; it'll skid loose."

The stern skidded loose. Billy back-paddled with a slight angle to the current. He didn't want it to shove them sidewise; flip the canoe. He checked real good for snakes; flip any snakes out if they dropped in. Neither noticed the other boat wedged up under the overhang until they bumped it and the current sidled their canoe up to it.

Hollings pushed against it, "Looks like it had a trolling motor at one time or another."

"Paint's worn off. Bow is stuck deep in the mud. Water inside about filled it up to the same level as the river. Likely sink if the river comes up. This far below the locks, it must'a pulled loose from its tie-down when the water was up."

Hollings grabbed the stern to steady them, pushed more branches out of their way. His hand slipped. At first he thought it was mud till the branches swept up a swarm of flies. "What the fuck's that smell?" Leaned over to push harder; jerked his hand back, "Oh shit!"

"What? You got a snake?" Billy trying to see.

Hollings looked again, "Looks to be a body in it."

"Body?"

Hollings said, "We ought'a call the law," grabbed his paddle to back 'em out.

"We'll take the cut through." Billy dug in his pocket for the scrap of paper with the phone number. "I know who we ought'a call."

Hollings frowned, "We gotta call the sheriff."

"There's a Bait and Tackle owned by Mister Sam and his wife. I bought colas there a time or two. He'll let me use the phone if I tell him it's a local call."

"That the sheriff's number you got there?"

"No."

"Who?"

"Someone I can trust."

They rowed hard. Banked their canoe. Hollings tugged, "Let's pull it higher so it don't float loose."

Billy said, "Highway's right up this hill. Bait place is up yonder. Not far."

Billy pushed through the squeaky front door of the Bait and Tackle, Hollings right behind him. "Afternoon, Mister Sam."

"Afternoon, Billy. Been a spell since I seen you."

"Mister Sam, I need to make a local phone call. It's kind'a of an emergency."

"Not a problem. Anything you need me to help you with?"

"No, sir. I just need to make a phone call."

Sam said, "Phone's right there. H'ep yourself."

"Thank you." Billy dialed.

"Ingram." Craige answered. Listened to Billy. Caught the calm urgency in Billy's voice. Asked, "You touch anything?"

"No, sir, 'cept for one of my stringers I used to snug the boat to a strong limb so it wouldn't float away."

"You by yourself?"

"No, my fishin' buddy Hollings is with me. We're at Mister Perkins' bait place on the highway. Flies all about the body. Smells like it's been dead for some time. Boat's got a Georgia number on the side. Lettering's so old you cain't read all the numbers or the date."

"You and your friend stay there. Let me talk with Sam."

"Perkins," Sam answered.

"Guess you heard," Craige said. "I'm on my way. Make sure the boys stay inside with you."

"I'll make sure. They'll be right here. Got any ideas on what they found?"

Craige said, "I'll have a better idea once I know more. Anybody else around besides the two boys?"

"Nobody except the wife. You expecting anybody to show up?"

"No, but you never know."

Perkins said, "That's a fact."

In no time Craige pulled into the bait shop gravel lot. He had no reason to suspect what the two boys had found had anything to do with Purvis. Still, the thought dinged in his brain when Billy mentioned he'd been fishing with Hollings when they found the body. Couldn't shake it.

Grannie came to mind. "Things happen like intended. A body never be give more than one can handle."

Craige muttered, "Never underestimate a mean skunk." Purvis had his fingers in a lot that was local and more that wasn't. Purvis didn't get where he was by being stupid. On his last pissin' contest Purvis was pissed before he showed up at Moccasin Hollow. Purvis was mad about something to do with Mort Raymond. Craige wasn't about to be caught off-guard; fail to spot pieces seemingly unconnected. That had killed a SEAL buddy under his command. Shivered from the somber recesses of unpleasant memories—Darrell's blood-soaked fist twisted in Craige's jacket as life drained away, the full-of-life eyes fading empty.

When they lost Darrel, Craige swore, "Never again."

Craige didn't want to think Dalugosh was in cahoots with anyone in Gray's Buckingham Parish bailiwick, but a river wasn't even a nuisance-trickle with bundles of cash flowing back and forth. He didn't have enough facts to checkmate any move from Purvis, but there was a backdoor he could use. He parked in front of the Bait and Tackle; pulled out his cell and punched the unlisted number on his quick-dial.

Mabel Struthars answered, "Buckingham Metro Law Enforcement Center, Investigative Support Team. How may I help you?"

"Must be your turn on the switchboard."

"Well Lord have mercy, stranger," warm lusty Mabel Struthars soft-hearted gushed. "Got something for the boss?"

"Only some hunches."

Her tone with Craige belied how hard as nails she could be when necessary. "A body would think you'd died and gone to whatever reward was waitin' for your backside. What in the world has my favorite good-lookin' PI been up to?" Always caught her breath when she was around him, and knew he knew. And knew he liked it.

"Trying to stay out of trouble."

She gave an earthy throaty chuckle, "You mean staying out of trouble until you find trouble you want to get into... and not get caught."

Craige laughed, "Something like that."

"You need to talk to Graysen? I think he's still in his office or in the lab with Fred. Want me to check?"

"It's your brain I need to pick. For the time being, since this is on my side of the river, I want to keep this unofficial. Gray's investigation doesn't need any boy-dog territory contest."

"That's for sure, but Captain MacGerald won't have a problem meshing gears with his counterpart over there."

"I don't want Graysen blindsided. It's the locals I'm concerned with."

"Mmm... so the scuttlebutt is right. You're messin' where some skunks don't want anyone messin'. Specially your kind of messin'."

"I'm not sure. So far I've not pinned names to the specifics. We got a dead body nobody knows about except the ones who discovered it. I want to make sure where the cowpats are so I don't step in one over my head. Be sure and jot the time and date stamp on your phone log with my name—just in case Gray needs a date-time proof."

"Consider it done. Sounds like it's getting tight and nasty."

"It could if the ones I suspect try to roadblock me—which is already in motion. You know any scuttlebutt about a trooper this side of the river, name of Purvis Dalugosh?"

Mabel's voice dropped a notch, "Enough to know you better be extra special careful. He's always been slippery—and a mean streak in seeing it stays that way."

"If you think of anything give me a ring."

"I'll do more than that."

Craige didn't need to ask Mabel anything else. He often thought she was better at digging in twilight shadows than he'd ever be. "I've got someone waiting. Tell Gray about this. I'll bring him up to speed on the details. I'm headed to the sheriff's department to file an official report on a body found on the river. I'll make hard copies for Gray and Dinkins, and bring them to you. No fax... no leaks."

"I'll brief the boss to expect you. Meantime I'll touch bases with some of the know-everything gals. You ought to pay a visit to the person on your side of the river that has fingers in the money pot of everything from squeaky clean to gutter smut."

"Zebulon Bergamot," Craige chuckled. "I was thinking about that, and Zeb would enjoy it."

"We both know he sure would." Mabel gave a deeper throaty chortle.

"Mabel, you are bad," short laugh. "Don't change. Gotta go."

"Watch your backside in River Disco. Don't need to remind a sailor like you that everybody else in there will be watching as well." She hung up.

Craige parked. Made a quick look-see around, and headed into Bait and Tackle. Billy and Hollings were waiting. He said, "Sam, I appreciate your letting Billy call me." Looked at Billy, "Okay. Tell me exactly what you two found."

* * *

Craige knew he'd set Purvis on a short fuse along with Mort Raymond's attitude helping to shorten it. He filled out the report, and walked the sheriff to his patrol car. "We have all we need from the boys." Craige said, "I'll see the two of them get home."

The sheriff said, "I'll keep you posted, and drove off.

Craige told Billy and Hollings, "You two keep this to yourselves. Maybe it was an accident." He knew Billy would do as he said, but wasn't so sure about Hollings. Dropped each of them home. Let their parents know what was going on.

All sorts of yellow jackets buzzed his brain as he drove to River Disco. Parked, and pushed through the leather-padded front door into the brassy loud glitz. Zebulon had given the bartender a heads-up that Ingram was on his way. Bartender recognized Craige. Buzzed Zebulon's office. Kept his eyes on Craige as he made his way through the red velvet settings surrounding the unlit runway. River Disco floorshows didn't start till sunshine was long gone, but the early crowd was already humming.

Before he could knock, the office door flung open to a chiffon vision in pink and pastel, "Goodness gracious, my faint heart slow down. Couldn't believe your voice on the phone wantin' to know if Zina Bea could spare you some time." Zeb looped his arms through Craige's, "You knew I would rearrange my schedule for my favorite shirtless soccer player. You come right on in here and sit yourself down." Gave a not-to-be-disturbed look at the bartender, and shut the office door tight-closed.

"I need your help."

"Anytime, anything." Put-on pout, "I could tell from your voice this was going to be about business. You know I've always got your back." Gave Craige a full-body leer, "And more anytime you want. We can always mix a little pleasure with making business more fun."

"Help if push comes to shove with Purvis Dalugosh, maybe some of your Bergamot muscle."

"Dalugosh!" Lisp and limp wrist, over-size lashes and garish lipstick masque were lost in the fierce look that flared from Zeb's eyes. "Fuckin' over that white trash son-of-a-bitch would be my undying pleasure. Comes in here wantin' favors; threaten to close Del down. Arrest me'n her if we don't do what he wants."

"He paid me an unannounced visit."

"That was a big mistake. Purvis Dalugosh is notorious for solving problems brutal and thorough, and covering his tracks with badge or threats or paid-for court-ready alibis." Lavender eye-shadowed eyes flashed fiercer than fierce. "You better keep eagle eyes in the back of your head wide open. Watch more than your backside."

Slow to ire, it took a lot to make Zeb Bergamot truly angry. It didn't happen often, but in high school Craige had first seen Zeb bullied too far and get savage-mean. Zeb's deliberate lisp and limp wrist campiness were meant to disarm. Most times it did. But threaten Craige or Deloma Pingley, then it was confrontation game-on, no rules.

Zeb said, "You investigating Purvis?"

"It didn't start out that way."

Zeb rolled heavy rouged shadowed eyes, "Believe me there's enough stink with Dalugosh and his gang for you and Gray and the Marine Corps with plenty left over."

"It didn't take long before things tensed in that direction. Things I hanker he doesn't want out in the open. I rattled his cage and got a response way beyond what I thought I was poking into."

Zebulon said, "Bury him under his damn cage, and keep on eye open to make sure he's not planning the same thing."

"What do you know about Billy Martel and Michael Hollings or their families? Any of them connected to Dalugosh?"

"Nothing much. But what's to know about a couple of high school kids? Billy's a scrawny kid. Had a rough life. He's street-wise. Smart, but not too keen seeing trouble coming and staying out of the way. Hollings is a little tougher, and dumb as a rock. When he gets legal he'll be hunky rough trade. I'd never trust him... something about him. I'll see what I can dig out. Shouldn't be too hard to find out if there's anything to be sniffed out."

"You be careful."

Zeb smirked, "I always am."

Craige stood, "I'll get back with you."

"That would be real nice, lighten up my whole day," Zeb batted the long lashes. "You cain't leave; you just got here."

Hand on the door handle, "I got things to puzzle together. It's not safe to give Purvis-types breathing room. He's already looking for ways to get the edge on me."

For his size rotund Zeb was quick at the door next to Craige. One hand rested on Craige's arm, "You need the help from any of my tailored-suits crowd, I'll make sure you have as much muscle as you need. More than that if you need it... anytime."

"Before it slips my mind. You wouldn't happen to know where I could find two bag ladies."

"Sallie Mae Drutherferde and A'gatha Ruth Hutchers," Zeb giggled. "Those two are a matched pair."

"And a big help in the past."

"Talked to them last week. They've settled into that abandoned building on the corner of Railroad Avenue. It's all weeded-up with no visitors poking around. Exactly like those two like it."

* * *

Craige crunched across River Disco's gravel parking lot toward his vehicle. Climbed in; cell phone out; pushed SEND for the sheriff's private number. Wanted to make sure the report was held in the sheriff's office for him to pick up, and get to Mabel and Dinkins.

Desk watch took Craige's call, "Hold on; sheriff's in."

Sheriff came on the line; recognized Craige's voice. "How'd you find out about this body?"

Craige said, "Let's just say an involved citizen. For the time being, that's namely me."

"When you're working a case, you're as tight-lipped as your grannie. Your SEAL buddy MacGerald said the same thing. I'm assuming there's details you're playing close to your chest. Details not in the report."

Craige chuckled, "Keeping my clients' names confidential till the body is in the morgue and we have a final forensics report."

"Dinkins already returned my call," the Sheriff said. "If it was anyone but you honchoing this I'd tighten the screws on this. Grannie set you with a good backbone."

"You're not the first to say that." With the cross-department support Gray had between his Buckingham Parish Forensic Team and the constabulary on Craige's side of the river, Coroner-Medical Examiner Dinkins would have his forensic van on the scene before anyone contaminated what recoverable evidence there might be. Dinkins would narrow any unknowns with an odds-to-even chance he'd come up with, if not a name, hopefully some useable DNA.

"Who you protecting?"

"More like staying out of any gun sights. Least till I come up with something solid instead of hunches. That's the reason I filed the report in my name. You wouldn't like any of my other reasons or the possible individuals involved." His name on the report could make for a red flag for Purvis or Dalugosh. "This way will keep the boys' names out of it, at least for a while."

Sheriff said, "You implying homicides? As in more bodies? I just took a look at the body. Looks to've been dead for a few days. I'll leave all that up to Dinkins as to whether it's natural causes or otherwise.

"I find anything solid, I'll make sure you know." Craige had worked with the sheriff a few times. Gray trusted him. That was good enough for Craige.

"You make sure you don't end up straddling a limb someone is sawing off."

Craige said, "If you're up for a boat ride, I'll check with Dinkins. Meet at my place; take my flat-bottom. Easier to get into the backwaters. Keep us from having to wade through bayous. Fred can spot details most of us overlook."

"Not a problem," the sheriff said. "Dinkins has been a real help to us."

Craige said, "You got my number." Ended the call. He'd make sure the outboard's gas tank was topped off.

While he drove, Craige tried on every reason Purvis and Dalugosh wouldn't have connections inside law enforcement on this side of the river. Billy and Hollings could end up two more bodies in the morgue. Wasn't the sheriff that left him uneasy. There were plenty other ears. Mabel was better than any covert agent. With her on the prowl Gray's department files would be sealed tighter than Fort Knox. Far as Craige was concerned, taking a kill-shot that missed was wasted effort. If the trigger-fingers were sweepers hired to get rid of witnesses or busybodies. If the body in the skiff was connected and the kill-shot was by the same person, someone was afraid he knew too much. Bailey could bring in unwanted Army JAG interference. Until he satisfied his own questions, he'd feed Bailey need-to-know details, but keep the need-to-know list short. Give Bailey enough to take up the command chain. Punched Bailey's number.

"Bailey," matter-of-fact.

"Checkin' in," Craige said.

"You sound a little tight."

"Been a busy day."

"Busy, as in serious busy?"

Craige said, "One of those few-to-none-answers kind of day. More questions with no answers... rumors and dead-ends."

"Anything I should know about?"

"I may have rustled up some connections with underage porn, but no ties with goings-on at the fort."

Bailey dropped his own eye-opener. "Carolina Bureau has been working that angle for over a year. Keeping it under wraps. The brass prefers not having that splashed around... even if personnel at the fort are not involved."

Craige stayed the Mister Cool, "I didn't spot that in the info you gave me."

"It wasn't in there."

Craige said, "You asked me to help, and you didn't think that little snippet was important for me to know?"

"Our investigation isn't after the small fish."

Craige said, "Your bosses may not want a lot of things splashed around, but it could come whether anyone wants it or not. 'Specially if it involves transporting underage across state lines."

"Our investigation is after the big boys in the state legislature, the ones lining their pockets and providing the legal cover."

"Your bosses better hope this has nothing to do with anyone on Defense appropriations committees—which could make for a media tsunami." Craige was more than a little aggravated at Bailey's hiding facts with all sorts of potential repercussions. "Raymond's daddy has connections in the local counties with good ole boy connections that could be messy... the nasty kind of messy. Any law enforcement figures involved on my side of the river you know about?" Wondered what other bury-the-details Bailey had been ordered not to tell him.

Bailey said, "None we've dug up. This side of the river is a lot more convenient to the fort. You ever thought this could involve blackmail?"

"If it does, it's by someone other than Mort Raymond. Raymond likes things nice and quiet. Blackmail takes up-front balls, and can get rough. Like being dead-rough. Not something Raymond would cater to being a part of."

Bailey said, "I'd probably want to hide, too, if I had that kind of heat coming down on me."

* * *

Craige pulled up behind the coroner's van parked a good ways up from the boggy slough. He called down to Fred and the photographer, "Need any help?"

A cloud of flies swarmed up as the photographer pulled the skiff up onto the sticky kaolin-thick mudflats. "I think we about got it." The photographer made sure the lens covers were snugged tight; he didn't want mud or watery blurring in still photos. "Doctor Dinkins, since this is where the body was found and likely only part of the crime scene, unless you want some special close-ups, I think we'll have what you need."

Dinkins stretched his back. He peered over the top of his black wire-rim glasses propped precariously on the end of his nose, "I think we've got it covered here." He brushed a hand through thin white hair, "Cause of death will have to come from the lab. We might be able to get partial prints for the DNA index CODIS databank. Doesn't take long for a dead body to recycle in these parts. That's a big *if*. Depends on how degraded the remains are. Connective tissue beneath the dermal ridges might contrast just enough with the overlying epidermis for it to clean up digital images for possible CODIS matches. It appears we don't have an intact *corpus delicti*. Seems we're looking at a felony murder with body parts moved, the remains ending up in a skiff minus its head. May have been a hurried attempt to prevent dental comparison. If it was a hurry-up situation, something interrupted the hurry. Fingers weren't removed—not like the other one those fishermen found a couple of days ago."

"Other one?" Craige looked at Dinkins.

"Skiff with body parts found along the river bank, only not enough to use for identification." Gave the sheriff and Craige a nod, "I'll hold the body till we get some answers, and let you know when I've studied the prelims."

Chapter 8

Winona's video-making hangover lasted all next day. Her frazzled brillo-pad bleach-burned hair looked blitzed. She and Janella slumped at the breakfast bar, empty beer cans and liquor bottles in the sink, trash bags overflowing.

Janella said, "We're about out of coffee."

"Crap. We cain't be out'a coffee ag'in," Winona nagged. "My butt'll be draggin' the rest of the day."

"I feel like mine already is."

The trailer reeked of stale sweat and the smell of unwashed clothes. Janella's smart phone buzzed. Its pounding heavy crash-bang buried somewhere behind her eyes. She grabbed for the gawd-awful hammering gadget, "What!" Purvis's raspy words grated at her headache that wasn't yet a migraine but was getting there. She listened, then blurted, "Today? You got to be kidding?" Her fingertips pushed hard at her temples. It didn't help.

Purvis said, "You just make sure everything's ready with enough blank tapes and disks so we have duplicates. No dumb screw-ups like last time."

"How you going to get him there?"

"Don't worry about the details," Purvis said. "You and Winona just make sure you got everything ready."

* * *

Craige tilted his head back to let the shower spray jet across his face. Other than the wife's afternoon bridge party with her Sunday school clique, his thirty-six hour stakeout at the Raymond house had

119

come up with a bunch of nothing and no sign of husband. He let the show spray a few minutes. Shut off the water; shook his head in a spritz of droplets; toweled his hair and snugged a bath sheet around his waist. The damp towel felt good. In his computer room he off-lined his prototype QuBit software, and accessed the memory chip for updated input from the bug in Raymond's office. He hoped for something. There'd been no phone calls, only the shuffle of papers and background street noises, and still no Raymond. The office could be a front. He thought of the body in Dinkins' morgue; whether or not it was Mort Raymond. If it wasn't he was more curious, who it wasn't.

If Daddy Raymond found out Purvis killed his son, Purvis knew he had a problem. He'd solve it or have it done. Whoever set the body adrift in the river likely figured boat and body would go over the spillway. Gators would do the rest—no body, no investigation, no questions. Which meant whoever disposed of the body knew nothing about the river currents. Craige knew he could be barking up a blind alley to nowhere with his investigation of Raymond and Purvis separate from Bailey's. His thoughts came back to the knot of who was pulling whose string. He couldn't see Dalugosh taking orders and not being top dog.

Craige's secure line buzzed soft. Saw it was Gray's ID. Like times when he was Craige's ComOfficer. Direct lines up and down any chain of command always made a better game plan to stay chess-move jumps ahead of under-the-table shenanigans being cooked. He grabbed it before it buzzed again, "Dinkins has an autopsy report."

"I'm glad you can't read my mind all the time," Gray said.

Craige reached for his keys, "I can come over now if the time's good for Fred."

"He said tell you anytime."

"On my way."

* * *

Craige nosed into the Employees Only precinct lot of the Buckingham Metro Law Enforcement Center's nondescript red brick building and parked bumper-to-bumper to Gray's dinged, well-used sedan. Took the rear entrance steps two at a time, then down to the lower level to the big sign FORENSICS – *Authorized Personnel Only* above the double doors leading into the green and cream tiled expanse. When he pushed through the right half of the gurney-scarred doors, the ever-present sterile formaldehyde-phenol-hypochlorite prickled a sting to his nose.

Dinkins, sitting at his corner-squeezed desk across from the empty trio of autopsy tables, glanced over the top of his glasses when Craige came in. "I estimated it would not be long before you showed up." He scooted up a chair for Craige, "Have a seat," and handed a folder to Craige.

Craige said, "Tell me some good news," and opened the folder. He'd hoped for more, but with the condition of the body, it was odds on probable the lab prelims weren't complete. Dinkins was too thorough to leave it at that.

"That's about it `till the toxicology report comes back." Dinkins' initials were at the bottom of the single sheet. "Besides MacGerald, you're the only one who's seen that. I'll include a copy in my official report to the sheriff."

"Don't put a rush on it."

Dinkins said, "No official paperwork or digital files leave this office without my making certain it's complete. A bit of a downside I anticipated in establishing a time of death... *Calliphoridae* blowflies." He pushed his black wire rim glasses off the end of his nose and onto his forehead, "Considering the high temperatures and humidity variables contributed to the severe decomposition of the remains, I'm waiting for the entomological breakdown. That will give us the *Calliphoridae* species, and allow us to make a count of species instars, pupae and pupae cases. Bottom line—It'll give a better idea of the Post-mortem Interval time. There's another interesting item. A missing person report on a graduate student came into Buckingham Metro Law Enforcement. Body was found tangled in logs and brush downriver; wasn't booked as a felony until we began the autopsy. An entomological *Calliphoridae* DNA request has been submitted. No reason to expect it's related to your investigation except the missing person report came in a couple of days after a skiff tied up to a houseboat was reported missing. The boat was moored at the marina, and the student was a part-time sitter for the houseboat. We managed to get a fair number of prints. I expect those back from CODIS anytime now. Blood types are noted in the files there. Cause of death is somewhat more intriguing."

"How so?"

Dinkins said, "For one thing the head was removed postmortem. A thorough resection of the stump of the neck along with adjacent bone and cervical tissues revealed the hyoid bone was not intact. The fractured ends of the hyoid show severe trauma with portions of the bone missing. There were grooved cut-marks on the *in situ* bone showing it had been cut or chopped. Rather crude, as though the killer was in a hurry. Only a few small clots inside the damaged hyoid and adjacent small vessels. A couple of bone splinters were clot-free—an indication blood pressure was low or absent. The trauma likely was *post-mortem*. Decapitation of a living victim results in a considerable effusion of blood. This victim was dead or bleeding out before being decapitated. Tissues show few areas of extravasated blood in the surrounding muscle and connective tissues. Low power microscopic samples confirm that. I'd venture an educated guess the hands not being removed indicate an unpremeditated killing. One that was interrupted."

Craige nodded, "Our perp didn't want to risk being caught."

Dinkins pulled down his mask; tucked it under his chin, "Got to shower and change; get over to Gibson. Constabulary wants me to have a look at a pending situation." He stripped off his autopsy scrubs, carefully folded them, and dropped them in a NON-STERILE container. "Soon as I know anything more, I'll bring you up to speed."

Craige went back to his vehicle; sat in the parking lot. He flipped through the pages of the prelim files Dinkins had given him. He poker-shuffled the slender leads he had and the empty spots in the lab analysis Fred was waiting on. Odds-on tonight was a good a time as any to stir the pot; chase some of his suspicions. He would let it get on toward dark, dial Raymond's office. If no one answered, it was a safe bet the bubble-chewing secretary was gone for the day—or never came in. Taking DNA swabs in Raymond's office was probably a waste of time. If there was any truth about Gum Chewer's under-the-desk quickies for her boss, he'd have DNA for half the people from both sides of the river.

His old flip phone charger he kept plugged to the jeep buzzed. He didn't recognize the no-name number. "Ingram."

A whispered, "You want to have a talk with Mort Raymond?"

Besides the phone being beat-up and old, he was barely able to make out the hushed garble, "Who is this?" His suspicions bourgeoned.

"I can't talk. Meet me in the parking lot at Mother's Bar at eleven tonight. And come alone." A click, the voice gone.

His clandestine visit to Raymond's office was forgotten. Craige fired up the engine, backed out, and drove home. The whole thing had the earmarks of a setup. The small roadside parking lot of out-of-the-way Mother's Bar was not the spot for a clandestine meeting—but it was a good setup for a ready-made shooting gallery. All manner of gut-warnings wrenched at him. So did the off-chance it was someone wanting to get back at Purvis or Raymond. He'd been in rougher dives than Mother's Bar.

Once home he tried to relax. Not a chance in hell of that happening. Even the refreshing snap-feel to the sweet damp-cool of the evening's river air didn't help. He grabbed a lightweight mackinaw in case he ended up being sent to wait on some side road or waiting half the night for a no-show. He knew the bar; had been inside a couple of times. Rough crowd, hard workers, hard partiers. The split millisecond after he pulled in, everyone inside would know he was outside. Odd choice to meet for someone who didn't want to be overheard, which meant the bar crowd already knew.

He glanced at the time. There was still time to sandwich a look-see in Raymond's office. He could get done what needed doing. Pick up some random DNA samples to take to Dinkins, and be at the bar ahead of the scheduled meet for a look-see of the layout. He checked his messages and found one from Terri for a late wine and cheese tête-à-tête. He jotted the date-time on a pad. He always felt good being with her.

* * *

Craige hung a right at the light that gave him a clear look at the unlit rear private entrance of Raymond's office. The lot was empty. He parked in the side lot of the restaurant across the busy thoroughfare of Old Trolley Line Road. He could see the entrance to Raymond's rear parking lot and had a good view of the front of the office. Reception room curtains were open and there was a single lamp that had been left on. The curtains were drawn on the side windows, and no lights. Purvis would have a field day catching Craige on a breaking-and-entering. He would use some bogus charge then keep if off the books for leverage to muddy the investigation.

Craige waited, as a silver-gray sunset deepened to purple and black. The streetlights didn't add much. He scrutinized the intersection for eyes that stood out before getting out of the jeep; casually crossed the street to the office where he swept his scanner for security fields. It wouldn't take much to get past the old lock on the rear door. He reached in his pocket for a pair of Fred's autopsy gloves. The lock was no problem. Once inside he moved cougar-swift through the front office and into the shadows with a thumbnail-pen light gripped between his teeth, sticky tape and plastic bag for fingerprint-DNA sweeps. He pulled Raymond's desk chair back. As he made quick swipes under the desk he spotted the second phone line running under the carpet inside the unlocked lower file drawer. Inside the drawer was a base unit to a landline and USB smartphone charger. He took Raymond's phone off the hook and followed the line to the wall with a flashback of a few SpecOps assignments. Would never forget the chill of fear-sweat. On his belly probing for antipersonnel mutilate-and-kill nasties. As he stood by the secretary's desk, he glanced through the front window; listened, nobody in sight. He meant to keep this swift and short—lifted the secretary's phone, tapped the mouthpiece. There was no echo in his ear—this line and Raymond's weren't the same. It had to be a renegade line. He'd checked phone numbers before he left the house and found only one number listed for Raymond's Sales Brokerage. His sweeper software would do the trick. He pushed TALK and REDIAL at the same time, and inserted his code. Three pulsed beeps followed by two quick ones.

The recorded message was clear. "The number you dialed is out of range or not in service at this time. Please try again later."

He pushed CANCEL before it could FLASH for a dial tone. He'd been inside long enough. With a cautious check of the back lot, he relocked the office door from the outside leaving no sign of it ever being opened. There was still plenty time to make his move at Mother's Bar. He would get there an hour ahead of when he was expected; check the bar patrons; let his gut feeling talk to him.

When he drove up to the bar, he made a mental note of the five vehicles parked in the lot: one dually, some pickups, and a stump-jumper four-by. A mud-covered motorcycle leaned at the side of the building next to a garish orange pickup with a bent rusty blue fender. He pushed through the door. Except for the bar, the interior showed dim outlines with a couple of rough looking beer-bellies leaning across a scruffy pool table, cue sticks poised in mid-shot, eyeing him.

The cigar-chomping bartender looked about as rough. With a crusty gruff, "What'cha want?"

Craige had a thirsty hankering for one of his favorite Artois lagers. He had discovered it during his homebound refuel leg from a Kamchatka round-trip and overnight outside Brussels near Leuven. Since he had cargo space to spare in his private jet, he prepaid the duties and flew several cases straight to Moccasin Hollow.

He knew Artois was way beyond this bar. Instead, he ordered, "Long neck Corona." Nursed it as he took in the all-in-one-bar, tables and chairs, neon Bud sign and smudged mirrors that looked like they'd fall apart if they were cleaned beyond a quick wipe. His boot gritted the unswept floor.

Barkeep jarred the bottle down on the bar, "That'll be three dollars." Suds foamed over the lip. The price had been upped for this interloper.

Craige thought of the skin smorgasbords and cheap motels of navy-times in Kings Bay and Jacksonville. Friday-Saturday-niter beer, booze and prêt-à-porter ready-to-wear orgies for sailor boys and horny marines out for skin-and-suds lost weekends. Servicing whatever was available, mainly freebie wives whose fly-boy or ship-driver husbands were deployed. Old urine-sweat smells brought back disjointed pleasures, the good parts and some of the not-so-good memories. He'd been in worse bars.

There was a jukebox at the end of the bar, bubble light decor broken, a weak glow from the ancient 78s inside. The nickel slot or five for a quarter told him how antique old could get. Grannie never fit into that sort of *old*. Beer in hand, he leaned, pretending to read the titles. Across from the bar he heard the click of the cue ball break the silence.

He said, "This thing work?"

Bartender glared, "This place don't got nuthin' that don't work. You gonna play it or what?"

Slapped a dollar bill on the bar, "Quarters."

"Big spender."

Craige fed the machine a quarter. Nothing. He banged it. Act too civilized they would get suspicious. He fed it another quarter, punched five selections. It whirred, squeaked, innards moved. A record dropped. More scratch than music. Craige picked a booth; slid into it. Balls on the pool table clicked across the torn green felt under a ceiling fan that hadn't moved in years.

The beer got warm, then flat. Two men came in. Craige sized them up somewhere between retarded and skewed mid-twenty-pushing-forty bodies. Two girls followed, cutoffs so tight they had to be pinching everything. All four squeezed in a shadowed booth in a back corner. One dirty fingernail hand so far up between once-upon-a-time-cutie's thighs, it looked like he was fisting her. Craige wasn't a voyeur, and sure didn't enjoy watching public-crude no matter what kind of show they were or weren't putting on. He checked his watch, coming up on forty-five minutes had passed. He ordered another Corona. At three bucks per long neck, he hadn't brought enough folding money, and he wasn't about to risk plastic in this joint.

A few minutes later two others came in. They started cleaning glasses, smearing greasy leftover french-fry crumbs around on the tabletops. Filled the ice bin. Bartender disappeared toward the walk-in cooler; came out rolling a frosted barrel. Craige wondered how many roach-homes he'd disturbed. It'd be better to leave the bugs alone; least they wouldn't be running around with the customers. Not that any of the current clientele would mind but it seemed cruel to treat bugs that way. Blondie came over. The closer she got, the more Craige could see.

She sidled up in her best version of swivel-swish. "Need anything?" Crackled lipstick grin didn't know how to smile. Mileage tracked across a face way beyond its years.

"I'm fine. Thanks."

"Waitin' for someone?" Working girl come-on tried one more smile, looking worse from the only kind of effort she knew.

He tried polite showing-no-interest, "Supposed to meet them here."

"Any real woman wouldn't stand up a good looker like you," meat market cut rate conversation her tried-and-true expertise.

Craige put on a neutral smile; might as well be civil without becoming her customer. Wet his tongue with beer, pretended to swallow.

She said, "Maybe I'll check back later."

Quarter past eleven—Craige was getting the same feeling it had been a setup from the start, but he wanted to find out some names. The pool table duet was now a foursome; teen quartet in the booth looked like a stacked twosome on top of one another.

Barmaid brought him another Corona, "Saw you were about empty. This one's on the house. Feel sorry for a big fellow like you all alone on Friday night. Ain't no justice in the world." Slowly set his half empty warm bottle onto her tray. Read Craige well enough to know he wasn't buying tonight.

Craige's hunch told him he'd waited this long, but he'd give the phone caller more time. Fingers curled around the dripping bottle and raised it to his lips.

* * *

Well after ten Terri decided night-owl Craige probably was either out of town or on surveillance prowls. She'd put off a grocery run. Didn't want to go this late. Do it first thing tomorrow. She would call him early in the morning; make up for it with a twosome breakfast-stop. The week had been full of details that seemed to never end; nothing bad, just busy.

127

* * *

Craige's blurry-eyed fuzzy gawk at his watch said midnight. He tried to remember when bars closed—eleven, maybe after midnight. Something wasn't right. The pool table was deserted about the time the rumble of the motorcycle roused him. The motor growl roared away, grew distant. Blondie Barmaid was nowhere in sight.

Craige tried to clear his head. The booth of occasional arms and legs and skin was still occupied. The face of a child rose out of the skin-tangle with an odd empty gaze at Craige. Then stood on rubber legs. Last thing Craige remembered was his weightless body folded onto the floor in a slow-motion fall. A sweet nothing face among a phantasm of unfamiliar voices and grotesque sloppy faces that was at times rough and pleasant. Last thought—*you stupid fuck*—you know better'n to accept an open drink from someone you do not know.

A faraway voice barely penetrated his conscience, "Get the pool balls off the table, and lock the goddamn front door."

"I don't see no rope."

"There's two rolls of duct tape behind the bar."

"Make sure you put the recharged batteries in the camera. We don't need to waste time with batteries that're rundown. Charger's plugged in. Spare batteries already chargin'."

"Get his shirt off."

A raspy female voice said, "I want his pants off."

Blondie giggled, "Winona, you're a dirty ole broad," swirled somewhere in Craige's stupor.

"Here's the tape."

"Pants are all tangled up at his knees."

"You make sure the doors were bolted?"

"Locked tight. Back entrance, too."

"Tape his hands and feet good an' snug. Don't want him workin' loose if he wakes up."

Craige half mumbled, "What's going on?" Tried to clear his thoughts, couldn't make sense of where he was. Remembered the motorcycle roar and the smell of the place.

Recognized Purvis's voice, "Do another wrap with the tape. He's not completely out." With a bad-tempered gravely snarl, "Hey kid!"

There was a hurried shuffle from the booth, "Yeh?"

"Get your butt up here! You think I made sure you was here for you to sit back with your sister while we do the work?"

"Yessir." The kid hurried.

Purvis said to Blondie, "Camera working?"

"It's on," through the eyepiece. Date-time glowed blue green, tracking reset; digits of the counter showing 0000.

Purvis said, "Bring that painter's drop cloth. Cover his ankles and wrists. Don't want the tape to show that... not yet anyhow. We want this to look like he was in the middle of fun and games." Purvis spit, "Ain't nobody gonna want to be around this bastard when we get finished. Much less believe anything he says. Okay kid—strip."

The kid shivered, "Ain't never done nothing like this."

"You're about to git on-the-job training. Do do as I say or I'll see you go cold turkey in jail after you get roughed up for resisting arrest. That the way you want it?"

"No sir."

"Then get your goddamn clothes off before I knock the shit out of you." Purvis yelled, "Winona, after the kid's in the frame get the girl over here." Purvis stood behind the camera, "Make sure this thing's focused. We ain't doing a second take. He's coming around just enough to make this look good." Squinted through the viewfinder again, "You sure them lights is enough?"

She said, "It's the same settings we used the other night. You said those shots looked okay."

Purvis looked at the boy, "Get up there. Face away so the back of your head is toward to the camera. Least that way it'll look like he's enjoyin' it."

Kid squenched up his face, "I don't know if I can."

Purvis tightened one hand at the boy's throat, genuine threat, "Want me to show your daddy how I caught you snortin' with the preacher's daughter? How you made us a movie with her in exchange for more crack? Give daddy a copy? Even better—give the preacher a copy. Daddy'll be damn sure to keep his mouth shut. Cut his supply 'cause his son wouldn't do another favor for us. Huh? Like me to tell him that? Rest of you be quiet while we run the leader."

The kid remembered not to look into the camera. He was afraid of Purvis and wanted to be sure Purvis wouldn't cut him off. He hated Purvis.

Winona gave Purvis a nod. Purvis said, "Ever'body quiet down." Lowered his voice, "Audio's coming on. Get the girls ready. We'll edit later."

A god-awful hammer pummeled somewhere between Craige's ears and a far-off squealing giggling noise like cats mewing. He tried to make sense of it. Like in a nightmare, his arms or legs wouldn't move. He could smell old garlic on someone's breath.

* * *

Terri still got no answer on either of Craige's private lines. Something was wrong. If he was called away on the spur of the moment and couldn't reach her, Craige made it a habit to leave a message. It was either that, or thoughts she truly didn't like. Whichever—he hadn't answered since late yesterday afternoon. She refused to give in to a persistent anxiety, which didn't make it go away. She shampooed and dried her hair. Tried again—still no answer. Put on a pot of coffee. Call the police? The sheriff? Craige had said something about an investigation. He was one of the most private men she'd ever met, and he hadn't change from the day he first walked into her office. She was determined she wasn't going to be the cause of complicating things for him. By the time she'd had her third cup, Terri decided she wasn't waiting for bad to go too worse. She grabbed her keys.

Tail-wagging Lucky recognized her car and bounded around the car till Terri stopped; got out and let him lick her hand. Quickly glancing around, she noticed the four-by wasn't there. If he took the jet the four-by could be out at his hangar.

She got another wet-tongue lick. "I know... I'm worried too. If he was at the hangar, you'd be with him." She scratched the ears, "Your being here tells me wherever he is he didn't take you."

She fidgeted with her keys; unlocked the mudroom door and immediately spotted the empty coffee pot and no cup in the sink. A widow having raised a son after her husband was killed, Terri made herself slow down. She checked the fridge door for notes he might've left but found nothing except a grocery list. And there was no note on his roll top desk in the den, nothing to tell her where or when or how. It wasn't like him. On the corner of the desk she came across a manila folder with the single word *Bailey* scrawled on the outside in Craige's handwriting. Inside were several telephone numbers, no names, some local prefixes, an 803 area code with a number she didn't recognize, and a note to *Call Gray*. Next to that there was another note quickly jotted—*Call Fort Gordon*. She wasn't about to call someone she didn't know. She glanced at the note with Gray's name. She knew Craige trusted Mabel and that Mabel would get a message to Gray.

She dialed the number next to Gray's name and breathed a relief at Mabel's familiar voice, "Buckingham Metro Law Enforcement, Investigative Support Division."

Chapter 9

Beleeza Norton dialed the unlisted cell. She chewed her lip as she listened to the rings, her breaths coming in shallow jerks until she heard him pick up. Her words tumbled out.

The voice soothed, "Leeza, calm down. I can hardly understand anything you're saying."

Leeza said, "Something's going on with Purvis."

"Something's always going on with him."

"I'm scared," she said. "I saw this letter with a list of names on the sheriff's department letterhead."

"Where'd you see it?" His tone changed; interest perked.

"It was on the kitchen table after Lela left for her afternoon class. It was right there on the breakfast table by the coffee pot."

"Everything is all right," the voice answered as it tried to reassure her.

"It's not alright." She was adamant.

"Leeza, calm down." This time the voice was firmer, "I can't talk right now. There's someone waiting for me. I'll get back to you as soon as they leave."

"Once he sets his mind to something, Ingram don't ever quit, and I know what Purvis can do when he gets mad. I'm scared."

The response was harsh, "You've had too much coffee. You know how you get when you've had too many cups."

"I need my coffee," she sniveled. "What you want me to do about the letter?"

"Leave it where you found it."

"My nerves are shot."

"I warned you about drinking too much coffee. Where are you?"

"I'm still at our apartment."

"Stay there. With rush-hour traffic it'll probably take me about two hours down the interstate."

She asked, "You promise you'll come?"

"I'll be there. Just stay where you are. You'll be fine."

"What if someone starts asking questions about it?"

He said, "No one's going to ask question about some letter in the middle of someone's breakfast table."

"Might be a good idea if I stuck it in a drawer."

"Get hold of yourself." He wasn't about to be drawn into an argument over the phone.

"Ingram is buddy-buddy with lots of the uniforms, military and local. He can find out anything. Purvis is the same. I don't want Purvis knowing I called you."

He knew Leeza too well. Spotted her as one of those cutout paper doll, flip-your-hair types. Not enough common sense to look ahead much less think about what she was doing. College was her playground. She stayed in school for the action-parties and the rich kids—too flighty for her own good, too lazy to work for what she wanted.

He said, "Don't talk to anyone on the phone. You have this number. And make sure the battery to your phone is charged."

Leeza felt some better after she hung up, and she couldn't take her eyes off the clock. She paced and fretted, stayed away from the coffee, paced some more.

* * *

Craige's eyes were blurry, body sluggish, memory fuzzed, head ached with a dull thud worse than the concussion from that mined booby trap. He knew he'd been drugged and tried to make sense of his surroundings through the fog in his brain. He wasn't sure where he was, but for damn sure he wasn't in the bar or its parking lot. He wondered who moved him out in what had to be the backcountry boonies on this dead-end of an old logging road. His Jeep was less than ten feet away nosed into heavy underbrush. A starless black of night was waning into the deep purples of coming daylight.

Honeysuckle and hedge-high wild azaleas crowded the windshield; tangled all around him, wherever he was. He slapped at a mosquito buzzing his ear.

He stumbled over to the jeep, and fiddled with his dangle of keys into the ignition. Vague phantasms danced in his being naked with other naked bodies in garbled recollections flickered with strange faces. Was it a dream? He looked down; wasn't bare-ass. His pants twisted, shirt was open, a button missing. Red marks that didn't break the skin looked like scratches from one shoulder across to his belly. He could smell garlic, and his skin felt sticky. He rubbed his wrists, raw like a rope burn—remembered tight duct tape. He stumbled against a small clear plastic case next to his feet. Inside, he found a DVD with a folded tear of paper stuffed in the edge of the case.

With his head throbbing, he grabbed it; fumbled with trying to open it. Squinting, he wiped sweat out of his eyes. The handwritten scrawl was barely legible; the paper smeared with a muddy shoe or boot print. The harder he squinted, the blurrier it got. His head buzzed, and he felt drowsy. He let the paper flutter to the floorboard. He fought the urge to climb in and lean the seat back, close his eyes, sleep. Instead, he forced himself to turn the key, motor caught; wasn't sure he ought to try to drive.

"Hell with that." He shifted into reverse and slowly gave it gas; made sure not to gun it as he backed out of the tangle of vines. He shifted again, this time easing off the brake, and let the vehicle take it slow in the direction of what he hoped was a road or highway. The cool breeze helped some, and he soon recognized the Aiken-Beech Island road. It wasn't long before he was nosing down the drive toward Moccasin Hollow.

Lucky had heard the jeep and met him at the highway. Terri heard him pulling in. She hurried out; saw him slide his legs out; slump back against the fender. She ran to him in a flash, "You look gawdawful."

"Imagine I look worse than I feel, but I'm not so sure about that either." His hand gripped her shoulder. "I'm glad you're here."

"What happened? You look a mess and smell like stale beer or worse. I tried several times to call you. When you didn't answer, I came out here. The longer I couldn't get in touch with you the more scared I got. You look like you've been through it."

He said, "Need sleep."

"A hot soaking bath and a good scrub first. I'll run you a Jacuzzi full for a good hot soak." She disappeared into the master bath then hurried back. "I'd better call Mabel before she calls out the state militia and turns out the whole of Buckingham Parish looking for you."

"Need a cup of strong coffee," he sagged against the kitchen counter.

"What happened?"

Craige held up the cover and its DVD, "Make sure the disk and this note stay together." He reached under the sink, "I don't know what's on it. Use a pair of rubber gloves. They're under that sideboard. Handle the plastic cover and the note by the edges. Won't smear any fingerprints. I may have smudged some when I picked it up out of the weeds and vines."

"Coffee's already made," said Terri, relieved he was alright. She poured his cup brim-full.

He chugged it. Unbuttoned his torn shirt, "Reach me a plastic grocery bag."

Terri frowned, "A grocery bag?"

He smeared a hand across his sticky chest—tore the shirt away. Held it in one fist, "Dinkins may want to have a look at the rest of my clothes as well." Stripped naked in the kitchen; shuffled toward the master bath and the hot soak of the steamy hot tub.

Terri put on gloves; half-fold his clothes got into two bags. Followed him into his bath. His head rested back on the folded towel, eyes closed, the steamy soaking his aches. She made sure he was okay, as she laid two big bath sheets within easy arm's reach next to him. In his master bedroom she pulled back the comforter on his bed; turned down the sheets. Back in the kitchen she reheated the kettle and set a pot of hot strong tea to steep. Then she called Mabel. When Mabel didn't answer, Terri left a voicemail. She heard Craige splash out of the bathroom. By the time she got to his bedroom he was sprawled across his bed, towel crooked around his waist, muffled half-snores buried in the pillows. She tugged away the damp towel, and pulled covers across this butt and thighs and drew the drapes.

Back in the kitchen she fixed a cup of fresh hot tea and took it out onto the porch swing and sipped slowly. Tail-wagging Lucky gave her a lick as she ruffled between his ears, "We'll wait till he wakes up." The dog tilted his head to one side as though he understood every word she said.

Terri tried to relaxed and calm her exasperation at Craige's penchant for sometimes playing raw things too close to a raw edge. Her apprehension not totally settled, she was touched with aggravation at Craige, at herself, at neither of them, at no one, at whoever did this to him. She thought of her late husband, Paul Wofford. He'd been almost as secretive as Craige. Their son Jeff took after his father. When Paul was deployed, she was never quite at peace. The dog sensed a thing wrong; licked her hand.

"It's okay." She stroked the silky head; got another slurp-lick.

She hadn't noticed the figure carrying a fishing pole walk into the yard until Lucky's ears perked, and he bounded off the porch to greet Billy and his stringer of Blue Gills.

At first Terri was startled, "Who're you?" She'd had enough surprises for one day.

Billy hadn't seen Terri. "Oh... hi. I'm Billy, Mister Ingram an' me are friends. I just caught me a mess of fish for supper. Clean 'em soon as I get home. You must be his girlfriend. The one he likes so much." Lucky nuzzled at Billy's hand.

"You've certainly got the dog's approval. That's something not just anyone can do. Craige doesn't invite many to fish on his place."

Billy grinned, pleased at having such a special invite. "Mister Craige told me I could come fish anytime. He sure has been to lots of places. Done things I'd like to do some day." He sat down on the bottom step and laid his cane fishing pole next to the steps. "I thought you were awful pretty the day I saw pictures of you on the shelves next to those of that old woman."

Terri said, "The elderly woman is his grandmother."

The growl of a pickup truck coming down the drive interrupted them; Lucky bounded out to meet it, as Sam Crawforde swung into the yard. Crawforde turned off the engine, and climbed out dressed in faded coveralls and a pair of well-worn, second hand army boots that were Crawforde's version of snake boots. "Well now, Terri, you're a sight for sore eyes. It's been a spell since I've had the pleasure of seeing you."

"It has been a while." Terri gave a nod toward Billy, "This is Billy, an acquaintance of Craige's who fishes here."

Crawforde asked, "Craige here?"

Terri said, "He's inside asleep right now. He had a long night."

Crawforde propped one foot on the bottom step, "I'd like to sit a spell, but I have several things to take care of before heading back to my office. Tell him I dropped by. He might want to come down to the dig and see some of the things we've uncovered."

Billy, excited, "Find any arrowheads?"

"There's lots of them," Crawforde said. "Lot of Indian sites around these parts."

"My dad had some. All kinds of things, one axe head. Got two bowls. They're broken but we have the pieces."

Crawforde said, "You know where they come from?"

"My dad said some come from Edisto Island near the shell hills back in the marshes. My uncle has a farm up near Aiken. Sometimes when he plows, he'll turn arrowheads all over the place."

"If the broken pottery hasn't been meddled with, the shards can help date artifacts. Once a site is dug through, it's spoiled for dating. If you like to know how people used to live, you might want to give some thought to studying it beyond high school."

"I guess," Billy sort-of replied.

"You could study all about the Indians."

"That what you do?"

Crawforde said, "Been doing it longer than you are old," to him his work as fresh as ever. "You can tell what tribes lived where; where they moved; who they traded with; how they reused every-day things. How their pottery designs changed, different axe heads like you found. They didn't throw away much. Recycled most of what they had. Couldn't run down to the nearest hardware store and buy a new one."

"We just finished studying about the Cherokees."

"Sad, the way they were treated."

Billy said, "Cherokees had newspapers."

"That kind of stuff interest you?"

"Sometimes."

"What year are you in school?"

"Senior."

Crawforde said, "Keep your grades up. College is your next step."

"USC Columbia. My Dad went there."

"What's your GPA?"

"Little above a three point."

"SATs?"

"English 550, math 600"

Crawforde smiled, "Sports?"

"Football, but I like baseball best."

"You going for a scholarship? Either football or baseball?"

Billy sighed, "Probably not. You got to be a spotlight quarterback or pitcher to get that."

"What you got to lose by trying?"

Billy thought for a moment. "Nothing I guess."

"Don't say no to yourself. Go after what you want. I've served on several university admissions' boards. When other folks say no to you, treat it as a roadblock to be overcome."

"Or go around," Billy said.

"You might be surprised how most people want to help. You won't have problems with USC. If you'd want, maybe one of these days you could come in the field with me. Look at some of the mounds discovered last month by one of the grad students from our department. We covered it back up to protect it."

Billy's eyes lit up, "I'd like that."

"Hope nobody dug it up since then."

"That happen much?"

Crawforde said, "It's a big problem. What's really sad is how some museums pay big money for cultural artifacts with no questions asked." Glanced at the sky, time of day was moving on, "Got to get going. Use what daylight's left." Gave a nod to Terri, "Nice seeing you again."

Terri watched the pickup disappear through the trees and down the curved drive toward the highway. Summer's darker green leaves were already tinged yellow-green around the edges along the drive.

Billy said, "I better get on home. Tell Mister Craige I dropped by. If I get my errands done I'll come back tomorrow or the day after. Nice meetin' you, mam."

"Nice meeting you, Billy." Terri watched him leave; finished her tea.

She went back inside and checked on Craige. He hadn't moved. In the kitchen she looked through the cupboard and fridge; scribbled a grocery list; grabbed her purse. She'd have him a hot supper waiting. Knowing Craige, he'd wake up with a roaring appetite. If anything would wake him up, the smell of home-cooking would. Just in case he got up before she returned, she left a note on the fridge saying she'd gone grocery shopping and to get hungry for his favorites.

She grabbed his keys and checked inside her purse making sure she had enough mad money tucked in the side pocket. On the way toward the farmer's market, she spotted the little mom-and-pop roadside seafood place. It smelled like it had brought the coast inland with it. Thinking it must've gotten a delivery of fresh seafood, she pulled in.

"Just got 'em unloaded," Pop said. "You picked the right time. My regulars know today is when I get the fresh deliveries. They'll have me cleaned out 'fore sundown. Seafood, 'specially shellfish, don't keep their fresh-caught flavor long."

Terri picked several of Craige's favorites, a Spanish mackerel, two dozen jumbo shrimp and the same number of oysters.

"Use this." He grabbed two big handfuls of the saltwater seaweed that had been used to pack the catches. "If you steam the mackerel or oysters, pack 'em with this. Gives just enough sea salt and flavor you cain't get no other way." He stuffed two plastic bags with the seaweed and threw in over a dozen sand-flecked empty oyster shells, "No point letting them go to waste when they'll add to the flavor."

"I'll try the seaweed," she said. "Thank you." She thought of the spices she wanted for the mackerel. She'd fillet it, then steam it with sautéed onions and lemon pepper. Maybe fix a jumbo shrimp salad with plenty horseradish. She grabbed a few condiments Craige liked with his shrimp, oysters on the half shell, maybe Rockefeller with steamed spinach. "Glad I stopped in," she said as she paid.

Ocean-smelly Pop said, "Appreciate you stopping by. We're open same time ever week."

Terri stacked the bags in the back of the jeep, and strapped them snug with the tie-down clips so the wind wouldn't blow anything out. She hadn't meant to get so much, but the fresh seafood was too tempting. Snugging her purse between the seats, she shifted into reverse when her brief look in the rear-view mirror caught the driver and vehicle easing into the parking lot. She took a second look. It was more the way the car pulled to the side of the lot—and stopped. The driver turned, as if watching—as though recognizing Craige's vehicle.

She kept her foot on the brakes so the brake lights came on, but didn't shift into gear. "I'm getting as suspicious as Craige," she mumbled. "Okay—two can play this game." She wanted the driver to know she was watching.

Terri wondered exactly what Craige's night-owl trek had been about. Foot on the brake, she shifted into park. Turned and looked directly at the driver. It was a woman. Through the glare of the sun off the windshield Terri couldn't see enough to recognize her, and she could see no one else in the car. The cream-colored sedan slowly eased forward; passed behind Craige's vehicle to the far side of the lot, and stopped again.

"Get a grip," Terri groused at her own cat-and-mouse impulsiveness. "You're driving a car that's not yours. She's following the car. Enough of this wait-and-see." She shifted into reverse, and slowly backed out. Groceries forgotten, she turned back in the direction of Moccasin Hollow. More certain the other driver had recognized Craige's vehicle, she did another quick check in her rearview mirror. The sedan was following, but holding back. She sped up. So did the other vehicle, keeping the distance between them. If she didn't turn into Moccasin Hollow, it was several desolate miles to the next fork onto the split four lane to the Savannah River Site.

"Forget that." She wasn't about to let herself be put in that situation—it would've been smart to have called Craige from the market. She nudged the accelerator, already past the speed limit. If there ever was a time to get stopped for speeding—this was it. Where was a cop when you needed one. The sedan stayed with her. Craige's turn-in was coming up; let her speed fall off on the slight rise of the highway. It would be a skidding tight turn; she'd brake for it at the last-minute. Glad there was no traffic, she hit the brakes. In a spew of gravel she nosed into the drive, nudged the gas pedal down the long drive, and skidded around behind the kitchen side of the house.

Her first impulse was to hurry inside. Instead she hunkered down and waited in case the sedan had followed. She didn't hear any vehicle. Nothing. She got out; moved to the corner of the house, and tried to see through the trees, but couldn't see the highway.

The entryway screen door from the kitchen-mudroom swung open to frame a frazzled Craige wrapped in a half-clutched crumpled bed sheet, "What the hell was that? You roared into the yard like a barn afire." Saw the look on her face; hurried to her, "You alright?"

She gave another quick look toward the highway, "Someone was following me."

"You sure."

"Yes. I'm sure."

"Who?" He yanked at the wrap of the sheet at his waist.

"I have no idea. Some woman, I didn't get a good look at her."

He said, "Anyone with her?"

"If there was, they were down where I couldn't see them. I'd stopped at the seafood market. The sedan pulled into the parking lot and stopped three or four car-lengths behind your vehicle. After I pulled out she followed, and kept a steady mile or so behind me, even when I sped up. When I turned in, and that's when you heard the gravel."

"I heard the motor growling when you skidded the turn off and hardly touched the brakes."

"I don't know if she saw me, but she must have driven on by. I don't know if she turned around and came back by."

"No reason why anyone would follow you. Had to be the jeep," Craige said. "Not much traffic on this road this time of day. The driver either knows where I live, or spotted the jeep at the seafood place." Craige looked toward the highway, "There's nothing in that direction except SRS, the road to Johnson Crossroads, a few back roads." He frowned, "And Ardochy. Which doesn't make any sense."

"The McGiffern place?"

"Or someone from the bar." With an absentminded faraway wary look, "Not taking any chances." Jerked the sheet away from his naked butt, "Key's still in the jeep?"

"Yes."

Craige made a mad dash back through the kitchen to his bedroom. Came back buttoning his cords, sockless loafers, light cotton sweater, camera bag slung over his shoulder. Lucky wagged close behind, tail wagging. "Lucky... " Craige fixed him a look, "Edoa." Lucky loped onto the front porch; drooped soulful eyes back at Craige. Lay down by the door, muzzle plopped on his paws.

"I want to check Ardochy," he said. "It don't make sense, but no crazier than someone you don't know putting a tail on someone they don't know at a fish market. The face in this mix is definitely wanting to stay out of the picture—which makes me want to know who and why."

Terri said, "What in the world did you get into last night?"

"That's only one of the questions I want some answers to about things that are way beyond control." He started the engine. "I woke up half naked with only bits and pieces of what happened. Bits and pieces I don't like. Get in. I don't want you here alone."

A few miles farther he slowed at the small sign on the corner post off the shoulder, *Redcliffe Road*. Its washed-out letters were hardly legible through a fencerow of twisted shrubs and thick purple-berry stalks of pokeweed. Craige eased up the gravel path of a road into the Old Yard approaching the two-storied wrap-around-porch house—old Redcliffe.

Terri said, "That looks like the same sedan. Why would it be parked by Redcliffe?"

"That's what I'd like to know. Redcliffe has been closed for repairs." He braked to a stop at the bottom of the drive. "Ardochy's across the way on the same land. Whatever the reasons, it don't strike me as being here for a neighborly visit."

Terri said, "You're not going in there? You said the caretaker carries a shotgun. That he didn't take kindly to trespassers snooping around."

"At one time the caretaker was the family footman. Worked for the McGifferns his whole life, and very protective of Theosia and her mother. In her younger days Theosia rode jumping horses. During the rough lawless years, the caretaker always carried a shotgun. Still does. By the time I knew him. Theosia's mother wouldn't let him drive her buggy. He was almost blind. Her mother drove the buggy. Both buggy and coach are still in the carriage house under heavy dust covers. Her papa last drove the buggy a week before he passed. Said automobiles were the ruination of the land. Parked the carriage in the stone shed out where the barns used to be." Craige unzipped his camera bag, "I want a photo of the license number." Searched for any movement in and around Ardochy, "Get close enough, a shot of the VIN number. If we're lucky, some registration info. If it's stolen, VIN tags may be missing."

Butterflies fluttered her stomach. Spotted basement cellar doors on the side of Redcliffe that reminded her of her great grandpa's cyclone cellar. "I have no intention of staying here while you get out of my sight and into no telling what." From her earliest memories Terri had hated that dreadful cellar. It looked to be a perfect place for snakes and other creepy crawlers. She wasn't afraid of snakes, but she wasn't in love with them either. It reminded her of a Scottish oubliette-tomb hole in the ground with outside winds moaning and shaking the door covers. Now as a grown woman, storms often reminded her of that cellar. Grandpoppi had kept a cot-like bed she made sure she never sat on, much less slept on. She would always stand in the middle of the cellar or sit on Grandpoppi's knee.

Craige eyed the doors and dirt and dust unwashed windows along the front and one side of the great house, and wondered if the best approach might not be to walk right up to the car. Decided against it. No telling who might pop up, including the caretaker with his ready-to-blast cannon.

Terri slid out of the Jeep. "I'm right behind you."

"Stay close," Craige hissed. He knew her too well to think there was a snowball's chance in a hot summer dog-day of changing her

143

mind. He made sure the camera lens was in place, and removed the lens cover. Focused. The shutter's whir and click of several shots the only sound. "That'll do it." With Terri right behind him, he quick-stepped to the far side of Redcliffe, his attention fixed on the whitewashed corner of Ardochy's thick stonewalls. What outside windows he could see were shuttered. He glanced at the potato-bin cellar, "That cellar is out of the dark ages. I can't remember the last time I was down there. It leads to meandering tunnels a body could get lost in. First ones dug back in the seventeen hundreds during the Revolution to smuggle arms. Confederates stored supplies in them."

Terri thought of that awful tunnel across the river, where she and Gray thought they'd lost Craige. She didn't want to ever see another tunnel much less be in for the rest of her life.

"Grannie told me stories how kegs of white light'nin' corn squeezin's got smuggled to the river. Channels change. Small parts of Georgia left in South Carolina. And while we're at it," his unyielding words and face deadly serious, "You're not going home tonight."

"Jeff's finishing exams, he'll try to call me when he finds I'm not home."

"He'll try your cell if you don't answer."

"I made sure it's turned off."

"We're not making this a debate. You're staying at my place tonight. Jeff, too. Neither of us would have any peace of mind if we knew he was alone in the house." As far as Craige was concerned, that was the end of the discussion.

Terri looked at Ardochy with a *déjà vu* vision wholly different from her first visit at Ardochy, right after she first met Craige. Craige Ingram, successor trustee of the McGiffern estate, had blown into her office like a renowned Texas blustery winter blue-norther; bigger than life and right in the middle of her new job with the Trust Department of the Landmark Bank. The McGiffern trust files were stacked and waiting for her on her first week at the bank, and she had hardly begun digging out the details. Theosia Ambarella McGiffern, regal Grande dame of Ardochy, had graciously invited Terri and Craige for tea at her beautiful home. Meeting Craige Ingram was full of firsts.

Craige seemed at home at Ardochy, "No sign of the caretaker," he'd told her on that first visit. "He could be anywhere on the grounds. No point our waiting around. Theosia's likely out gardening."

Terri hadn't been surprised when Craige pulled out keys to the massive solid wood double doors of the main entrance, or that they swung open with no sound on heavy brass hinges. She was, however, totally unprepared when she entered. "Oh my goodness," she was mesmerized by the great oil portrait just inside the entry; a gentle face framed by gray hair on a waif of a very dignified figure, as if the portrait itself would speak. In the subdued light, Ardochy not only looked like a museum to Terri, it was a museum. It engulfed her. Her gaze lingered here and there—a gold embossed teapot, cups, saucers, sugar dish with its pressed glass lid still on its assigned place on the baroque sideboard next to an arrangement of fresh flowers and a breathtaking tea service.

The gracious voice had startled Terri. "I'm Theosia McGiffern. Do come right in. You must be the young lady Craige has told me so much about. Ardochy is near a second home for Craige. His Grannie, Corinthia Ingram, and I were quite fond of one another," she had told Terri.

Even now, it was as though Theosia was still welcoming her to Ardochy as Terri remembered bits of conversation from that first visit. "The tea service you were admiring was a gift passed on to me from my Uncle Roynane—a name shared by Craige. He was quite the family bachelor and the family's raconteur scoundrel. Something of a black sheep; traveled all the time. I enjoyed being around him, and for whatever reason I seemed to be his favorite. Perhaps it was the little gifts he made sure for me to have," Theosia had explained. "Years would pass without any word from him. Then unannounced he'd walk right in the front door, as though he'd never been away."

Theosia also noticed Terri studying a fine water colored coat of arms. "The coat of arms is from a branch of the Russian Imperial Navy," she explained. "Uncle Roynane served aboard several of their vessels. The Czar gave him that tea service. He was a fine figure of a man, big strapping thing that would have made any woman happy. It was whispered that several eligible young debutants from other plantations tried hard enough to entice him. There were also some whispers of a scandal with some preacher's daughter. He had to leave sudden-like. The girl's mother never spoke of it."

"Southron families keep our skeletons," Craige had said, the wisp of a slight smile crossing his face. "Gives us something to talk about on hot summer afternoons. Theosia seldom mentions him."

Terri never forgot that first visit, and how Theosia seemed to be so much a part of it, even now. Unspoiled treasures, antiques, and unquestioned taste. "The library is Craige's favorite," Theosia had told her when they walked through the beautiful mahogany and black cherry wainscoted library with its massive library table and leather bound, embossed first editions. "I often find him crouched in one of the Chippendale chairs, lost in the pages." It was soon after that when Theosia passed.

Ardochy was the past, lived in and treasured with its long-receding times and places. Terri felt herself suspended between those first memories of Ardochy and now, here in the quiet emptiness that only death can leave. She had an overwhelming desire to know more about Redcliffe and the place Theosia called home—Ardochy.

"Theosia was born on Redcliffe plantation," Craige said, as though sharing her thoughts. "Lived there all her life. Her grandfather built Redcliffe, the main house at the center of a working plantation. But Theosia preferred Ardochy Lodge."

"Ardochy was considered a lodge?"

"Theosia called it a lodge. For Theosia the main house wasn't homely like Ardochy. Redcliffe was drafty, too formal, humid in the summertime, hard to heat in the winter with no fireplaces on the second floor. She seldom went inside Redcliffe. She loved her fireplaces. The rooms in Ardochy had big iron and stone fireplaces, like they had in Scotland. She said her great-grandfather's and her grandfather's finances were a bit strained after the 'Late Great Unpleasantness.' Even with money tight, selling the land was never considered."

For Craige it was the same as Grannie. Grannie scrimped and stretched what little money she had, often going without. But selling any part of Moccasin Hollow was never to be.

"It is such an old-fashioned phrase—the 'Late Great Unpleasantness.'" Terri had thought of "Unpleasantness" as Vietnam or the Middle East and her late husband, Paul.

Craige's gaze wandered far-off, "For most that survived that upheaval it was a struggle, as if the war was in the near-past. Theosia once told me her father called it "The War of Northern Aggression." After I was out of the Navy she asked me to come by Ardochy to discuss matters. She showed me the papers and arrangements with the governing board of the State Heritage Society for Redcliffe and its adjoining land grants. Papers and timeworn documents from the time of George the Third. How poor Farmer George had been treated shabbily. That he wasn't such a bad sort, only poorly advised about the colonies. She once said Ardochy seemed empty without children, without a family living in its walls, and that a house became desolate when it wasn't loved. It was the only time I ever saw Theosia a touch melancholy. Her words stuck with me. How Ardochy would become a museum haunted by times gone; haunted with its own tenant apparition." Craige with a wisp of a smile, "Several who've visited Ardochy swear they've seen *the ghost*, an old Cherokee chief wandering the halls and on the stairs. Theosia didn't believe the Cherokee spirit part. She said if there was a ghost, and he ever paid her a visit, she was going to ask him if he was perhaps searching for his Westobou daughter DeSoto kidnapped, and if that dreadful DeSoto ever found their treasure. And if the daughter escaped, and if the Westobou did bury treasure near Silver Bluff. She went to the small alcove of shelves and pulled down the small blue leather bound volume. Rubbed away the dust. Called it a very old first edition and she wanted me to have it. It was rumored the treasure had been bound with leather, covered with reeds, buried and never seen again. How exciting history might turn if an old blue book buried on these shelves of bygone lives proved the legends to be true."

Terri wondered what other stories lurked in the secret corners of Redcliffe and Ardochy. Craige snatched her from her thoughts, "You alright?"

"Yes."

Terri Clung to his arm, as they made their way down the hollow creaky hallways, and entered the library with its high shelves and roller-ladders, reaching up to rows of volumes on shelves near the ceiling. Less than half filled with oil, the Tiffany lamp was still where it had been when its last incandescent mantle threw warm softness dancing patterns across paneled brocade walls. Terri caught a very faint whiff of kerosene with a touch of a camphor after-smell. She imagined the worldly small-framed Theosia reclined on the burgundy velvet settee, her teapot steeping hot tea on the tea service, a cup in one hand, the other across a favorite book in her lap. Her slender fingers reaching to turn up the brightness against an outside world that had changed in so many ways.

From Craige's expression, as he moved through its rooms, Terri could tell he felt an unease, as though Ardochy had been somehow violated. Back at Moccasin Hollow the DVD disk in its plastic case lay on the corner of the table.

* * *

Bernice Raymond marched into Purvis's office, cornered him behind his desk to block him from even standing up. She was in no mood to let him sidle anywhere. Faced down at him.

He started to get up, "I didn't know you were in the office," trying to sound believable, like he hadn't heard her come in.

"Where's my husband?"

He was cornered. He blurted, "I haven't seen Mort. You're his wife. You see him more'n I do."

"I'm not here to exchange empty words," she said. "Mort and I have an understanding. We sleep under the same roof, and that's it. Your fingers are in just about anything that's shady." She didn't mention the rip-offs in their insurance schemes, but she wasn't about to let the likes of Dalugosh stop her. If you don't know where he is, you know someone who does know," her words steady, her eyes prickled like an agitated wasp. Lots of folks were afraid of Dalugosh. She wasn't. "He's one of your poker regulars, and don't even make me go there."

Purvis wanted to shut her up. He knew he wasn't getting away from this one, "Why ask me? I already told you I don't know."

"Purvis Dalugosh, I've known you all your life. You aren't stupid, but that's the dumbest thing I've ever heard you say. I want a straight answer, or I'm going to start making noise, and the first stop will be with my church crowd. Grandmothers are very good at getting the word out. I expect an answer before this day ends."

It wasn't an idle threat, and Purvis knew it.

Chapter 10

Craige rolled over; slid a lazy arm across the warm coziness spooned into him, the blanket and sheet twisted between his thighs. Nuzzled his nose behind Terri's ear.

She murmured, "... mmm... " Cuddled tighter against him.

He nosed behind her ear; inhaled her tantalizing smell mixed with the lingering fragrance of her perfume and warm skin. It felt good, a fuzzy muddled lethargy buzzed between his ears. He stumbled out of bed in a wobbled gait toward the bathroom, towel around his waist, shirt, cords, shorts tangled across the bedroom floor in scruffed piles. He stiff-armed the john; wondered what time it was. He had tried to put together the mismatched pieces of that whole evening at the bar. Night, morning blurred amid fragments and flashes of things that did and didn't seem to go together.

Lowered the commode lid and tossed the oversized bath sheet across it before stepping into the rough-tiled shower. Cold water jetted full-on. Vague aches pestered his muscles. He closed his eyes and faced into the shower jets pulsing against his skull letting his body relax into the hot steaminess. He recalled coming off maneuvers—and a hot shower as his hands slicked soapy bubbles across his chest, soaped everywhere-bruises, one raw nipple, armpits, around thighs, butt, unable to wash away the lick and nibbles of unknown lips and tongues. He lazed a moment longer, then shut off the water; buried his face in the towel and swiped his hair damp. The steam and the jets left his skin prickly. The more he tried to remember, the more he wanted to forget. The memories didn't swirl down the drain with the soap bubbles. His blurry streaked intense emerald eyes glowered back at him as he toweled away the steam and dribbles off the mirrors.

The damp freshness of the towel around his waist felt good, as he padded into the kitchen with his usual craving for boiled bilge-coffee. Instead, he punched the coffee maker; tripled-up with his strong coffee; checked the filter, added water for several refills in case Terri woke up coffee-thirsty. As the coffee spewed and sputtered, he grabbed a quick morning-refresh of grapefruit juice. He caught a trace of her favorite lilac bath oil as he walked out onto the screen porch.

Terri had said something before he hit the bed about who was or wasn't following her. He didn't believe it was the shooter. Professionals don't do a repeat... unless it wasn't a professional. It could've been a snitch's eyes and ears for the shooter. He had played his following the car to Redcliffe like he was an amateur. Going to Redcliffe made no sense. Still, he was glad he had. The photos he took might provide a license or VIN match, the vehicle either legal or stolen. Taking the photos to anyone this side of the river was way too close to Purvis's turf. He'd funnel them through Gray.

A fresh coffee smell tugged him back inside. He poured a raw cup, then picked up the disk from the dining table. Careful not to wake Terri, he kept extra quiet through his bedroom and sat down at his main terminal. He used his stamp-tweezers to carefully lift the folded piece of paper and then the disk. Eased the disk into the tray; punched PLAY. The camera wobbled on its fixed tripod along with a raspy sound of metal against metal until the draped dull gray background view steadied. Lighting was dim, bad and way beyond X-rated, but damn well focused on his face. He recognized the mucky green of the pool table, but wasn't sure it was Mother's Bar. The video went screen-snow blank; blinked back on. Craige watched the whole sequence. The two giggling females showed everything except their faces and made sure they didn't block the camera, hands, thighs, bellies and him on grand display. The video flickered; ended. He punched REPLAY. When he heard Terri shuffle in from the bedroom, he paused the grainy skin flick.

Her warm voice whispered right next to his ear, "There're better pictures of you."

"This is a bad copy. Wish I remembered more of what went on—whoever has the original can make any number of copies. My first guess would be TV stations, newspapers, anyone wanting to grab the couch-potato crowd."

Terri didn't miss a beat, "My guess is blackmail."

"Or it's intimidated threat. The kind of behind-the-scenes leverage Purvis likes." It wasn't the splash of his own naked skin that bothered Craige, "The young stuff looks to be underage." He'd seen his share of slick professional skin-and-sex, good lighting, fair looking models. "It's one of the biggest cash crops all over the world. Next step is skin-for-rent posters." Could take or leave skin games as long as it was between consenting adults. This was someone's slipshod quickie. Punched OFF. "I don't think you want to see the last part. I don't like seeing it. Skin-for-sale in some countries is a cash crop for the closet spectator."

Terri said, "You're eyes are half closed. You look groggy."

"'Drugged' is the word. Thoroughly hammered... most of the recording I'm out like a light. It's all foggy." He squinted then rubbed his eyes, turning a number of possibilities of sniffing out some river rats. "This piece of paper was in the sleeve with the disk." He used tweezers to unfold the wrinkles; spread it, and slipped it inside a plastic sleeve. The penciled scribble was almost illegible.

The way the scene was framed and filmed from a tripod was almost identical to the video showing the killings in the barn. He recalled holding his breath the first time he saw it. He wanted to believe it was play-acting. He'd replayed it frame by frame. The rear-side view of the kid's face and neck, the knotted garrote slid over the kid's head. The cord buried deep into flesh; a flick of the tongue gagging for air. The camera bumped and jerked, the same as this one. The shadowy motion of a pair of arms pressing down on the kid's shoulders, and at the end a shadowy someone walking in front of the camera wiping off a bloody hand. Neither of the videos was about sex.

"I think your blackmail bit about this video is right on the money—except it's not about money. Be interesting to see how they go about using it," he said. "The snuff video was an S&M for revenge, but pain, too." He wondered what other details he could've missed.

He pictured Purvis, "Only consistency on both videos are the faces. He made sure mine was center-screen." DVD showed nothing that would connect it to Purvis. Later, when Terri wasn't within eyeshot, he'd go through it frame by frame, then feed it to his software to see if he could pick up any background noises; see if it was good enough to pin down any voice IDs. If Dinkins didn't have the facilities for video voice analysis or other bits and pieces that could be recovered, he'd call in some favors from Atlanta. Let the Georgia bureau give it a thorough look-see.

Waiting for Purvis was a chess move that didn't suit Craige's reconnoiter-attitude. He preferred to delve amid the shuffle of his own versions of Machiavellian, stir things and see what happened. It wouldn't be the first time Craige had seen money blind a fool. SpecOps gone wrong and Gray's local files proved that. Disgust swept Craige's misgivings. He knew a rush to action could be premature, and Purvis would have no problem getting rid of the unidentifiable underage T&A in the video. He wondered how Mort Raymond fit into this. The forensic exam Dinkins was doing on the body from the boat might prove interesting. Craige turned the bar-angle in his mind. He wanted a closer look at Mother's Bar, any witnesses, the barmaids and bartenders along with snapshots of the pool tables. Pick up random DNA; compare it with what Dinkins could come up with. Blustering in wasn't the answer. Legal rigmarole and good ole boy's politics would bury circumstantial evidence—and that wasn't good enough. His inbred kill-training fought against his warrior's call for action, but first he wanted to pick Zebulon's brain for Purvis's underbelly.

He played his own devil's advocate. Muttered half-whispered, "Cool it, Ingram," a braced disciplined bulwark against hurry-up-before-you're-ready. Still, his tone sizzled with the same scorched blizzard when a SEALmate buddy got hurt—or worse. Raymond wouldn't sit still for being cut out of the loop. From experience, Craige had seen cornering a scared rabbit wasn't the only impetus that led to weak people doing the unexpected. Like father, like son— that what got the kid killed? He knew Purvis wasn't above putting his hand to blackmail; force Raymond to knuckle out of the picture. Purvis might use it to threaten Daddy, but a fried-brained kid who expected Daddy to cover his ass was a whole other ball game. If he wanted to put the screws to Raymond, Craige would plot it from a direction Purvis might not expect.

Seeing how far he would make Purvis jump could get risky. He had seen the best of plans go out of control with a cornered beast. It went beyond that. Try to blackmail him, threaten Terri—at this point Craige was ready to take a few dicey gambles.

* * *

The frame-by-frame replay ended. Sprawled back into his well-worn computer chair, Craige stared at the blank screen. Reran each frame through his mind's eye.

Terri came in. She caught his hardened expression fixed on the nothing-screen. She had seen that look those times he'd mentioned the SEAL on their team killed during one of their unit's operations gone wrong.

She asked, "You want an extra hot mustard on your turkey sandwich?"

His lips tight, Craige was lost in that other world in an inner search just short of dark-night savage. As though he hadn't heard Terri, he said, "It sounds stupid to say it out loud, but I can't wrap my mind around how some people can treat kids."

Terri's hand moved to her throat, "Maybe you're trying too hard. Try to take your mind off it, maybe parts of it will come back. It's like the dreadful emptiness of losing Jeff's father. It never quite goes away. With time it recedes. Then in the middle of something that has nothing to do with Paul, flashes of our lives together come flooding back. Events and times, that if I were asked about it, I'd never have remembered."

Emerald deWorthe eyes swirled arctic frigid, "They used the kid like some useless throwaway that was no longer needed." His jaw clamped tighter, "I can smell Dalugosh behind it." He reached for his scramble cell phone and jabbed the air with it, "Never makes sense to me how drugs and prostitution get such a hold on people that they'll do anything."

"Money can make people do horrible things," Terri said. "Most often to themselves."

Craige said, "With drugs in the mix people see more money than most only dream about."

"You're not the first person to question that."

He grumped, "But most folks muddle through without throwing lives away like an old pair of shoes."

Terri wanted to comfort this worldly sailor that sometimes could be guileless and vulnerable to the profane. She wanted to hold him, soothe his hurt, but knew his pain and the warmth that birthed it was caged in meticulously protected inner recesses. "Most of those kids probably never know anything but abuse... emotional or physical or both. Taking what their world deals them so they won't have an empty spot where love's supposed to be. More kids in this world live like that than I like to think." Her words so soft they were near silent.

Craige rubbed his eyes; slewed a faraway sadness, "I've seen too many." Angrily punched the quick-dial on the landline handset attached to his console.

A slight click in Craige's ear, and Bailey's recorded voice came on the line, "I'm away from my desk and unable to answer your call. Please leave your name and a message after you hear the beep."

A cranky Craige snapped the connection, no point leaving a voice mail. He grumped deeper into his chair, eyes lidded with a panther's primal prey-fixation. He forced himself into a stalker-calm, "Purvis likes to bully. Intimidate to get what he wants. This video is both threat and bait." Fixed on Terri, "So I let him think I'm backing off. Keep digging until I hear from Dinkins, and in the meantime pray like hell he doesn't string up Raymond."

Terri said, "And if it goes beyond Purvis?"

His eyes didn't budge as he pondered all manner of ramifications, "I'm crossing my toes those cards don't fall."

"That is one heck of an open-ended gamble," Terri sighed.

"It sure is." Phone rang. Hoping it was Dinkins, Craige grabbed it, "Ingram."

Bailey said, "You just called. I recognized your unlisted number."

"I need a federal arrest warrant for Morton J. Raymond. And a possible second one for one Purvis Dalugosh—but hold that one for the time being."

"Why federal?"

"Fort Gordon is federal land," Craige answered.

"You found something?"

"Some hunches I want to narrow down once I have me a good look-see at a coroner's reports."

"Dinkins give you anything?" Bailey not sure Craige or Gray was keeping him in the loop.

Craige said, "Nothing on the lab test, but I want to smoke out a few skunks."

"You can't use a federal warrant to go on a fishing expedition."

Craige said, "Why not? Feds don't blink using the flimsiest of flimsy."

"Personal or property searches and the rules of preponderance of evidence are required by a grand jury predisposing whether charges will be filed. Fourth Amendment. You'll hang an anchor around your neck and prejudice any evidence you obtain without probable cause for search and seizure—it won't hold up in court."

Craige couldn't keep from seeing Bailey stuffed to the gills with lawyer-speak. He wasn't about to argue with this don't-think-outside-the box, by-the-book core of Alpsworth Bailey. "I didn't say I was going to use any evidence I found."

"What?" Bailey stuttered.

"I'm looking to stir up some fog and dust that could become probable cause. But not with the warrants. I want the warrants for their stampede-effect. I've got a nasty video. I doubt it's an original. Just get me the damn warrant."

Bailey said, "Send me the video."

"All in good time."

"What?" Taken aback by Craige's shortness.

"Right now the disk is being scrutinized for any usable forensic evidence, starting with finger and palm prints. It's got my face in it along with some illegal camera action I won't discuss."

"That's plenty probable cause."

"Not if there's not much on it except my face."

Bailey pushed, "So what's the illegal part?"

"It has all the marks of a rigged blackmail along with kidnapping minors and taking them across state lines for illicit prostitution, and homicide."

Bailey gulped, "Ingram, what the hell you stirring in?"

"More than you want to know. Along with more unsavory garbage than I'd like to have. Just get me the warrants. By tomorrow morning would be nice. I'll let you know if I get anything definite." Craige hung up, paced a step or two, stopped. He held a centered look out across the river; didn't like being sunk into this kind of mood.

He thought of Grannie's, *"Things happen as they should,"* and, pacing harder, muttered more to himself than anyone, "Maybe it's for the best, letting Bailey talk me into this. Dalugosh is a fucking pervert."

* * *

Dusk light was fading fast. Stars began to show through the deeper purples-to-night. Terri showered early, made sure her hair was dry, and slipped into bed. The cool sheets felt good against her skin. She snuggled into his pillow with its soft fragrance of his Sandalwood cologne. Sleep wouldn't come. Her restless thoughts buzzed at her along with the steady pad of his footsteps pacing the wide expanse of the den. She heard the front screen door screak, then creak open and shut again.

Night-hours later he finally came into the bedroom; shucked shirt, pants, shorts, and slid gently into his side, one arm across his fitful no-sleep eyes. Terri listened to his tossing catnap breathing. Somewhere in the time of night she felt the wonderful warm skin of him roll next to her. At first she thought he wanted to hold her. He liked to sleep spooned. It wasn't unusual for him to wake her in the middle of the night. She pulled him closer, letting his head slide into the curve of her neck and coming to rest between her breasts. His breathing settled more regular.

As he dozed deeper into a stilled half-sleep, he mumbled a garbled snore and his body tensed, "Darrell... " More of his mumblings only garbled in grunts and moans.

It brought her full awake. The name and other words she'd heard come out of other dark venues and war-dreams. She held him the rest of the night, her heart going out to this very private man, her arms around his broad shoulders, wanting so to shield him from some appalling sorrow that racked his memories only to be brought to the present by tensed body-jerks in his broken sleep, as if he was stalking some same wild-card game as Dalugosh. Cornered predators on the stalk for one another.

Chapter 11

Terri and Craige piddled at their half-eaten breakfast. Craige downed two robust mugs of stand-alone boiler sludge coffee. Didn't touch his toast. Terri found herself pondering about Ardochy and Theosia McGiffern. His fork rattled his plate as he pushed his baked grits to one side, then the other on his plate. He wasn't trying to ignore Terri, but he wasn't at the table with her either. Half-hearted, his mind was in recon mode. He willed a silent phone to ring with Bailey telling him what was holding up the warrants; evaluating, shuffling, reshuffling, reassembling, puzzling at as many patterns as he could rally.

When the phone did ring, Craige bounded out of the chair jiggling the table; slopped a glass of juice, and snapped a gruff, "Ingram."

Bailey said, "Your warrant forms were posted by special courier. Will be delivered to Moccasin Hollow sometime this morning."

Craige said, "I'll be waiting."

Bailey repeated his usual, "Keep me posted."

"As soon as I have anything definite." In one gulp he drained his juice and quick-dialed Gray's direct line.

Mabel answered with her usual proficiency, "Investigative Support Division Homicide, Captain MacGerald's office."

"Gray in?"

"Hey there, good lookin'," quick retort. "Not this morning. He's down-country with the Jenkins Parish sheriff at some site with a body. He should be back about two. Said it might have something to do with what you are working on and was planning to get in touch with you when he got back. Anything I can help with?"

"How about Dinkins?"

"He's with Gray." She caught the tense edge to his voice, "Anything wrong?"

"Checking to see if Dinkins has heard anything on the DNA of that other body the boys found."

"There's some special deliveries for him I stacked right here on the corner of my desk ready to put in his hands soon as he gets back. "Hang on a minute." She shuffled through the packets. "There's three." She reached for her razor-edged knife that passed for a letter opener, and slit all three open. "Yes, one is a paint sample analysis on an arson incident. The other two are DNA lab results coded to Dinkins' case numbers. I remember logging those into Gray's files before Dinkins packaged them for shipment. I'm right sure one is the Raymond autopsy and the other was tagged to the missing person report. You want Gray or Dinkins to call when they get back?"

Craige thought a moment. "No point their wasting time playing phone-tag. I'll call them."

"You sound uptight."

"Lots of things on my plate." He heard the crunch of tires on the drive gravel. "Must be the courier. I'll get back to you."

"Oh, by the way. Before I forget," Mabel said. "We received info on that VIN number, make and model you spotted at Redcliffe. Vehicle reported stolen off a lot in Spartanburg."

"Spartanburg?" Being stolen didn't surprise him, but he'd expected it to be local. It could be one of Purvis's devious sidetrack shenanigans.

"Another vehicle on another lot was reported vandalized for speaker systems. Fingerprint reports didn't match anything we have on file."

"Interesting."

Let me know if I can help," Mabel said.

"Will do," hung up and got to the door before the courier knocked. Craige signed for the special delivery. He jerked on his no-socks running shoes; slipped a cotton V-neck over his head, and headed out the door.

Terri brushed one hand through a wayward curl, coffee cup stilled in midair, as she watched him bound off the porch. Heard the growl of his jeep fade away before sitting on the big sofa in the den with her feet curled up underneath, the book about Ardochy in her lap. The musty aged pages bound in soft blue, still-supple leather seemed almost warm to the touch.

* * *

Craige parked right up front at Raymond's office. Step One, he strolled unhurried through the front door. The first thing that hit him was the stifling overload of her cheap perfume.

Chirpy gum-smacker secretary looked up; saw who it was; kept filing her nails, "I ain't seen him in days." Didn't want to be bothered with small talk banter with this troublemaking SOB that already done caused enough trouble.

"Any idea when he'll be in?"

"Ain't talked to him in days neither," continued with her cuticles and nails.

Craige was in no mood to waste time on her. He had already decided on Step Two; left her smacking her gum and filing her nails, and drove to the Raymond house. Raymond's wife finally answered his repeat thumbing of the doorbell.

"My husband isn't here," white-knuckled twisted fingers fumbled the front of her blouse.

Her abrupt odd answer left Craige with a feeling somewhere between *isn't home* and *isn't here* that she was telling the truth. Without words, she was admitting she had no idea where he was. "You expect him anytime soon?"

"Please leave us alone." Her undecided look darted up and down the road in front of the house.

Craige sensed danger bristling the hackles on the back of his neck. A sixth sense made him follow her glance, "Mrs. Raymond, what's the matter?"

"I don't want you seen here."

"Have you talked to your husband?"

"No."

"Has anyone threatened you?"

Her fingers twisted tighter into the front of her blouse, "Please go." Backed farther inside and started to shut the door.

Craige used his heavy boot to block the door. "I'm not a law enforcement officer, I'm a private investigator." He recognized how distraught Bernice Raymond was. "Who's threatened you? Is your husband dead?"

Bernice Raymond's eyes darted back and forth at him and beyond, "You already know who I'm talking about. He said anyone who helps you will be next after he's finished with you." She gnawed at her lip, "I told him I hardly knew you. My husband hasn't been home the last two nights."

"When did you talk to Purvis Dalugosh?"

"Yesterday. He called. Warned me that he had proof you were a child molester. That you were dangerous."

Craige knew he'd get nothing out of this troubled woman. Far as Craige was concerned, Mort Raymond was an unreported missing person. His sinking feeling reinforced his fear that the body Billy had found was Mort Raymond. Somebody was going to a lot of trouble to make sure Raymond's disappearance stayed a non-event. Craige was sure—if a weasel like Raymond was dead, it was because he might've been cornered and he knew too much. Killing him was an easy way out to solve a problem and muddle up complications for anyone's investigation.

* * *

It was too early to go to Mother's Bar. It made for a good time for a social call on Sallie Mae and A'gatha. It took him a few retraced steps on parish back roads with no street signs to find the weeded-up lot surrounding the Victorian-styled pumping station and the old unmarked brick-and-shingle warehouse. He left his jeep in a semblance of what had once been a parking lot, but wasn't sure which of the weathered metal doors to the left of the loading platform to knock on. As he raised his knuckles to knock, a metal-to-metal rattle and clank of a sizable chain scraped along the grating slide of a hand-bolt, and the solid door creaked open a mite.

With another shove, the door swung wide revealing Sallie Mae Drutherferde with a big toothless grin. "Lawdy mercy, Mister Craige. You bring yourself right on in. Me'n A'gatha can hardly believe you be payin' us a visit. Zebulon passed the word how we might could be of some he'p."

Craige ducked his head to miss the single light bulb hanging down from a twisted wire extension they'd stretched over a steel I-beam. "I figured Zebulon would get the word out, and you two would hear soon enough."

Agatha said, "Done put you on a boiled pot of that rotgut coffee. Strong an' black just the way you like."

Sallie Mae's sky blue eyes took in Craige square in the face, "Been way too long since we put eyes on you."

Craige said, "Time has a nasty way of slipping gone without a body noticing."

"Sit yourself right there on the sofa. You brung us luck. Few days ago we come across them good cushions what somebody dun throwed away. Fits the sofa jus' fine," A'gatha said, "knowin' you'd show up like Zebulon said. Them's new covers for the whole set Sallie Mae just finished makin'." She got more serious, "Zeb said you be buttin' heads with that no-count sorry excuse for what passes for the law, Purvis Dalugosh."

Sallie Mae added, "Ain't no law 'bout that sech trash. Likes to hide more'n his share of skulldugg'ry behind that badge. What he up to now?"

Agatha's eyes flashed at Sallie Mae, "What ain't he ever been up to?"

Craige said, "Haven't figured all the angles."

"He heavy into passin' on drugs," Sallie Mae said. "Not takin' hisself, but makin' sure others got the cash to line his pockets. Sell 'em all what they got money to throw 'way. Snort up their nose or stick in their arm."

"Pimps too," Agatha huffed. "Pimps young stuff." Wiped her lips with the back of her hand, "I don't take to meddlin'. Ain't to buttin' into what ain't no bizness a'mine, but any growed-up what take advantage of young'uns or boys or girls needs a good public leather strappin'. And that be for starters."

"Can't argue with that," Craige said. "But he's up to something more than drugs and pimping."

"For sure ain't good at makin' videos," Sallie Mae giggled. "That one he made of you is plumb awful."

Craige blushed beet-purple, "You've seen that?"

"Practically ever'body 'bout seen it." Tittered. "It's a dilly."

Sallie Mae said, "Didn't watch it all." Giggled harder, "Lordy sakes, more copies in the trash than June bugs in August. We don't computer an' fancy gadgets none, but I sure 'nough recognized your name on the plastic cover. I showed it to A'gatha. We knowed your face; couldn't be nobody 'cept you."

"It was me alright," blushed so hard his face felt hot. "Not by choice. But it's me."

"Didn't figure you took money to do it," Agatha said. "You did look a mite tied up," with a girlish smirk.

Craige said, "Purvis is up to something, and getting rid of any that gets in his way, or anyone that looks to become a problem."

"Wouldn't be the first time," Sallie Mae said. "He the kind that makes problems disappear."

"Any word on the street of who's helping him?"

Sallie Mae said, "Zebulon said that what you be needin'. We been keepin' an ear out. Ain't heard nary a tetch."

"I smell good coffee," Craige said.

Sallie Mae said, "It be on the hotplate. Should be good an' ready. Won't take hardly no time to fetch you a strong pour of it." She brought back a big steaming mug, balancing it precariously on its cracked saucer. "Careful with a first swaller. It be b'ilin' hot 'nough to set the tip of your tongue to blister." Gingerly set it on the rickety tray next to the sofa and iron bedstead and accidentally bumped the tray. The propped-up lamp waggled, its split shade bobbled. She steadied the lamp, "This here onct had good legs, but they done got wobbly." Made sure Craige had a good hold before she turned loose the saucer, "See how you like it."

Craige took a slow sip. The thick bite of ground raw coffee stung his tongue with the special kick he savored, "I don't know a saltwater sailor who could make a better brew." Licked his lips, noticed there were no bars on the lone too-small-to-break-in window with its polka-dot hand-stitched curtain. "How you two find this place? It's the one of a kind you two are comfortable with. Back out of the way. Nobody to bother you."

"Right the way we like it," Sallie Mae said.

Agatha said, "A couple'a them living under the bridge told us about it."

Sallie Mae said, "We checked it out. Watched it for a goodly couple a weeks. Nobody come around. Knew it was safe when a family of wrens settled in, and around that far corner of the building a pair of redbirds nested in them scraggly flower bushes. Raised them broods. Had to run off some feral dogs out'a the big workshop area. We never go in there much. Mean dogs, full of ticks. Likely never vaccinated. Them kind ain't afraid of people. Bite in a heartbeat, an' you'll come down with the slaverin' rabies."

"Best coffee I've had in a long time." Craige drained the last dregs.

"Want a refill?"

"I'd better not if I don't want to have to make a quick side-of-the-road stop."

Sallie Mae couldn't keep from asking, "You still seeing that sweet Terri?"

"I am, and you're right. She is sweet."

Sallie Mae wrinkled her nose, giggled softly, "You ought'n make it so long 'fore your next visit."

A'gatha said, "We'll keep on the look-see for you. We pick up on anything we'll git the word to Zeb quick-like."

They walked him to the door and stood just inside waving till he was out of sight.

A'gatha said, "Mister Craige be one fine gentleman."

"His grannie raised him that way."

* * *

After leaving Sallie Mae and Agatha, it was still too early for the bar. Craige pulled a U-turn at the cracker box mini-mall a mile away on the opposite side of the road from Mother's Bar, and drove to his hangar where he left his jeep. Took the work pickup back to where he had U-turned between the mini-mall and Mother's Bar, and backed the bed along with most of the cab into shrubbery and vines. The windshield was barely visible in the overhang; the hood buried in a layer of green. He'd scouted the lay of the land around the bar two afternoons before. The only vehicle parked to the rear side of Mother's was another pickup with a blue left rear bent fender. He'd checked an old high school annual, and confirmed his suspicions with county voting records. Janella Dalugosh, the barmaid that stiffed him, was Janella Whipple in high school. He argued back and forth with himself whether to wait outside for a possible no-show of Purvis or Raymond, or show up inside with the downside of losing the element of surprise along by putting himself in a viper's nest with the pipeline-to-Purvis eyes and ears inside.

When he got closer, he could hear Purvis blustering loudmouthed noise, "Ingram ain't got no legal grounds for staking out the bar, staking out any business without due process. It's legal grounds for revoking Ingram's PI license." Purvis could contrive a charge to hold him overnight, likely in one of his so-called "safe houses" where he could easily become maggot food. Leave no paper trail and no witnesses. When he moved, he wanted a watertight indictment and charges that would stick. If forensics came up with anything solid, there was a chance he could use the shoddy video as evidence against them. Assuming Mort Raymond was still alive, if he could spook Raymond enough—Raymond might try to save his own skin by giving up Purvis for drug trafficking or porno or prostitution or god-only-knew-what. Once he got them selling out one another, tying the murder rap onto Purvis could fall into place.

Craige sat back, dogged down tight on his SEAL training, "One thing at a time."

* * *

At her office desk Terri nibbled at her lunch; absentmindedly played with her salad. She fiddled with her watch. Time was coming up to half past twelve. The morning had been filled with the tangle of details involving two estates. The paperwork was a mess. She never understood why people didn't take care of legal affairs before things got to the mortuary. At least Paul had made sure it was all neat and tidy for her. Craige usually called before she left for work, but he hadn't that morning. He was probably tied up. Knowing his spur-of-the-moment impulses, she tried to dismiss the ramifications of her thoughts.

* * *

Craige kept his distance from Mother's Bar. Let the last smudges of dusk fast-fade into formless navy-blues of night. He had recognized only one face, Janella Dalugosh. After-work and late-afternoon rowdy patrons came and left into the early hours of the night. The bar wasn't showing much promise. He'd spotted Janella come out to her car; fiddle in the front seat; go back inside. The night looked to be a bust. He reached to turn the key; fire-up the truck. He might as well go home, catch a shower and get a good night's sleep, when the idea hit him.

If his bar vigil remained zero, Purvis's wife might be another possibility. Nothing to lose. He glanced toward his duplicate of the blackmail disk in the seat next to him and started to stuff it under his snake boots behind the seat. Instead he slipped it into his vest pocket. Contrived or not, the video could make him as well recognized as some *leaked* celebrity tapes. He didn't particularly want to think of himself and his all-togethers going internet-viral, but didn't much care what Purvis did with the original—some of the tapes his SEAL/CTU gang had made of each other were raunchier.

Two guffawing beer bellies stumbled out of the bar; climbed in their fancy spotlights, mud-spattered truck; gunned the engine, and swerved off down the highway. Craige gave them a disgusted look-see. Two reasons why auto insurance was so damn high. He didn't want to think about times he'd gunned pedal to the metal, only cold sober. He yanked the keys out of the ignition, and climbed out. Made his way to the bar. Let the door bump shut behind him. The same stale beer smell enveloped him like unwashed armpits. Here and there couples sat at the tables. No one else bellied up to the bar except for Janella, her back to him, two empty beer mugs in one hand and a dirty towel in the other mopping at the bar. He wondered where the owner of the pickup was.

He took in the threesome pool group, knowing that could be the same table in the video. Legal push come to legal shove, Dinkins could match fibers from his clothes that he'd bagged—if and when they were ever needed. He spotted the large plasma screen TV, the two older-than-ancient VCRs sticky with a mix of spilled beer and whatever, and one unplugged CD player.

As Janella turned on her barstool, she saw him; walked toward one of the tables slopping a pitcher of refill on the way. On her way back to the bar she put on a bored lie, "Didn't expect to see you in here anymore." With a guess-we-showed-you leer, "What you want coming in here anyway?" Her eyes made a giveaway back-and-forth quick look toward the rear door at the end of the bar.

"Maybe save your life."

"What?" Fear quivered in her voice, afraid of what this unpredictable navy juggernaut was about to do.

"Who's going to get your party favors for you in prison?"

"What's this prison shit you're talking about?" Headed behind the bar, "I'm gonna call my husband. He'll take care of you quick enough."

Craige pulled the edge of the disk from out of his inside pocket. Baited her, "Before the dust settles on this piece of amateur crap, he'll get rid of you, too." Casually slid it back into his pocket, "You know way too much." Another sliver of fear crossed her face and stayed there a touch too long. That and the tightening of her lips told Craige he'd hit dead-on center. Tapped his pocket, "He may have convinced you there's nothing to worry about, but a friendly suggestion would be for you to think exactly how clear your face shows up on this." He coolly reached his business card to her, "I wouldn't wait too long, and I wouldn't get careless and leave this laying around. He might not let you get to a phone. Don't call the police. Call me. I'm not talking about the tinker toy camera games you play in your trailer. God knows what the fine god-fearing folks in this town will think when this gets out."

"Your face is all over that video." The half-light in the bar glanced off the pummeled veins in her neck.

Craige flat-faced serious, "I don't need a video for anyone in this neck of the woods to recognize my face." He walked over to the disk player; reached for the unplugged cord, "Want me to plug this in?" Didn't keep sarcasm out of his voice, "Let everyone in here watch it right now."

"No." Glanced around. afraid someone was watching. The bartender was.

Craige didn't need to ask if she was scared. He could see she was. Knew he'd pushed about as much as more push would budge her. He tapped his pocket, "Your husband probably counted on you not being able to testify against him, but you're not the only one involved. Won't take much to put names to those in this little production; those alive and those that aren't. With the right encouragement they damn well will sell you down the river to cover their butts. Killing one or two people doesn't take much time, but getting rid of the bodies takes planning. Planning that needs solid alibis that'll hold up, and I don't intend giving him the time he needs."

Janella murmured a garbled moan, "... gawdamighty... "

Craige walked over to the pool table. Tapped it, "Table showed up real good." He fingered the whittled graffiti where his left elbow was tied. He'd confiscate the table before Purvis got rid of it. It would be a nice touch of evidence. When the time came he'd have the probable cause for Bailey, and more than enough for Gray. He let the silence grow deep. Then dead serious, "Call me. While you still can."

Gut-fear bugged Janella's eyes, "I don't know nothin' about what all went on."

"Maybe. But you know who does, like you know about a lot of other things. Things I know about."

She swallowed hard, "I didn't know nothin'."

He took one step toward her. Leaned close to her, "You know anyone who'd believe that? No matter how you think this will play out, one way or another you're an accessory. You keep silent, and someone will make you real silent. Dead silent. Dead or running from the law or running from Purvis or both, you're still an accessory."

The corner of her mouth quivered, "I didn't have nothin' to do with no killing."

"All you do is roll lonely horny drunk soldiers. Spike the drinks you're told to spike, and help tie them up for center frame in kinky films. Blackmail is a profitable business long as everybody gets their cut and keeps their mouth shut."

Janella whined, "I never had nothing to do with no blackmail. We just get together for a good time."

"Good times with underage kids?" words tight and slow and vicious. "And what happens after Purvis is finished with them?"

"I don't know what you're talking about." Her cowed look searched for an out.

Craige said, "You stick to that line."

"Janella!" The bar went morgue-silent. Purvis Dalugosh stood in the rear entrance, "Shut your goddamn stupid mouth! You never did have enough fuckin' sense to keep from running your mouth. 'Bout all you're good at is with your thighs spread." He kill-glared at Craige as he strode forward, "What the fuck's a pervert like you doin' in my bar?"

Craige liked the pissed-off expression all over Purvis's face and would've enjoyed puttin' some whup-ass on this sleaze. "Who would've ever thought you'd be brain-dead stupid enough to make a snuff film in a place everybody knows you own. I always thought you were dumb, but your little video scenario proves it."

"There's a warrant out for your arrest."

"I doubt that."

Purvis's grip set around the handle of his revolver, "You calling me a liar?" Janella backed away.

Craige was quick, brought the two men nose to nose, "You pull that gun out any further and I'll show you how to get a broken wrist so fast you won't believe it."

"You resisting arrest!" Purvis blustered.

"There wasn't any warrant as of this morning, and you're interfering with a licensed private investigator exercising a legal investigation in a public business. Doesn't matter hog shit whether you own it or not." Craige grinned right into the fury-red face, "I have contacts I can depend on. Which is something you don't have."

Purvis's weapon stayed holstered. Hissed like a hognose adder, "You piss arrogant sonofabitch."

"Arrogant and good at it and a meaner sonofabitch than you'll ever be." Craige smiled right into the smelly face. "That's why you like me so much." His down-deep gut told him not to push too hard, didn't want to panic him. "Smarter, too." Craige knew Purvis was on the edge of losing control. He could use the video; toss some loose cash on the floor; claim it was a robbery.

Janella looked at Purvis, "You didn't tell me about no killin's." Cowered against the bar with a feeble quick look at Craige.

"I told you to shut the fuck up! You think you can remember that or you want me to knock it into you?" He turned at Craige, "I ought to break your fucking neck."

Craige grinned a relaxed sneer at Purvis, "Go ahead. I need the exercise." Postured a relaxed stance. Waited for Purvis to take the next step. He wanted the wife to see that husband's intimidation was mainly bluff. At the same time, he knew that, for this woman, being threatened was one of the few real things in her life. Craige caught the flicker on Purvis's face and baited him a touch more, "Maybe you ought to take a copy of the video to the newspaper or to some of your cronies in law enforcement. They might want to ask both of us some questions. Mainly, like how you got it. Answers would make some truly interesting department reports. Let me know when you make up your mind." He walked out of the bar and got into his truck before Purvis recovered enough to realize that his little blackmail scheme was backfiring in directions he hadn't intended it to go.

Purvis stood in the shadows of the bar; caught a low snarl from deep in his belly. He had to stop this goddam PI bastard before it was too late, but couldn't quite get a grip on why the usual rules didn't apply to Craige Howelle Graeme Roynane Ingram. He never considered the simplest answer of all. The rules never had.

Chapter 12

Purvis in a foul smoldering temper. His focused scowl fixed on sonofabitch Ingram as he walked toward the jeep, and he stayed in a dead sweat that whole night and into the next day. He wasn't about to put up with this, or let Ingram keep poking around. He'd cool the drugs. Let demand push the street price up, but he was bothered by those he didn't want Ingram to find out about. His head-on skin movie idea was useless.

He snarled like a cornered marauding pirate, "Problem solved if that goddamn shot had taken Ingram out."

He tumbled through names of anyone close to the buttinsky PI; anyone he could use to squeeze Ingram. His heart pounded; knew he had to tread careful. Ingram wouldn't bluff. The threat would have to be real, and that made a ticking bomb. Whatever it boiled down to would have to be done out of sight and thorough and no fingers pointing back to him. Ingram would take a threat to his friends as deadly personal. MacGerald came to mind. Damn homicide cop with a Dragon Lady secretary would have every state in Dixie after his hide. Fat slob Zebulon Bergamot was a possibility. The first impression of Zebulon Bergamot was a quickie limp-wristed pushover. Purvis knew better. Bergamot had a rap sheet thick as a stack of books, along with the hired protection muscle to go with it.

He remembered something Janella had said. Most times he never paid much mind to nothing Janella rattled on about. Janella and Lela rambling on about Ardochy, something about Ingram and the McGiffern estate. Ever since the old woman died, word had been around how Ingram and the university in Columbia were arranging for the libraries in Ardochy and Redcliffe to be on permanent loan from the foundation. Redcliffe would make a good spot. Out in the country, isolated with only an old caretaker. All he needed was the bait.

* * *

It was near sundown. Purvis pressed against a back wall of Ardochy, the chalky whitewash dust smearing the back of his shirt. The caretaker had made his rounds earlier. It wouldn't be long before he turned in for the night. Drapes were drawn on the tall downstairs windows with the exception of only a couple of windows in the butler's pantry, and the servants' back stairwell had nightlights. Purvis looked at his watch, then cautiously opened the canted storm door to the cellar and vaults, and eased it back against the side of the house. He went back to the front corner of the house to make sure no one had come up, then returned to the open cellar-vault door. He spooked himself thinking about a face glaring back at him from the cellar—never had liked places like cellars. The stone steps down were cracked and crumbled. He took care as he stepped into the basement shadowed in the dwindling light. He wouldn't need much time—just a quick hustle through the libraries. Grab any of the old books. Scatter pieces of rotten bookworm pages. He didn't need bait; the caretaker would do his dirty work for him. Ingram would get the word and show up in no time. All he needed to do was stay in the cellar and wait. He eased one foot in front of the other, feeling for the cement-brick step up to the hallway off the kitchen. He stopped; listened; heard shuffled steps upstairs. The caretaker hadn't turned in; wasn't following his usual routine. "Trigger-happy sonofabitch is still inside," he muttered, eyes on the rim of light under the hallway door at the top of the steps.

His sweaty hand fumbled with the small penlight as he swept each step—it wasn't the time to get snake bit. He roamed the narrow beam around in his catacomb-like surroundings, across the overhead sills and heavy beams. He spotted no rotten lumber or loose electric wiring. He heard the back kitchen door thud shut tight, followed by the bump and creak of the screen door; then voices not very far from the outside cellar door. The old man never had visitors. He hadn't

173

counted on anybody being around. There could be others. Witnesses he didn't need. He waited for the voices to fade before he took a look. Not seeing anyone, he slowly lowered the door, making sure it didn't slam. It was dark as he crept from the house toward the highway where he'd hidden the sedan.

* * *

Leeza never paid much attention during high school history classes, and her classes in government were wearisome. She distracted herself by emory-boarding her nails or doodling monograms. University tuition plus books was more than her parents had, and her grades never came close to getting a scholarship. Near the end of her freshman year, a classmate in her boarding house said, "I'm changing schools next year. My job transcribing notes will be open, and you've been looking for part-time job."

Leeza snapped it up. Transcribing Doctor Crawforde's notes and translations of old manuscripts into computer files wasn't that hard. Many of his notes were single-line scribbles; others referred to tagged pages from stacks of books and heaps of references. She had to step lightly in his cluttered piles of oversized folios—papers, letters, hurried drafts being readied for submission or rewrites. She made sure the updates and backups were ready and in the small INBOX on his desk by the next morning. She couldn't understand how anyone could spend week after week digging in the centuries-old trash and graves. To Leeza stuffy academia was a boring life buried amid musty shelves of crumbly papers. Most of his notes were lists of names, dates from the past, trade routes through the wilderness and along rivers, diseases, treasure ships, skirmishes and native's ambushes. His notes on *The Chronicles of Fidalgo, Gentleman of Elva* were thicker with more pages than his original of the thin volume in Portuguese. Fidalgo's travels in the new world and the aborigines encountered, including several tribes, and one tribe of Westobous he'd underlined. She seldom read any of the boring stuff she transposed.

One afternoon when she came in, she found his notes paper clipped to the folio on the corner of her desk. She opened it to collect his notes, and found the most graceful elaborate swirls of letters on the embellished originals. When she asked, Crawforde said, "It's calligraphy. Greek for *beautiful writing*. Very decorative."

She said, "I can hardly recognize some of the letters in that big folio."

"My translations are in that back folder in medieval Germanic and English," his words ear. "The originals have footnotes annotated with the signature of the Royal Recorder with its Imperial Seals. There's an affidavit of DeSoto's private secretary Rodrigo Ranjel along with Ranjel's diary. The 1557original's are in the Prado in Madrid with the Imperial Seal of Charles V amid the flourished supporters of the Imperial Coat of Arms. The loose sheets in the back sleeve are copies of prints and wood etchings and early maps of Florida. Some have crude southern portions of the Georgia colony claimed by Spain, and the Carolina upcountry border with Georgia, the Westo River, and a rough sketch of the crossing of DeSoto."

She noticed he'd penciled-in a question mark next to *El Dorado*, Silver Bluff and an Indian settlement—*Cutifachiqui*. She wondered how anyone could be interested in long-dead smelly sailors and Conquistadors tramping through bug-infested wildernesses. There was one hand sketch in Crawforde's scrawl she did recognize— *Ardochy collection*, and he'd added *gilded city, jewels, furs, trade goods* with another question mark and more marks in the up-countries of South Carolina. She wondered what else was on the shelves in that rundown Ardochy House.

He said, "These are photos of hand-wrought native gold pieces, decorative strings of beadings, and a list of museums."

Crawforde's notes about Desoto teased Leeza. For sure about the jewels. Leeza wished she'd paid more attention to her history lectures. When she came to work the next time, instead of transcribing, she read through the oversized bound folio he'd made, skipping the long and flowery stuff of royal titles and dynastic intrigues. Her attention was caught by a blurry drawing of a young beauty. Crawforde had scrawled one word... *Queen*? Leeza recalled playtimes of hide-and-seek or olly-olly-oxen-free, and playing Indians with her friends. Sometimes Daniel Boone or cowboys and outlaws or Yanks and Rebs. She wondered what cowboys and Indians would be like with

Cherokee and Crawforde's Cutifach. She wondered who wore the jewels.

She hurried to finish transcribing his batch of notes. Instead of rushing off to her local pub for beer and pizza, Leeza stayed late. She brought up earlier files she'd transcribed, and quick-tabbed through the pages. She kept seeing notes with *C. Fidalgo* and *Elvas* with other names scribbled in the margin and came across more maps of landings and river crossings squeezed between the oversized pages. Carefully she turned through the oversized folio pages She closed the large volume and was re-shelving it when she noticed a crumpled piece of paper with jagged edges stuffed between the spine and hard cover. Curious, she pulled it out and unfolded it. She was surprised it felt thick like a very dry piece of shammy cloth or parchment. There was writing, and she expected it to be in the same cursive lettering with words she couldn't read. It was in English, and it wasn't about DeSoto.

"There has been wasteful burnings of homes, barns, and entire towns. Sherman's bummers came frightfully near to us. The libraries in Redcliffe and Ardochy House would certainly have been sacked or burned had our gallant arms near Aiken not prevented intervened. There is likely to be more fighting. The rarest titles have been packed. Once this missive is finished it will be added to the last crate, and hidden in the tunnels with the others. River entrances will be filled to prevent flooding, and entrances in Ardochy bricked up. The kitchen cellar entrance and its adjoining wall have been resurfaced as though solid. Family heirlooms of silver, china and the brooches and necklaces are in the smaller tunnel Grandpoppa prepared after the firing on Fort Sumter. Poppa is more concerned about my most-defiant sister. She detests the invaders. She refuses to leave. The treasures must be moved away and well concealed. They will loot or maybe torch everything. If the rumors are true, I feel a great consternation for Columbia."

Leeza couldn't make out the name written at the bottom. Her fingers lightly brushed the raised `W' on the off-white parchment and the Coat of Arms. The name looked like it spelled *d'Worthe*, but she wasn't sure. Startled by the bump of a tree limb across the roof, she folded the paper and stuffed it back where it had been.

Could there be more in other books? Over the following days she caught herself thinking about what she'd read. The paneled library, its shelves crammed with books and a large smoking room on the main floor. She remembered one of the notes she'd transcribed: "*... family papers in the upstairs reading room...* " With a reticent smile, *I wouldn't need much time.* Her mother would never believe she was actually reading about history.

Leeza picked one of her days off when Crawforde was out of town. She second-guessed herself as she thought how to go about it, and found herself making the turn onto the curved weeded Ardochy drive and parked next to the old granite buggy steps. She walked around to the front door and turned the ornate brass bell ringer; listened to its clang-ding echo. Waited. Nothing. She gave the brass knob another twist.

The door opened a crack, "Who're you? What you want?" The door opened slightly more, "What you doin' on this property? Radcliffe and Ardochy is closed for renovation. Won't be open till restorations are complete."

The gruff bushy-brows startled her. A bit of sweetness couldn't hurt, "I wanted to visit Ardochy."

"Both are private property. I asked you what you were doin' here?"

"Are you the caretaker?"

"I don't see that's none of your business. Ain't your place to ask questions. You're on private property."

"I'm doing a research paper for my history professor at the university in Columbia about the confederate battles near Aiken."

"The Battle of Aiken?" The door opened wider.

"The McGiffern family and the name of Ardochy has come up several times. The university librarian told me most of the McGiffern papers were still in Redcliffe and Archochy."

"Far as I know they're all still on the shelves, but they're book-wormed and full of silver fish. Pages are rotten. Fall to pieces in your hand. Ink faded, barely readable. I think the fellow handling the McGiffern properties is making arrangements to move them."

"I'd be ever so grateful if you could show me. I know it's imposing, but I won't take long."

Grumpy face disappeared; the door opened, "Only for a few minutes. I got things to do."

Leeza gushed, "Thank you ever so much." In the stifling afternoon humidity she felt a twinge uneasy as she followed him up the age-worn creak of solid wood stair steps that spoke of by-gone years. The long hallway talked to her, and she caught the slow steady tick-tock of a great clock somewhere.

"Library is right in here," the caretaker ushered her in.

The moment she walked into the smaller room Leeza was bewildered, near to the point of being overwhelmed. Crawforde's office had nothing like this. The narrow shelves were crammed with frayed folio volumes and stacks of handwritten papers and letters. "I expected this room to be bigger."

He said, "This isn't the main library. This room was Miss Theosia's. Where she took her afternoon tea and sit and read."

On the small desk with its rickety chair lay large leather-bound volumes, one trimmed in blue. Too big for her to hide and sneak out, "All these books and papers."

"Still laying right where Miss Theosia last left them. Nothin' fake about this place. Old man Virgil told me once when the landings flooded and the river got high, how he saw pottery and bones sticking out along the washed-out river banks. When the water went down Virgil went back and reburied the bones. Never told nobody what else he found. If he found anything he wouldn't have told nobody. Folks talked about him. How Virgil was a dumb field hand. He wadn't one bit dumb. Times when Redcliffe was a workin' plantation and when the field bell rung after supper, I'd often see him sitting in that very chair with one of these books on his lap, readin' away. He read every one of these books, sometimes more'n once." Quick look at the shelves, "Some got wet during times they was hid in the tunnels and caves along the river 'twixt here and Savannah. Tunnels are older than Redcliffe. Indians likely lived in the first ones. McGiffern's been hiding things in the tunnels since before this place was built." With a wicked chuckle, "Early on it was corn squeezin's bein' shipped to Savannah Towne. Ain't safe to go in them no more. All soggy when the river's high. Timbers gone rotten. Most clogged with cave-ins. Lots of critters, turtles and snakes. Easy to get buried; no one'd ever know. Mud an' river an' rot can make a body disappear real quick if'n gators don't take it first."

"I'm terrified of snakes."

He said, "Plenty of them about."

Leeza recalled what her fifth grade teacher once said—how a book's value comes from what's inside. Leeza said, "One of my teachers knew about some of the tunnels."

"She must'a been one of your old teachers."

Leeza said, "Could I take just little look inside one or two of these? History of people's lives right here in these pages." Same as Crawforde had her do with his old volumes, she slipped on a pair of soft white cotton gloves, "I'll be extra careful."

The caretaker said, "A professor once looked through these books. He put on a pair of gloves exactly like that."

"The professor I work for uses gloves when he's handling his old volumes."

"I'll leave you be. When you're done, I'll be at the lower landing." He shuffled out, Clomping down the creaking steps down one step at a time.

Leeza had used FIND and parts of the filename to locate the one she wanted with its small colored snapshot he'd taken. When she found the note, she printed a copy.

"*Confirm El* Escorial title *printed in Madrid* – check Ardochy *library – name on the spine with embossed Coat of Arms – list of kings and queens, consorts and mistresses, madness and intrigues, courtiers, notables of each reign - Cortez, Portuguese Magellan - Fidalgo y Ranjel - Cutifachiqui – Westobou treasure – DeSoto –*"

She turned to the endless shelves. Her eyes searched for the title with Madrid on the cover. Leeza had heard old-timers talk about Indians and their settlements along the Savannah. She reached a smaller volume down from the shelf. Several loose handwritten pages fell out. The flaky edges crumbled. Across the top of one page, "*Westo tribes centered along upper Savanno River.*" More faded words inked or penciled along the margins, across the top of the fragile sheets. "*Traded mostly with Edisto and coastal tribes - bartered furs for sea treasures-*"

There were more words in cursive she couldn't read or understand; more scribbles in English, but the faded ink was almost unreadable. "*DeSoto kidnapped a Chief's daughter - Chief died from the sickness the medicine man had never seen -*" Underlined one word, "*smallpox*" Followed by, " *- fear for her people. Daughter gathered tribe's sacred objects - hid them near the burial mounds of their forefathers.*" She flipped through the folio pages for any other notes. Nothing shook loose until her fingers trailed the uneven bumps between the last folio page and heavy back cover, and found more notes between the original binding and the newer binding laid over the original. Leeza turned to the spine. She could just barely make out *Madrid* underneath the later cover.

She took out the pages she'd printed, and opened the book with the blue trim. The stylish handwriting scribed so many decades was long gone. She flipped through a few more pages, then eased closed the aged cover, and took the stairs back down.

The caretaker was waiting at the foot. Leeza said, "It was so nice of you to let me have a look at the books. I appreciate it."

With a faraway gaze he said, "When I was a youngster, I was up to the university in Columbia a couple of times. Used to be crowded with horses and buggies. Last time I was up there a body still couldn't find a parking place for all the automobiles. After that, 'bout the only time I ever saw a horse and surrey was someone wantin' to show off here when Miss Theosia used to have her big Redcliffe cookout every July Fourth. I hear the campus is grown way bigger." He opened the front door for her.

She gave him her best smile, "Thank you."

* * *

The microwave timer showed half past twelve. He grabbed a cold bottle of Artois and guzzled a heavy swallow; then shucked out of his shirt and kicked back out on the side screen porch. Mosquitos whined against the screen. With all their summer rain, mosquitoes were bad. By the time he finished the beer it was well after one. He stood and stretched; idly scratched his chest, and headed for the bedroom. Got out of his pants.

Thought of Terri. Muttered, "You've sort'a let this case push her to one side."

He plopped onto his bed. No sooner had he muffled several pillows around his head, than his thoughts were wrangling possibilities. He drifted into sleep with in-and-out variations of prying Janella loose from Purvis, but the odds were against it. She'd been emotionally battered too much, too often, and cowed beyond being much help.

* * *

Leeza slid into the driver's seat of her car. She heard the front door of Ardochy shut with a solid thump. She fumbled through her purse for the keys.

The rough hands came from behind. With cold harsh words, "Looking for these?" Keys dangled in her face; the stink of his breath in her face. "Start the engine. You're gonna drive nice and easy. Try anything stupid, it'll be the last dumb thing you do."

Leeza screwed down her fear. She didn't want to rattle this son of a bitch, "Where you taking me?"

"Just drive nice and calm, and stay under the speed limit. Plain dumb luck, you being here." Purvis tapped the muzzle behind her ear, "Figured by now you'd've cozied up to that private investigator." He cut his eyes toward the side road where he'd parked away from Ardochy.

"What are you talking about?"

He kept her on the highway until they crossed the bridge. "Turn here, and drive past the docks." Agitated, he glanced around to make sure there were no other cars and no cops. "Turn around."

"What?" The palms of her hands were sweat-slick against the steering wheel, her mind spinning with no idea what to do.

"Don't get mouthy." One slow word at a time, "Do like I told you, and turn-the-fucking-car-around." Pointed, "Park over there."

She pulled in, "What do you want?"

He said, "Kill the motor, and stay where you are."

Leeza did as he said. "What are we doing on this side of the river?"

"If you don't shut your mouth, I'll shut it for you."

"Why should I trust anything you say?"

Jabbed the gun barrel up under her ribs, "Cause I'll shoot you right here if you don't."

"No you won't." She figured she didn't have much to lose, "You're scared. I don't know what about, but I can tell you're scared."

"And jumpy. And don't forget it."

"You going to kill me?"

"If you don't do as I say.

"That's not the reason you waited at Ardochy and brought me here."

"Why throw away an opportunity? You could be just the bait I need."

Leeza said, "And get rid of me when I'm no longer needed."

"I could do that now. Nobody around. Car windows are up. Down here by the docks in this part of town nobody'll pay attention to a little noise. When I don't need you any more, you can go where you want."

She said, "With you pointing a gun at me, it isn't exactly a reason to believe you're telling the truth." Scared as she was, letting him intimidate her wouldn't help.

"Don't push me. Right now you're less trouble dead."

"And a dead body would make it easier?"

Your pokin' around Ardochy got me to thinkin' how you could help me solve a problem." He opened the rear door. "Give me the keys. Stay where you are till I tell you to get out."

Leeza took notice of the lightless, two storied restaurant with its tattered for-sale sign. Except for the hiss of bug lights on the city docks, across the empty parking lot there was the one houseboat along with several street lights not working.

"Get out. Nice and easy," he grunted. "Walk straight toward that houseboat."

She gripped the handrails on the wobbly boards of the houseboat's ramp, "I can't see." Each of steps set the ramp in a shaky wobble.

Purvis said, "Back against the wall," motioning with the gun he pushed against the rusted lock on the glass side door of the houseboat.

When it gave way, he slid the door open. "Inside." Feeble streetlight shadows through the heavy curtains outlined bulky furniture. "Get back yonder toward the bedroom." He closed the sliding door with a metal-against-metal scrape.

With what little she could see, Leeza measured her odds with a knee in his groin and grab the keys to the time it would take to reach her car. This fool was capable of doing exactly what he said. She wouldn't be risking much, but she read the odds being definitely against her.

His face pressed to hers, he pushed the gun barrel against her cheek. "Sit down. Keep quiet, and don't make no problems, or you'll be gagged and hogtied. Or a bullet where you won't be a problem."

She reached out, felt with her hand toward what looked like a rumpled bed. As she did, he walked out of the bedroom. She heard the sliding door thud shut. Outside the bug light buzzed and crackled amid the swarms flickering around it. She glanced toward the front. The private investigator Purvis mentioned had to be the Craige Ingram she'd heard about. The sliding door opened, then closed. She could hear his heavy footsteps pace back and forth. Leeza tried to stay calm, silently questioning herself why Purvis had been sneaking around Ardochy. She had no reason to think he'd followed her there.

* * *

At Ardochy Craige gave three hurried knocks on the *porte cochère* door. From inside, he heard the shuffled footsteps of the caretaker, the rattle of latches, and the door opened. "Mister Ingram, right this way." Craige followed him. "Them papers you wanted to have a look at are in the upstairs library. Sure been more folks than in a long time looking at stuff in them books. Yessir, more folks than there's been in a long time. Folks keep coming, I'll have to set up some chairs. Some of Miss Theosia's books still be on the table. Take all the time you want. At the top of the stairs, "They're right there in that room. Anything you can't find might be in the big library."

"Any left in the Redcliffe library?"

"No, but they might be some in them big boxes they moved from over there."

"Any of the boxes sent to Columbia?"

"They won't be moved till you give the say-so."

Craige scooted up to the table, "I won't be long." He noticed one of the large folios was open. It wasn't left like that last time. It took a good three-quarters of an hour to give the shelves, binders, spines, and covers a thorough look-see for any dust that had been disturbed. The book with the blue trimmed cover was still there. He met the caretaker at the bottom of the steps.

Caretaker said, "Take longer than you expected?"

"Longer than expected. I appreciate your help."

"Anytime." He watched Ingram drive off and wondered what in tarnation was so-all-of-sudden interesting about books what'd laid around all these years.

During the drive home the disconnected ifs pillaged a ragbag of Craige's suspicions. Pulled up next to the house; killed the motor; punched Bailey's number. He had heard zilch with his skin video ploy attempt at blackmail. He figured Purvis had expected more. He also figured Purvis was up to something else; threw an uneasy glance toward the front porch where the bullet-shattered flowerpot once hung.

A sleepy Bailey answered, "Bailey."

"Be at my place in twenty minutes."

"Damn Ingram, you ever call at a reasonable hour?" Gruff, "You always were a creature of the night. I'll be there." Hung up.

The time it would take Bailey to dress and drive to Moccasin Hollow would be enough for him to pick on some loose ends. Craige restarted the engine, backed out, and drove the several miles toward the dirt road cutoff. He wanted to get a look at the vehicles parked there. A couple of miles ahead he caught a glimpse of a dark-colored sedan—dark blue, maybe black—there were no other vehicles. The Dalugosh trailer was less than mile farther on. He let the jeep edge to a bare crawl, and eased on by the trailer. He suppressed his BlackOps instincts. It was a made-for *carte blanche* invitation for Purvis to use a shotgun and then claim it was self-defense against an intruder. There wouldn't be anything in the trailer Purvis hadn't already hidden. There was one other place to check. With jaws clenched and muscles tensed, he pulled a tight three-sixty and headed for Mother's

Bar. The parking lot at the bar was empty; neon sign in the window turned off. He considered checking Raymond's office. Nixed that. Purvis was definitely keeping a tight cover on things. The thought occurred to him as he drove home that maybe he had overplayed his hand.

In his study he loaded his favorite snub nose and one high-powered hunting rifle. Then made himself stop. "Slow down." It wasn't hard getting inside Purvis Dalugosh's mindset. He kicked in his cunning—deceit he understood, devious he had down pat. He'd done it enough during SpecOps. Muttered at himself, "Purvis isn't coming after you. All he's got to do is get rid of potential witnesses." It was time to make a pot of coffee for Bailey.

He made a pot for Bailey way weaker than he liked, then set it to perk. Then boiled himself a separate pot.

He slumped onto the sofa. Got up, fidgeted, sat down again, the coffee maker spewing the filtered brew. Got up again, this time took long strides back to the gun cabinet where he lifted down the shotgun. He checked it over, then shoved it back in the rack. Covert stealth was his game, his rules. He just hoped he wasn't figuring this wrong. He slouched back on the sofa.

Soon as he heard the tires crunching down the drive, Craige was at the door. "Wasn't sure you wouldn't decide to make it later."

Bailey got out, said, "I thought about it. I need coffee." As they walked into the kitchen, "Why you got a hornet under your saddle blanket at this hour of the day?"

"Coffee's fresh. Dishwater thin like you like. You want anything stronger, there's a pot of mine you're welcome to try." Craige grabbed two mugs and poured, "I got a burr under my saddle blanket because things aren't adding up neat and tidy."

Bailey downed a hard swallow, "With the way you dig into the rot I'd expect things would never be tidy."

"Porn and drugs is one thing."

"That tape you gave me was something else." Bailey's eyebrows up, "I remember a few times seeing some pretty wild R-and-R videos that made the one you gave me look tame."

"S-and-M and fake snuff films are never tame. This isn't about tapes and videos. That one I sent you is about underage kids being bought and sold. The pieces don't fly."

Bailey's mug stopped halfway to his mouth, "What don't fly?"

"I'm damn certain there's something else Purvis is trying to hide. I just don't know what."

Bailey shook his head, "There's not much else a bunch of soldiers could get into."

"In this case I think it's more like stumbled into."

"Why you dodging around Dalugosh? He's a sonofabitch and the crowd he runs with is worse."

Craige growled, "Including his political connections."

"What makes you so sure there's more to it than porn and drugs? That combination has always made cozy bed partners."

"A gut feeling."

"All you're going on is a gut feeling?"

Craige said, "That and reliable scuttlebutt."

"Your limp-wrist contact from River Disco?"

"This case isn't about which zipper you like to play with or tits and ass, and it isn't about porn-for-profit." Fixed Bailey eyeball to eyeball, "It's more than that. This has one thing in common with porn and drugs... money. Young skin brings a premium price. By the time witnesses or used-up underage merchandise is rotting in some swamp or being shark bait off the coast, it's too late. You and your bosses thought this was tied into local trafficking and Purvis's buddies in the Highway Patrol. It is, but it's bigger than that. My gut tells me it involves not only names you and I don't have, but pieces and panicky witnesses that don't add up. Purvis used that video to try and shut me up. He should've known better, and by now he does." Craige had a nasty squint, "And there's an ugly touch of desperate in his panic, and that always makes things unpredictable."

Bailey said, "Here's a piece you might find interesting. According to his office Purvis is in Columbia for a district Highway Patrol conference."

"That's why there were no cars at his trailer and the bar was closed."

"He's been up there for three days. Spent one night a motel in Lexington in bed with two women and one of the husbands... a state senator. We got the surveillance tape."

"Now you're wiring motel rooms?" Craige shook his head, "You're in an exciting line of work."

"We've had Purvis under surveillance for over a year. Extortion, vote scamming, influence peddling."

"Other than murders on a military base, why are the feds so interested?"

"Interstate commerce. Purvis is a little fish in a big picture that reaches all the way to South America. If Purvis is up to anything along those lines we'd know about it."

"I doubt some of your group has the imagination to cover everything. Drug mules don't worry about state lines and small-time problems. They find out, they take care of them." Craige studied Bailey, realizing he'd depended on him more than he wanted to admit. "One thing we'd better not screw up is running around with no one knowing where we are or how to get in touch with us."

"That may be more to the point than either of us would like." Bailey caught the look from Craige. "Purvis hasn't been seen in or around the motel with the women in two days, at his office or at the conference."

Chapter 13

The star-bright night was beginning to fade in the murky eastern sky. The red numbers of the bedside clock glared half past four. For Leeza the night seemed to stretch in a never-ending forever.

Purvis stomped into the bedroom, pig eyes darted a squint out the window. "Get your butt up against the headboard." He waved the gun like it was a small hammer, then jerked her up and shoved her back against the creaky headboard. "I ain't puttin' up with your wigglin' around. I'm hungry. Need me some coffee and somethin' to eat. Not taking you with me, and sure ain't leavin' you not tied good. You can scream your head off, an' nobody'll hear." He yanked more cords off the floor and snugged them tight around her feet and her hands to the bed.

Leeza coughed at the smelly cigar smoke, "That hurts."

At the sound of a heavy engine Purvis went dead-silent still. From the window he saw a delivery truck rumble by. Folks were waking up. He yanked Leeza's cords tighter for good measure. The doughnut shop off East Boundary wasn't that far.

Leeza heard the sliding door scrape, then bump shut and the lock click. His footsteps shuffled along the dock-boards and across the creaky gangplank. She worked at her wrists. She wasn't about to just sit here for him to do whatever he was planning. She didn't think he had a plan but couldn't figure out what he wanted, and he was jumpy enough to do anything.

* * *

Purvis stood by her car, Leeza's car keys clenched in one hand, other hand on the door handle. He squinted at the houseboat and then back at Leeza's car wishing he'd left her car at Ardochy and taken his. Hers parked in the marina parking lot was trouble waitin' to draw attention. His vehicle would'a been as bad though. At least it was hidden. He eyed the delivery truck down the road where it had stopped. Nearby he heard a door slam. His mouth felt sticky. Coffee and doughnuts forgotten, he wanted to be back inside in case anybody come nosing around. He should have gone out while it was still dark night—damn streetlights were blazing bright. His body stiffened statue-still at the growl of the truck as it came up the road.

Breath short, his armpits were soaking wet. She ought not'a been nosing around Ardochy. He needed time to think. Fumbling with the keys, he hurried back toward the houseboat but not fast enough. As the truck passed, the driver looked straight at him, and drove on. Purvis tried to convince himself it was his imagination that the driver looked at him. Maybe the driver didn't see him. Once inside he peeked toward the road through the water-stained shabby curtain and saw only the dusty swirls left behind; the truck hadn't stopped. There were no other vehicles nowhere. Across the weedy field he could see the tops of early traffic on the highway. The truck driver probably didn't amount to nothin' he told himself.

He would make Leeza-bitch tell him what she was doin' pokin' around Ardochy. No way was he cutting Ingram more slack. He would do what had to be done, and do it hisself. He had followed this Lela Etzigge. Being Leeza's roommate, women talked. Leeza might've talked about Ardochy with her. He could grab Lela, but didn't want the both them holed up in the houseboat. Holding two women would be like juggling nitroglycerine, but with the two of them he could use one against the other. He felt stupid not thinking about it sooner. Lela was dumb enough to tell anything to save her own butt. He ruled out Janella. She didn't know nothing about Ardochy. Neither did Winona. Raymond's wife was making noises about Mort being missing. He had checked out that suit-and-tie type he'd spotted with Ingram; smelled like some fed from the way he was dressed. He could hold Lela and Leeza on the houseboat and move the boat. Tying up a houseboat back on any of the creeks made a perfect place to hide. Then he could get rid of them when he got what he wanted. With Ingram out of the picture, nobody'd poke around worth worryin' about.

He sat down at the main console up front, the ignition keys dangling in the switch, put one hand on the throttle. The engine hadn't been started in no telling how long. Batteries were likely dead. He turned the switch—heard the starter engage. The engine coughed; rumbled; settled into a steady thrum. Console instrument lights flared bright; dimmed; brightened again. The motor continued to run steady as the anchor warning flashed orange.

Purvis swallowed hard. He had never handled a boat that was more barge than boat and bigger than his garage. For a split instant he considered shutting it down. Maybe pulling away from the dock was a bad idea. That changed when flashing blue fishbowl lights of a patrol cruiser crossed over the railroad tracks through the levee to the marina side. "Damn... nosey cops I don't need." Blue lights slowed. Stopped. Its spotlight seemed to light up the whole world.

He was glad the anchor was still in place. Like a cornered animal, his only idea was to make himself scarce. Jawed gritted hard, "That damn bitch scream, there's no way the cop won't hear." Panic tightened his chest. He had to do something before she found out the cops were right outside. It looked like they were gonna come aboard and search. She'd hear for sure. Without thinking he eased up the throttle; engaged a notch into the gear, and another notch higher.

He tightened against his grip on the wheel; added throttle. The engines roared with more power. Slowly the ponderous bulk began to move. The anchor warning buzzed, and its warning light blinked off and on for a few seconds, then turned solid red. The blunt heavy bow skewed inward as hawser bowlines snugged taut and drove the hull into the metal and wooden dock, splintering a piling. The dock crumpled like a folded deck of cards. Dock line and metal cleat whiplashed; smashed through one foredeck picture window. Too late for caution, it was get out or get caught.

Purvis rammed the throttle full-on. Dock planking groaned; splintered. Mooring lines fought the ponderous drag in a white-hot screech of metal and power lines. The two uniforms examining Leeza's vehicle jumped out of the way. Hands on their weapons, both backed away from the roar and plunder of the decking and metal shards. The dock planking rippled and tore away. One hawser parted, and whipped against deck. The bow line parted. Dock and whipped a light post and side of the houseboat. The houseboat yawed, then gave a sluggish lurch, dragging both stern anchors. Anchor ropes parted. Purvis leaned hard against the wheel to hold it from slamming back into the dock. The bow end of the houseboat torqued and carved along the dock, as it skewered toward the massive steel bulkheads of the oil storage tanks, and grazed a deep slice into the side of an old Bayliner cruiser. A party barge pontoon bobbled in the midst of the melee— untouched. The Bayliner's broken hull sagged below the waterline, settling by the stern. Bow up, the wrecked cruiser disappeared below the water.

Purvis caught glimpses of the twisted heaps of wood and metal of the dock. The forward motion of the houseboat wobbled as the prop thumped against wreckage banging against the hull. Purvis spun the wheel to lever the houseboat away from any underwater tangles. The two uniforms waved their hands, shouting as the gap between dock and boat grew wider. The houseboat inched into mid-channel and gained momentum with the current. He prayed the water was high enough back in the creeks and cutoffs so he'd have alcoves and side-branches to shove her into before anyone got out the word. A glance at the fuel gauges told him the tanks were about half full.

He played with the throttle to hold the boat steady in mid-current, but he didn't want to stay out on the river. He wanted to get it back into the heavy overhangs of some unmarked channel, and he didn't care if the river dropped and stranded the damn thing just so long as it was hidden. Using the boat's floodlights in the dark would make it easy to spot, so he had to get it hidden before daylight faded. At the river bend the downriver bridges came into view. There wasn't much in the way of logjams and trash to snag in and end up a nightmare in tomorrow's headlines. Under the towering railroad trestle he guided the houseboat toward the Georgia side and good creeks and forks ahead. Their poker barge was several miles ahead. The bass boat once tied there was gone, but if he was in luck, one of his poker-crowd might've left their fishing boat. He could ram the houseboat up on a mud bank. Any trouble from the girl, he'd weigh her down with anything that wouldn't float and dump her overboard. "More trouble than she's worth," he muttered. He would leave the houseboat as a decoy.

Once he got rid of her, he'd take the fishing boat back upriver beyond the tore-up docks. Walk out, nobody the wiser. The more he thought about it the better he liked the idea until the sound of a small outboard caught his ear. A fisherman putt-putted lazily up the far side of the river. Paid him no mind. Purvis breathed easier as the ramshackle house barge came into view, its lone bulb burning at the corner. He was alone on the river. He shifted the engine nearest the bank to neutral; drag increased; the hulk slewed toward shore. With a bump the houseboat drifted against the creaky poker barge. A few cedar shake shingles skittered off the roof, and plopped into the river.

* * *

Bailey tried Craige's number again; listened to the burr of the rings and wondered if bloodhound Craige was on a surveillance for some two legged animal.

Bailey was about to punch OFF, when Craige picked up, "Ingram."

"Your local Buckingham constabulary found a car in Augusta's River Front Marina parking lot. Registered to a Leeza Norton. Call logged in by the midnight-to-four watch. Message was on my desk when I arrived this a.m. after leaving your place."

Craige sensed Mabel's watchdog touch, "On the Georgia side?" He didn't mention that angle to Bailey—didn't want him asking.

Bailey said, "I've been trying to reach you."

"Been on a watch-and-look stakeout. Any sign of Norton?"

"No personal effects and no sign of a struggle. They dusted for prints. Several sets belonging to Norton were found with partial smudges of several others. Took hair and fibers for DNA analysis. The Norton car hadn't been cleaned in some time. They've got it in impound for a more thorough going-over."

"Damn."

Bailey said, "What's going on?"

Craige said. "Could be I stirred significantly more than I expected."

"There's more to the Marina situation than locating the vehicle owner. There's a missing houseboat, a damaged pontoon boat, a high speed V-hull sunk dockside, and one badly damaged dock. Tie-down cleats ripped off, decking splintered. Couple of Buckingham Parish deputies were in the parking lot to check on the vehicle. Houseboat took off in a big hurry while they were there."

Craige said, "You figure whoever took the Norton woman took the houseboat?"

"Looks that way. The houseboat's been for sale for some time; owners moved away, and a local college student boat-watching hasn't been located. His campus friends haven't seen him in over a week. His family lives in Connecticut. They can't locate him either."

Craige thought of the body Billy and Hollings found. He told Bailey. "Odds are it's the missing student. Obvious question... where's the houseboat? Wouldn't take thirty minutes to check upriver for it. Craft that size couldn't pass the rapids. Has to be somewhere downriver. Could've come by my place while I wasn't here."

Bailey said, "A Fort Gordon chopper overflew the river between the dock and the downstream three-o-one bridge. No sign of it."

"Could be it's underwater. From the air you can't see all the streams and creeks draining into it. There are sloughs and backwater bayous with good clearance and heavy overhangs for a houseboat to ease into. Make good cover. Houseboats aren't much more than thin walls on big pontoons. If it took underwater damage on one pontoon. If holed on an old pontoon, the center of gravity shifts. I've seen houseboats roll bottom-up, and not sink. The water-tight pontoon will belly-up like a beached whale. The damaged one hangs underneath."

Bailey said, "Something that big couldn't hide in shallow creeks."

Craige chuckled. "You sound like a dry-land sailor that swears there's no islands in the river. Anyone who knows this river, knows otherwise."

Bailey said, "Police have a witness, a local wino. Sleeps under the boathouse-restaurant. Claims he saw the houseboat pull out. Hit other boats right before the v-hull went under."

The bottom of his stomach churned. "Someone was in a big hurry." Craige didn't like the way this dance was jig-sawing. "We have Purvis into blackmail, drug running and underage prostitutions and potential witnesses disappearing." He had no reason to think the houseboat had anything to do with Purvis, but couldn't shake a certainty that it did. "Norton's car being where it was smells like Purvis." His thoughts zeroed to Ardochy at the center of it. Either somebody panicked or it was Purvis and he panicked. "Any sign of Purvis?"

"He's not in Lexington. Our eyes and ears at the conference have him as a no-show after that first night in the motel."

Suspicions surged through his feelings. "Was he ever there? Maybe he knew he was being tailed and needed an alibi?"

Bailey said, "We tracked a phone call made about midnight from the Lexington motel. Whoever made the call used his cell phone, and the phone was left on after the call ended. We followed it south on I-twenty. Phone was switched off as the vehicle approached the Aiken exit. Phone was never switched back on. And another interesting tidbit. The vehicle registered to Morton J. Raymond showed up in his office parking lot sometime during the same twenty-four hours before the houseboat disappeared."

Craige said, "The last time I was at Ardochy, the caretaker asked me if I knew a university student, name of Norton. She'd told him it had to do with a paper she was writing. I didn't think much about it. I want to check with him again." Craige puzzled the jumbled of what they had. "So, Raymond's vehicle shows up with no driver. Now we've got the Norton vehicle and no driver."

Bailey said, "With next to nothing tying it to Purvis."

"Purvis makes extra-sure there never is," Craige said. "Makes one wonder why Purvis wants the Norton woman out of the picture. Did he follow her to Ardochy, and what was she doing at Ardochy? If he took her, what does he need from her?"

"Because his little game with you center stage on a video didn't pan out?"

"The caretaker said she asked about tunnels along the river, and how old they were." Scratched his head, "Most of those tunnels are along old riverbeds that are filled in or dried up. They're deathtraps. Unless... " His thoughts stopped.

"Unless what?"

"Of what I might be digging too close to," Craige said. "If he followed Norton to Ardochy, and the caretaker spotted him, Purvis had to find a quick way to take care of witnesses he didn't want."

Bailey said, "What did you do to put a scare into Purvis?"

Craige didn't care what Bailey thought, "I threatened Raymond with already knowing Purvis couldn't be trusted. How Purvis wouldn't bat an eye getting rid of him. Tried to convince him he was safer cooperating with me than trusting Purvis. Looks like it might've worked out the way I told him, but not the way I wanted it."

"So you think Purvis has this Leeza Norton?"

"Or killed her, and hid the body." Craige didn't like Bailey's question one bit.

* * *

Leeza twisted and rubbed at the cords around her wrist until the skin was raw. She stopped when she thought she heard voices. She listened harder, but the rumble of the engines made it hard to be sure. As she strained at her bindings, a gravelly crunch rolled and bumped beneath the bottom of the houseboat. The bed jerked hard; walls torqued into odd shapes. Engines strained; coughed; strained harder. She heard the clatter of pots and pans falling, glass shatter. The ceiling above her head twisted uneven. The headboard banged against her head. Cabin walls, uneven, thudded and bumped; seemed to tip to one side. The ceiling light fixture dropped to dangle from its wires, then broke loose and bounced off the edge of the bed scattering in pieces across the floor. The bed skewed to one side. When the headboard bent, her arms came loose. The floor settled in elevator-jerk stops and starts. More thuds and bumps. Leeza's eyes widened fearful, watching water trickle under the door. The flow increased until it was a deepening flat sheet soaking the rug. She tugged at the ties around her ankles as the cane-back chair at the foot of the bed floated against an end table. Its lamp crashed to the floor.

The engines growled louder; the tilt of the walls steepened, and the floor buckled. There was a screech of metal and wood, and she smelled the stinging hiss of electrical wires. Then everything went silent. Leeza saw a puff of smoke through the ceiling vent. She wasn't about to get caught inside this wreck in a fire. Bracing her back against the wall, she sloshed over tilted furniture and kicked the window out. Using a chair leg she knocked away pieces of the glass pane. Pulling herself up she began wiggling through the opening. Branches and leaves smacked her face in a tangle of sunken trees, rotten logs and mud. The boat wasn't moving. She heard the sound of a snap and crack above her, and a rotten limb crashed onto the upper deck. The smell of oil and gasoline was overpowering, but the smoke had drifted thinner. She glimpsed a shadow stepping off the front of the boat. It had to be Purvis. Leeza jerked her head back inside, hoping he hadn't seen her. Through the window she watched until the figure disappeared into the thick undergrowth, then once again pulled herself onto the tilted side the houseboat and let herself slowly slide down until her feet sunk into soft ooze.

She didn't know where she was. Some distance away she heard a thump and a string of cuss words. She checked around for snakes. A big slippery log jutted from underneath the boat. She tested it with one foot to make sure it would hold her. "To hell with snakes." No way was she going back inside.

She took a careful step off the log into sticky black ooze that squished between her toes. With one foot she felt along the bottom, careful not to get tangled; grabbed at twisted vines, and pulled herself up on the bank. The stern of the houseboat was under water. Exhausted, Leeza sat down on a moss-covered stump, ignored the buzz of a mosquito, and brushed at the ants swarming her foot. Frogs settled back into their afternoon croaking. She glanced around to make sure Purvis wasn't sneaking up on her. She had to be on the South Carolina side somewhere below the airport. At the sound of something or someone moving toward her through the undergrowth Leeza froze. She wasn't about to let the Purvis get hold of her again. A fawn and doe emerged through the trees. Startled, the deer gave her a look; flicked her ears, and as quick they were gone.

Out of the corner of her eye she caught the half-hunkered silhouette hurry up over the slight rise of the riverbank. She crawled her way up to the top of the bank, and found herself at the edge of a hayfield. The figure was running with a slight limp toward a dirt road. It was too far for her to tell who it was, but the figure was tall enough to be Purvis. She watched as the figure waved down a car that slowed; stopped. The color reminded her of the sedan Lela drove. She heard the car door slam, and glimpsed the flash of cream color and chrome as the car sped away. Leeza made her way to the road. Wet, shivering more from fear than being soaked, she clutched her torn blouse with one hand and waited until the vehicle was out of sight.

With no one else in sight, she started walking up the road through the flat farmlands not knowing where the closest farmhouse was or if there were any houses near. Homes along this stretch of the river were few and far between. She plodded one tired foot in front of the other, then wondered if the driver of the car had been Lela. If it was, what Lela would be doing way out there? Purvis and Lela? She no longer knew who she could trust.

Chapter 14

Lela sat at her desk, the phone glued to her ear. She clamped the filter of her cigarette between her front teeth to keep it from smearing her fresh lip-gloss. "There's another one of those calls coming in. Call you back." Hung up. Mort Raymond's private line in his office had been ringing constantly. "I'm not about to sit here and listen to it ring all day. Somethin's going on." She never had trusted the seedy bastard. Things work out like she wanted, she wouldn't need this job. Wouldn't need any job. "He wants ever'body else to do his dirty work while he counts the money. Raymond needs to get his butt here and take his own phone calls."

A second line started blinking, the phone jangling away. Lela's knuckles turned white when she saw it was Purvis's number. He'd warned her about telling nobody about her picking him up. She wondered how he managed to run a houseboat up on a mud bank, then call her to come get him. Her hand dropped away, "Ought'a let it ring."

Even if it was Purvis, it had to mean somethin' had gone wrong with the deliveries between him and Raymond. She didn't want no part of that. Particularly not with Ingram snooping around. About ever'body knew trouble was brewing hot and heavy between Ingram and Purvis. Mort was afraid of them both. The phone stopped ringing, then started again. She let it ring.

She stubbed out her cigarette, scattering ashes across her desk, and grabbed her purse and keys. "Not sittin' here like a lonesome duck and wait for something to happen."

Her heart started pit-a-patting faster on her way home with fear and doubt crowding her thoughts. She fumbled with her door key, finally got her apartment door unlocked. Leeza wasn't home. She closed the door quick then peeked around the curtain of its small window to make sure no one had followed her. Her purse clasped tight in her hand, she slouched down on the sofa and rubbed her aching headache. It didn't help. She got up. Hands trembling, she lit another cigarette; paced back and forth. "Damn drugs and money." Her whole life was screwed up by money, mainly about not having any. She once asked Leeza, "How could it hurt digging around old Indian graves most don't even know about? How'd it get to dirty CDs and killing? Pillow talk the next morning where he started bragging about all he'd done. Purvis talkin' like he's dumping trash off some deserted coast or in the desert."

Lela thought about that afternoon helping Leeza load her car. Leeza hadn't said one thing about where she was going. Lela had puckered her lips, "I can tell by the way you're being so tight-lipped. You've met someone. It shows all over your face." She caught a flicker in Leeza's eyes, certain Leeza would be gone the whole weekend. "Where's he live? Charleston? A navy man from Kings Bay? Florida?" Leeza wasn't packing even an overnight carryall. "Oooo... a weekend quickie hookup with a sailor man."

Lela gave Leeza an incredulous look. "Lela, where do you come up with such silly ideas?"

Bug-eyed Lela's mouth dropped open, "Don't tell me it's Ingram."

Leeza snugged her laptop between her raincoat and umbrella so it wouldn't get bounced around. "I've got work to do." She hurried into her car and drove off.

At she lit another cigarette, Lela tried to shove their conversation away. ugly thoughts spun her brain like the swirls of the cigarette smoke. If Lela's in bed with Ingram—what if she's snitchin' for him? That thought scared her. "Mort just wanted me to do his dirty work." Fear oozed inside her. "No one was supposed to get hurt." Part whimper, part talking to herself. "Purvis could kill me, too." Her fingers twisted at wayward strands of red hair brushing her long pale neck. Fear tightened nastier. She remembered Mort mentioning some soldier from the fort. She never forgot his words to her, "He got discharged. Blew all his money, no family. He was the perfect score until he wanted more money. Said he'd go to the cops if we didn't cut him more money."

It gave Lela the shivering chills when he said *"we"*. Before it had always been about what *he'd* done. She knew then there was big trouble. She'd told him, "You promised no rough stuff!"

He said to her, "What was I supposed to do? If I paid him more money, he'd want more."

She'd said, "It was just money."

That was when Mort got right in her face, his threat-sweat stinking in her nose, "You didn't think it was just money when you were so hot about stuff you wanted to spend it on. You best remember you're in this as deep as anyone. One more druggie soldier amounts to nothing. World is better without him. If it had been done right, it would've never made the local news."

Lela didn't doubt for an instant it was a threat. For the first time in her life Lela felt truly alone in a knotted cobweb of her own making. Her Sugar Daddy had taken care of his sweet baby, and helped her with college. She hadn't been about to wind up like the rest of her family. Still, it wasn't worth getting killed. She could walk away. Pack a quick bag; grab her purse and be gone while she still could. Take what money she had and get lost in any big city. The idea to run tugged harder and harder.

Going to college was easy—sleep with the right teacher, keep her GPA up, now and then hookup with some lab assistant, or let some fat alumnus screw her doggie style in the locker room. Shop around for fun and games. She wasn't interested in graduate school. She wasn't sure she'd even want to do graduate school—too much work. Her high school happy-times cheer leading days were gone. She rubbed her aching head. How had it got so complicated?

In the kitchen Lela ignored the breakfast leftovers still on the table. Her throat clutched as she remembered how a few days earlier Mort had stormed into the kitchen without even knocking, cell phone in his hand, "You know a man named Ingram; lives on the Beech Island side of the river?"

She said, "Name's familiar."

"He's nosing around."

"Into what?"

"A damn SEAL, private investigator. Commanded his own unit. He's been asking questions about soldiers from the fort."

Lela said, "Purvis know?"

"If he doesn't, it won't be long before he does. Some smartass named Emmett Whitfield knows what happened. That the tunnels under the old Redcliffe are a safe place for the merchandise. Whitfield and Buddy Raymond are good pals."

The kitchen seemed to squeeze her into a tight box with running the only way out. She'd tell nobody. Get away from Purvis. Being from a small town, Lela knew no one ever did anything without someone knowing. She could see herself being dumped into one of those dreadful tunnels, all drippy and wet with all kinds of creepy crawly things. She shivered. She'd be a skeleton, only be her bones left in a tunnel forever. No one would ever know. She shuddered at the image of her empty eye sockets and teeth grinning up out of the mud. Some fisherman find it, and keep her bones in a garage or throw it back in the river. She'd heard tales of human bones found in the river.

Lela reached for a cigarette, her hands were shaking so bad she dropped it. She thought about her suitcase in the bedroom closet; didn't know whether to run or stay put. She dialed Raymond's office and let the phone ring and ring only to hang up. Fear seeped deeper, "You're being a fool to just sit here like an addled duck," but she knew she already was. The more Lela thought about it, if she didn't do something, sooner or later she was dead.

* * *

At the approach of a vehicle Lucky growled; bristled. Craige didn't recognize the car and he couldn't make out the passenger through the sun glare off the windshield and the tinted windows. There was a decal or lettering on the side of the vehicle, and the driver looked a lot like Purvis. If Purvis was serving a warrant, he might be looking for a confrontation—any reason to haul Craige off to jail. Anything could happen there.

Craige was relieved when Terri and Bailey stepped out of the car. "Bailey, you're looking all official with that vehicle." He could tell Terri was definitely not a happy camper. Put his arm around her shoulder. Caught a whiff of grease and oil and kissed the tip of her nose, "What happened?"

"Battery's dead. I'm not too much at tinkering with car engines that don't work. I let it sit for about thirty minutes, but it still wouldn't start. So I left it on the side of the road and started walking here. Bailey came by and recognized me, or I'd still be walking."

"You should've called me. Hank keeps his dually in my hangar. He'd do anything for you. We could've towed your car there. Wouldn't take Hank any time to know what was wrong, or give you the keys to one of the vehicles."

"Couldn't call. I forgot to charge the phone last night, and didn't have the car charger with me. Guess today isn't my day for batteries." She brushed at the front of his shirt, "I've gotten smudges all over your shirt," brushed again, "and I'm just making it worse."

He said, "Not the first time I've had grease where it shouldn't be. Won't be the last."

She said, "I smell awful, and I need a shower. This humidity puts a body in a summertime sweat with an attitude. The thought of your walk-in shower and its cold jets made it seem like heaven. It's so humid."

"If you get hungry Quidda Lovisa left me some great tasting roast beef when she came in to clean. It's in the fridge. Said for me to be sure and tell you that she asked about you." Said to Bailey, "Glad you came by. Either of you want coffee? Got a full pot of hot reboil."

"I'll try some," Bailey said.

"I've already had my quota for the day," Terri said. "I'm hitting a quick shower while you two exchange secrets."

In the bathroom, she put on the shower cap; she'd shampoo her hair when she got home. She stood under the shower for a good soak. Stepped out, and cuddled into the wrap of the bath sheet from neck to ankles. She tipped one shoulder toward the mirrors; examined the scraped bruise where she'd bumped the hood of the car. After taking off the shower cap, she ruffled her fingers through her loose hair and swirled it back up in a loose curled bun. She slipped into the robe she'd left in his closet, and padded back to the den where he and Bailey were finishing their coffee.

Craige said, "Your tea water is on boil, and there's a clean cup by the tea caddy."

Bailey set his mug down, "Seeing Terri on the highway surprised me. More surprised finding you staying put here."

Craige said, "You were right wanting me to stay cool and low key. You made a good point not giving Purvis any chance of concocting some bogus smokescreen charge for an arrest warrant. If he thought he could've made anything stick, he'd have charged hell-bent-for-leather out here long before now. Bogus is his middle name. That's why nobody gave any credence to my having stage center in that video. Be wary. It's a mistake he won't make again. Dinkins received DNA confirmation that the body found down-country in Jenkins Parish was Mort Raymond." Reached the info to Bailey, "He faxed me a copy. You've probably got one, too."

Bailey gave it a quick read with a stern look at Craige, "This adds a nasty fact to this fuzzy shuffle, and makes the situation a lot more dangerous. It doesn't mean Raymond wasn't involved though."

"True. But he sure got crosswise with someone," Craige said.

Bailey stood up to leave, "You mean, got in Purvis's way."

"More'n likely, but Purvis isn't the only one keeping back in the shadows." Craige and Terri followed Bailey out on the porch.

Terri said, "Thanks again for stopping for me."

"Glad I happened by."

They watched as he drove away. Back inside, Craige put his arms around Terri. Relieved she was all right. Glad she was there. Her hair smelled better than good; snuggled her against him. Kissed her slow and tender, "You know being around me right now is not exactly the safest of places for you."

She squeezed against him, "You mean I'm not safe here from Purvis or from you?"

"Both."

She said, "If one of those places is up against you, I think I'll risk it."

She kissed him back as he slipped his arms inside her robe, smoothed against the warm swell of her breasts. Her lips circled his tongue as her belly yielded against him; his arms tightened gentle. Their embrace a release they both needed.

"God, Terri... " muffled in her ear, her hair, against her lips; swept her up in his arms.

Terri played her hands inside his shirt, "I thought he'd never leave." A button on his shirt popped, skittered across the wide polished pine boards of the den, as her robe slumped to the floor.

Skin against skin, he wanted the rest of the world to go away. He crushed her to him, "You are my leavening."

Unable to touch enough of each other, they never made it past the kitchen. Her tongue in his ear, down his neck, his chest. After the first hurried crush he lifted her, and made it to the bedroom. The never-ending night drowned in skin-blistering togetherness.

Early next twilight Terri woke in the curve of him. A contented murmur slurred from deep in his chest. Terri slid out of bed, hurried to the den to grab her robe from the pile and slipped it on. In the kitchen, she opened the fridge to see what assortment of refrigerator-goulash she could come up with. Spotted the roast beef.

* * *

Lela looked at her watch, then mushed her half-smoked filter tip in the overflowing ashtray of smeared butts and half cigarettes. She started to pour herself a cup of coffee, but the coffee pot was empty. She started toward Raymond's office. Stopped. "To hell with this."

Waves of fright stabbed at her. She was prickly-positive she was being watched, a troublesome loose end to be tidied up. Her anger mixed with the awful fear. Neither Purvis nor Raymond never needed her. Purvis had called her dumb so many times she'd lost count. "Don't be a sucker and stay in this pace."

She picked up the phone, hesitated a moment, then dialed 911. There was a funny buzz-crackle on the line, one she'd never heard before. Panic jumped a notch higher; she almost dropped the handset. The phone was bugged. She was being watched for-real. She grabbed her purse; dug out the keys. Her lipstick plopped out unnoticed and rolled under the coffee table, then beneath the sofa as she rushed out of her apartment not bothering to close the door. Minutes later she was on the highway. Her heart hammered in panic. She couldn't run far with no place to stay. With little money in her purse and her credit cards maxed out, motels and hotels were out of the question. Sleeping in her car on the street or in a parking lot was not a risk she was taking. With Purvis's connections it wouldn't take him no time to find her. The only hope she could think of was the one person who wasn't afraid of Purvis Dalugosh. She had to find out where this Craige Ingram lived. She tried to think of who would know; who she could ask. She was running for her life, and Ingram was the only person she could trust.

Chapter 15

Terri said, "You want another blueberry pancake?"

"I'm stuffed," Craige patted his stomach.

"There's enough batter left for one more. Skillet's still hot. I'll split it with you. I hate to throw it away."

"Don't split it the way you usually do, where you make sure I end up with the biggest piece. Which I'll eat and don't need."

She gave him a puckered midair kiss, "How you do go on," and wrinkled her nose with a come-hither twinkle.

His cell buzzed. He recognized Bailey's number, answered, "Ingram."

Bailey said, "Sorry if I interrupted a lazy morning twosome, but I'm on my way to pick up Leeza Norton. She's scared. I could hear the fear in her voice. She has no car; called from some farmer's home on your side of the river, downriver from you."

Craige sat straight up in his chair, his fork clattered onto his plate, blueberry pancakes forgotten. His and Terri's midmorning reverie at an abrupt end, "She's scared of Purvis, and she should be."

"When I pick her up, we won't be far from your place."

He looked at Terri, "Seems everybody's decided to come to Moccasin Hollow."

"You get back to me within twenty minutes." Craige kicked his thoughts into high gear. "I don't hear from you in two-zero minutes, I'm turning loose my hunt-and-seek buddies along with your bosses at the fort," punched END.

Terri said, "I'll get the coffee started."

* * *

Craige straddled a ladder-back chair in the spacious front den of Moccasin Hollow while Bailey sat across the dining table from Craige. Both fixed on a withdrawn Leeza curled into the recliner. Crage folded his arms across the back of the chair, "Leeza?" He got no response. He tightened his words, "Leeza, you sure you heard another voice right before the houseboat grounded? Leeza! Answer me! Before you get us all in the gun sights!"

Leeza opened her eyes, "I'm not sure. The engines were so loud just before we hit something about the same time I smelled smoke."

Bailey's eyebrows lifted, "So far we only have the word of the homeless guy who saw the houseboat leave the dock. And there's more." "On my way to pick up Leeza, I received a jumbled phone text. Don't know whether it was canceled, but it looked chopped. Like it wasn't complete."

"Or interrupted."

Bailey said, "Phone ID showed it came from a Morton J Raymond number." Exchanged looks with Craige.

The den hushed. Craige broke the stillness, "Anyone text messaging using Raymond's number couldn't have been Raymond."

Leeza said, "No one's been in the office in days. No one knows where he is."

Craige said, "Maybe someone using one of Raymond's phones?"

Bailey brought up the message, "This is all that came through." Handed it to Craige.

"*Need to find out where Craige Ingram lives...* " Bailey pointed at the time-date stamp.

Craige fixed on the few cryptic words, "I paid a visit to the wife earlier and struck out. She made it abundantly clear, as far as she was concerned I was *persona non grata.*"

Leeza huddled deeper into the recliner. "Anyone could have sent it if they had one of the cell phones in Raymond's office. There were a couple of them in Lela's and my apartment. Purvis could've easily taken one."

"Or already had a phone," Craige said.

"The DNA was Raymond's," Bailey added.

"What DNA?" Leeza said.

Craige said, "Raymond's dead."

Leeza gulped, Mort is dead?"

Craige said to Bailey, "Purvis is going to a lot of trouble to stay below the radar."

Leeza said, "Holding me in a burning houseboat isn't my idea of laying low."

Craige said, "It would've been if your body and a flooded houseboat had been hidden back in some creek or swamp instead of being beached in plain sight on the river. No telling what panicked him... maybe the fire."

Covert-training Ingram sniffed at the footprints of Purvis-the-cornered-fox. He looked at Leeza, "Why go to the trouble of kidnapping you? Be simpler for him to get rid of you. Like it appears he did with Raymond. There has to be a reason. You have any idea why he did it?"

"No." Shook her head; pressed tighter into the recliner, "He made me drive to the docks. After he broke into the houseboat everything started to go haywire."

Craige snapped, "Haywire started when he shanghaied you."

Bailey said to Craige, "Maybe covering a killing we don't know about?"

"It's for sure we've never had the whole picture. Otherwise we'd have method, opportunity, motive and likely solid leads about the perps and likely, bodies no one knows about." Craige turned back to Leeza, "If it's about keeping victims from never being found, then the one reason for kidnapping you is to shut you up permanently."

Leeza said, "I don't know anything about bodies."

Craige said to Bailey, "She's right though. Stealing a houseboat doesn't make for keeping a low profile."

Bailey said, "Purvis grabbing her makes as much sense as some of the other things he's done. Purvis has a bullheaded ego that uses notoriety to intimidate. That may the reason he took her."

Craige turned his thoughts backwards and forwards, "Somewhere we're missing a motive behind this."

Bailey said, "Money and the uglier underside—power."

"For anyone to go to this much trouble, they're hiding something. Narcotics, kiddie porn, interstate gambling rings, or corpses with the single-minded intent to control all of it." Craige's eyes squinted mean, "Power and reputation climb in bed together more often than not, which fits neatly into how Purvis runs his activities with little to no interference. My actions are what has him spooked. That video was part of his hunting for any way to shut me off."

Leeza said, "I know plenty who would do anything to blame someone else. Not get caught," as though she could lock away the nastiness touching her.

Bailey said, "Certainly nothing that would hold up before a judge or grand jury, and there would have already been more subpoenas on the docket. This doesn't have a smell of vote buying or politics."

Craige said, "Which doesn't mean there haven't been payoffs."

Bailey said, "One of our prime suspects ended up a rotting carcass in a fishing boat. Janella Dalugosh has snorted so much she's no help."

Craige said, "To clean up loose ends, Purvis likely would've eventually had her on his hit list for catfish bait or dumped in a backwater slough for the gators."

Craige followed Bailey onto the porch. Bailey said, "I'll keep, as you put it, turning over rocks. See if anything crawls out." Started down the steps toward his car.

When Leeza stood up to go with Bailey, Terri put her hand on Leeza's arm. "Craige, don't you think it's safer if Leeza stays here tonight? There's plenty bedrooms, plus Lucky will make more than enough noise if any strangers show up."

He said, "Good idea."

* * *

Terri padded into Craige's bedroom, "I made us some snacks." She had a good grip on the breakfast tray with its cold cuts and juice before she set it right in the middle of unsuspecting Craige's naked belly.

"Jesus!" With a quick suck of his breath. He caught himself before he sloshed a big mess in the bed, and slid the tray between them. "That's enough to wake a dead man."

"If we get hungry for one of our midnight snacks, we can't mosey to the kitchen in our birthday suits." She lightly pecked the end of his nose.

He said, "I don't see why not."

"I like looking at all of you when you have nothing on, but that's off-limits for any houseguests." Slid her hand along his belly, beneath the sheet.

"Don't you ever get enough?"

"Not of you," Terri near whispered. "With a guest in the house you'll have to be quiet."

"I'm not sure I can do that with you."

"I'll help," swiped her finger through the whipped topping and strawberry jam, smeared it down his belly.

Craige shivered; pulled her belly to belly. The saucers and forks rattled on the tray. "Move this before we have a fork in uncomfortable places."

"Making a mess sounds like fun," scooted closer; felt him against her. A jelly dish clattered on the tray. She put the tray on the floor.

Later into the night Terri snuggled into him in a sound sleep. Lucky sniffed the bedside tray, then nudged Craige's shoulder with a cold wet nose and plopped down next to the bed. The German shepherd eyed the tray, but left it alone.

In the still of the night Lucky's low warning growl brought Craige full awake. Hair up, the dog fixed on the closed bedroom door and gave another low lip-curled snarl. In one motion bare-assed Craige rolled out of bed with his Glock in hand, safety checked with a full clip, and kill-ready in a heartbeat. Lucky gave another deep-chest rumble.

Bleary-eyed Terri uncurled from where Craige had been against her and propped on one elbow, "What is it?"

"Don't turn on any lights, and get down on the floor here in the bedroom." His muscles were bowstring tight, pupils wide in the dim light, "Someone's outside."

Oblivious to being naked, Craige's cougar-smooth shadow moved next to the bedroom door. The German shepherd, right by his side, stopped when Craige stopped. Craige pressed an ear to the door, keeping his body out of any line of fire to one side, as he listened for what seemed the longest. To his trained ear the silence was too still for the night. Night sounds, even the frog croaks, had stilled. He bent down. Face to one side, he pushed one eye to the rug and squinted for any shadow backlit by moonlight through the porch windows. Against the hallway nightlight nothing moved. When he eased the door eyeball ajar, Lucky gave a muffled soundless *woof*. One measured step at a time, Craige eased down the hall and into the den, and froze statue-still. Moonlight danced leaf-shadows across the porch windows. Lucky fixed on the door leading onto the front porch. The swallowed growls in the dog's throat didn't stop.

A swamp-monster shadow filled one windowpane, and as fleeting, disappeared. Craige resettled his grip on the Glock and whispered a Cherokee command. Man and dog became two hunter animals locked in unison. Lucky stayed by his side, as Craige made his way through the kitchen, and slipped out the back door to the corner of the porch. The hunched-over figure on the porch peeked in one window, moved to another.

Craige braced the Glock steadied with both hands. With flat even words, "Don't make a twitch or I'll splatter your head from here to the highway. Your body dead before it even knows it." Muttered Cherokee, "Guard." Lucky circled off to one side. "You make any quick move, the dog'll rip your arm off."

"Mister Ingram?"

Craige frowned. Unsure, yet the voice was familiar. He crouched low. Made less of a target, while keeping the figure in his sight, "Identify yourself. And be quick about it."

"It's Lela." Lucky growled. "You alone?"

"Lela? What are you doing sneaking around here?" His eyes swept his surroundings and across the yard; saw no vehicle. The vehicle could've been left out on the highway or off the road. "Stay right where you are." He patted his thigh and Lucky heeled to his side and sat, the dog not taking his eyes off the figure.

"You're naked," she said.

Motioned with the Glock, "Move into the light where I can get a better look at you."

211

"Please. No light," she whimpered. "In front of the window makes me a target."

"You didn't answer my question. Why are you sneaking around in the middle of the night?" Craige didn't like hearing *target,* "Why are you here? Who're you running from?"

Snapped a near-silent Cherokee, "Seek." Lucky vanished into the night-purples. "Won't take him long to find anyone out there."

"Anyone with you?"

In no time Lucky padded near soundless back to sit next to Craige. At least he didn't have to be concerned whether there was somebody flanking him from out of the shadows. Dog would've cut loose a free-for-all along with some skin. In the narrow spot of his light Craige saw a huddled shivering frightened woman that looked to be little more than a girl. "Why would you think anyone else is here?"

"I don't have nowhere else I can go. If they catch me, they'll kill me."

"Who? Who'll kill you?" Swatted at the whine-hum and sting of a mosquito.

"Kill you, too."

Craige squinted into the darkness, "Lela Etzigge? That who you are?"

"Yes."

"Who you think is trying to kill you?"

"Purvis Dalugosh or Mort Raymond. Or both. I ought not have to tell you how mean Purvis is. Leeza Norton, my roomie didn't come home yesterday. She's goes to the university in Columbia. I think Purvis might've already killed her."

Purvis's name was enough to raise his hackles hair-tight. Craige tried to make the tumble of thoughts slow down. She didn't know Raymond was dead. "Park yourself on the sofa. And stay there! My dog doesn't take to people sneaking around." He left the porch and went around toward the mudroom at the back of the kitchen where he grabbed a cotton pullover and a pair of old jeans. Slipped the Glock in the back of his waist.

"I don't like being near the window. It's so dark outside." She caught the blazing look from Craige and shivered terrified glimpses toward the window, her knuckles white-tight clenched.

Craige said, "Sneaking around outside a house in the middle of the night is a good way to get shot. And asking about anyone else being here don't quite set so well with me either."

Terri stuck her head out from the bedroom. Surprised by a face she didn't recognize, she threw Craige a worried look and snugged her robe tighter, "Everything okay?"

He said, "I'm not sure."

"I'm afraid something happened to Leeza." Lela sniffled and stood up.

Craige turned to the window trying to pierce the moonlit dappled undergrowth just as the nasty hissed-spitter punched through the corner windowpane, the shot spattering slivered shards across table, chairs, and floor.

In a blur Craige grabbed Lela by the arm, bodily flung her to the floor inside the mudroom. He hit the master switch for the outside floods, and in the same motion he dragged Terri down, shielded her with his body. Glock to the ready, he hissed, "Silencer." Nobody was getting past him or through the porch windows or door. Putting his lips next to Terri's ear, "Stay on the floor." Rolled a huddled tumble to a hunkered squat behind the frame of the mudroom door. Lucky whine-growled right with him as he half-opened the back door.

Cherokee, "Seek!" The dog was out and gone in a flash of claws and teeth.

Craige hunkered tighter, and let his eyes sweep along the front and side of the house. There was no movement between the drive and the dock. He froze at a loud snarl-and-growl crash of underbrush beyond the house toward the highway, followed by a scream and savage rip growling attack along the drive. He heard the slam of a car door, an engine gunned, and tires digging in.

Lucky limped back toward the porch, stopped, cocked his ears in the direction of the fading sound. Craige knelt, lifted the dog's paw. He found no broken bones, only a bullet-graze in the blood-matted smears. "Lay down." Lucky licked at it; licked Craige's hand.

Back inside Craige took no chances. He dialed Gray's unlisted cell. This late it would be next to his bed.

Gray answered before the second ring. "MacGerald."

"We've got shots fired."

"On my way. Boback's on desk watch. Will have him meet me at the overpass."

Craige warned, "Keep your eyes and ears wide open when you pull in the drive." Punched FLASH. Dialed Bailey.

"I heard voices." A yawning Leeza came into the den. Why are all the lights out?"

"Leeza, get over there with Lela away from the windows."

"Lela?" Leeza'a eyes widened as they adjusted to the dark. "What's Lela doing here?"

* * *

Craige made sure all inside lights were off and the outside floods still on, while Terri made a half-attempt to sweep most of the glass out of the way. "We need to watch out for broken glass until we get this vacuumed." She squatted on the kitchen floor next to the fridge. Leeza and Lela crouched behind the sofa. In the darkness Craige slipped back into the room to position himself to one side of the front door and windows where he could keep the yard between the drive and dock in sight. He tried to figure if this was Purvis Dalugosh. Still, he wasn't convinced Purvis had the guts to do his own dirty work. Later it might prove interesting to check the local ERs and find out if anyone paid a visit for a dog bite.

He frowned as he zeroed in on the glass pane crazes centered on the bullet hole and muttered, "Bullets aren't the same caliber." Teeth pulled at his lower lip; the tocking of Grannie's big dogtrot long-case grandfather clock was the only sound. "Caliber of the bullet that hit the flowerpot was smaller, a twenty-two. Different MO, different shooter, different weapon." Hairs prickled the nape of his neck. He looked at the two women huddled behind the bulky sofa, "What were you and Mort Raymond involved in with Purvis?

As if Lela was a piece of furniture, Leeza said, "Lela an' me have shared an apartment since my second year at the university. She's never said nothing to me about Purvis or Ardochy."

Lucky growled; stood at the sound of a car turning off the highway. Craige set his jaw. The dog knew Gray's car, and this engine sounded too heavy for Gray's well-worn vehicle. The squeal of tires, crunch of gravel, and the engine being shut off came about the same time. When the car door slammed, Craige thought of Purvis's muscle-engine patrol car. Reset his grip on the Glock when Lucky's growl softened; tail wagged. If it was Boback's cruiser Gray wasn't wasting time.

Craige gave a teeth-to-lip inaudible, "... whsst." Opened the front door; pointed. Lucky bounded through on a full-out run. Leeza stared bug-eyed from window to window while Lela whimpered; crouched lower. Craige looked at the two women. None of this was making any sense with the pieces standing square in front of him. Lela was convenient for running errands and fronting for Raymond. The main problem she caused was getting in the way."

"Least you got that damn dog out of my way," Crawforde stepped out from the mudroom.

The voice startled Craige. "You don't know the half of it." The look on his face was deadly dark sinister.

"That damn beast is mean." Crawforde rubbed his arm with the raincoat draped over it. No one could miss the business end of the snub-nosed handgun he was holding. "Get rid of the Glock." Crawforde saw Craige tense-up, "Don't be stupid." Craige put the weapon down, and kicked it toward Crawforde who quickly picked up the Glock; stuffed it in his jacket pocket. "Leeza, you do keep interesting company. Lela I don't give a damn about, but I've been looking for you. You and Purvis should never have tried your end-run game to cut me out of the picture. At least you'll be one problem solved." He closed and bolted the kitchen door. "It's a pity this has to end this way." Said to Craige, "It could've been much more pleasant if Bailey hadn't gotten you involved."

Lela said, "You told me nobody would get hurt."

"Nobody would have. Things were going fine until you started running your mouth to Janella with Purvis right there, wanting a cut.

Being suspicious of your roommate might be the only thing you were right about. Purvis getting you hooked on nose candy so you would keep feeding him details. The day you showed me how to roll a snowball in paper was the day I knew you were a problem. I'd never heard of a snowball, and you wanted me to try it. I wasn't about to put any of that shit in my body. That was about the time Purvis started having you cozy up to bored soldiers."

Lela wiped at her sniffles. Whimpered again, "You promised nobody would get hurt."

"Doing Raymond's son the way he did was way beyond being stupid. Plenty ways to stop Buddy Raymond from running his mouth. Could've shut him up permanently without broadcasting it. What Purvis really wanted was to make a point. None of Buddy's party-group could keep their mouths shut. Killing Mort even stupider, and you can put killing two soldiers under the heading of stupid. Killing them brought in the feds." He glanced at Craige, "I've learned how to cover my tracks, even from a dogged pro like you."

Leeza turned up a pert nose, "Without me you'll never find the package."

"You're not as cagey as I thought," Crawforde snickered. "How do you think I knew where to find you?" Bragged, "There were times it wasn't easy keeping track of you."

Leeza's anger spilled out at Crawforde, "You knew Purvis had me on the houseboat?"

"Purvis didn't trust Lela, and I knew he was shadowing you. I didn't know about the houseboat. I think the houseboat was done on a spur of the moment panic because he didn't know what else to do. Even if I had known, there was no point to my interfering. Purvis was handling a problem I wouldn't have to. Only he messed up."

"Is that what I was to you? A problem?"

"I've been shadowing you for some time. I didn't need to do much but stay out of the situation. My mistake was thinking Purvis would finish the job, and take care of you. Lela almost caught me going through your apartment," lifted the raincoat draped over his arm. The moldered stained chest was clutched tight in the curve of his arm. "I gave you more credit than to hide this in the bottom of the clothes hamper."

"What's that?" Lela said.

Crawforde smirked, "I saw Lela leave the apartment in way too much of a hurry. I should've hidden in the apartment; taken care of both you loose ends. It works out just as well. You're both here. Once everyone started poking through those old records in Ardochy, I didn't have much choice."

Craige's muscles tripwire quivered as he tried to control his hammer-cocked impulses. "You're going to have a nasty problem when the dog comes in."

Crawforde said, "I doubt that," made sure the weapon's safety was off. "Shooting the dog won't take much. Or shoot your girlfriend here if you don't make sure the dog behaves." He nodded toward his no-longer-useful college sophomore-meat, "I haven't gone to all this trouble to let some private investigator get between me and what I've worked for all my life. To someone like her it's pretty baubles and bling." He glanced toward Leeza and tightened his grip on his weapon, "Even though you managed to complicate things, it's not something that can't be put right."

Craige was afraid for Terri, and pissed as hell at Crawforde. He knew he was running out of time. "You're running out of options, and Dalugosh isn't around to back you up."

Crawforde scoffed, "Purvis doesn't even know me."

Craige said, "Like he didn't know Mort Raymond?"

"All Mort Raymond cared about was money. He was scared shitless Purvis would find out he was skimming the take off the drug trade. Purvis was small time. Thought he knew more than anyone else. He liked easy money; never quite put his finger on what was going down. To him it was drugs and porn. Anything else didn't make enough money. I never understood the porn trade, and they ought to castrate bastards that run kiddie porn. Lela never read a book in her life. Believed she could get anything by spreading her legs."

"Or pillow-talking the details of your treasure-hunting? Sounds like pillow-porn to me." Craige knew it was a gambler's risk goading Crawforde. "We're not haggling over what you are, just your price."

Crawforde's grin vanished. "She should never have tried to go behind my back when she found the chest in the apartment where

Leeza hid it. She wanted to run, but she wasn't smart enough to get a passport."

Lela put on a sulk, "You don't need a passport to go to Mexico."

"Where did you read that? The internet?" Crawforde with a slight shrug, "Need I say more? Even if you had brains to remember to take this chest, the minute you tried to pawn it you'd be dead. Your body dumped in some field, and the chest lost forever."

Craige said to Lela, "You try to pawn anything in that chest, the sun wouldn't set before the word got around."

Crawforde said, "That's her whole life... selling to the highest bidder."

"I don't see you being any better," Craige said. "It comes down to you being a common thief, and I might add, a somewhat clumsy one."

Laser-hot hate shot through Crawforde's eyes, "Good enough to keep you fooled."

"Fooling me is not a big accomplishment," Craige using any tactic to keep Crawforde off balance.

"Artifacts are worth a fortune with buyers all over the world."

Craige said, "Anonymous ones who never question a piece's provenance."

"Why should treasures stay buried and rot away?" Crawforde bragged, "Think what I can get for this. The dead don't have any use for them. Why shouldn't they be sold to the highest bidder? Universities don't pay enough. Even denied me tenure. Told me I was unprofessional."

"I don't agree with the egghead set most of the time, but in your case I do."

"Shut-up!" Crawforde snapped. "They picked on the wrong man when they picked on me. For two hundred years the Westobou treasure has been searched for, but I was the one who found it!" Spittle flew. "DeSoto never found it, but I showed them." Crawforde's arrogance snarled straight from the heart. "Nobody else found it. I put the pieces together. I found it!" He tightened his grip on his weapon. The small chest was almost too heavy for him to manage under one arm.

Chapter 16

A barefoot Terri had enough. One shot was all Crawforde would get before Craige was all over him. She could tell from Crawforde's bragging and the look in his eyes that he wouldn't leave any of them alive. She decided not to waste what time they did have. She judged the distance between her and the large vase next to the armoire; closed her eyes and prayed it wasn't one of Craige's priceless antiques but knew the odds were it was. She edged one quick look at an angry Crawforde waving the gun at Craige. To hell with the glass stabbing her feet. She swung her body in one smooth move, and gripped the heavy vase. Sucked in her breath, and swung the heavy vase as hard as she could into the side of Crawforde's head. The heavy vase shattered. The chest under Crawforde's arm hit the floor with a jarring thud knocking the lid loose and scattering its contents across the floor. Quick as a lightning strike Craige grabbed Crawforde in an arm lock and jammed his thumb between the trigger and the trigger guard. No way Crawforde could fire the weapon. Craige smashed the hammer-edge of his other hand into Crawforde's Adam's apple not caring if it was a kill-chop. Crawforde slumped into a heap next to the ancient chest. Craige hit the lights. The alabaster vase was now in broken pieces among the glitter of gold and pearls and jewels.

* * *

Leeza crawled on her knees, her trembling fingers clawing frantically at the treasures. Her eyes grew big and round as she tenderly brushed one tiny coronet; small green emeralds surrounded by rubies. The legend was true. Nestled in dark velvet wrappings was the mellow gleam of burnished gold and the sparkle of all manner of things. She unfolded the soft material, fingertips shaky. The graceful curve of the gold spur begged her to touch it. The metal looked warm with an elegance never meant for any rough man-at-arms. The goldsmith's filigreed handiwork was embellished with gems. Where yellow metal changed color to form an oval buckle toward the arch strap, there were large blood-red rubies fit for a royal crown, two on one side, one on the opposite with a mounting where a fourth had been. She caressed the exquisite bauble of Spanish glories past.

Her heart fluttered. Part of one translation from the *Chronicles of Fidalgo* had been about the armor of Hernando DeSoto. DeSoto had been renowned for being stingy with the yellow metal. He would've melted it down if he'd gotten his hands on such a treasure. Filled with greed and lust, he was on a hunt he never finished. He visited the Silver Bluff of the Cutifachiqui in his search for Chiaha. Leeza didn't care where it had been hidden, in drippy tunnels beneath Ardochy or in some hole in the ground. The chest was old, but certainly had been kept safely.

She picked up more gold baubles and jewels, when the light caught the interior of the chest. She laid the gold spur down. The small chest was deep. The young Cotifacheque Queen had saved more of their treasures. Gingerly, she lifted the soft cloth. A chill went through her. The chest was half full of pearls gleaming their soft grey. All sizes, some as huge as marbles, from dusky near white to black, perfect spheres mixed with ornate baroque ones.

Gray and Boback burst through the front porch door, their weapons drawn. "Didn't know what we were walkin' into. We have Purvis cuffed in the back seat of the squad car." Gray looked at a sprawled Crawforde, scattered pieces of the vase, a king's ransom of jewels, and Craige with his arms around Terri. Said to Boback, "Looks to me like SEAL Commanding Officer Ingram has things under control and his hands full."

Terri put her hand to her mouth and looked at Craige. "Please don't tell me that was a priceless antique vase."

Craige held her tighter, "What's to care about an old vase? You're safe."

www.ingramcontent.com/pod-product-compliance
Lightning Source LLC
Chambersburg PA
CBHW051501170626
46811CB00002B/581